KING ARTHUR

KING ARTHUR

A novel by Frank Thompson based on the
screenplay written by David Franzoni

HYPERION

NEW YORK

For Claire,
my own personal Guinevere

PREFACE

THE CLASSIC MEDIEVAL TALES OF KING Arthur and his knights of the Round Table have gripped the imagination of the world for centuries, for they are tales of chivalry and romance, heroism and betrayal, of knights in shining armor and their ladies fair.

The legends about Arthur are many, but the basic tale is this:

Long ago there was a great British king named Uther Pendragon. Knowing that rivals from all over the world hoped to take over the throne upon his death, Uther gave his firstborn son, Arthur, to a wizard named Merlin for safekeeping. Before Uther died, he asked Merlin to place a spell to make sure that Arthur, and only Arthur, would succeed Uther as king. Merlin took Uther's great sword, stuck it through a lead anvil which sat atop a large stone, and enchanted it with powerful magic. On the side of this stone was a plaque, on which was carved this legend:

Whoso pulleth out this sword
of this stone and anvil is rightwise
King, born of England.

Years passed and young Arthur grew up under Merlin's care. Eventually, King Uther grew old and died. As word spread of his demise, his rivals and would-be successors immediately began lining up at the stone, each pulling at the mighty blade with all his strength. But no one could remove it. No one could even budge the sword a fraction of an inch.

Young Arthur knew nothing of the spell or of his royal heritage. One day, riding by, he happened to see the huge sword stuck through a lead anvil atop a great rock and thought how odd it was. He liked the sword and, as it appeared to belong to no one, casually pulled it from the anvil and stone and rode on. When others heard what had happened, the surprised boy was declared the King of England.

Soon, Arthur encountered another, even greater sword: Excalibur, an awesome blade given to him by the spectral Lady of the Lake. Merlin told him that Excalibur's scabbard was even more powerful than the sword itself, and that as long as they stayed together,

Arthur would never lose any blood, no matter how seriously he was wounded.

Soon Arthur fell in love with and married the beautiful Princess Guinevere, the daughter of the king of a nearby principality. His father-in-law gave Arthur a large, round table as a wedding gift. Arthur decided that each of the table's chairs would be dedicated to one of the greatest knights in the world, and he set about gathering twenty-eight such men, including Sir Gawain, Sir Galahad and the gallant Sir Lancelot.

Together, Arthur and his knights of the Round Table fought many battles and won many victories. But their all-consuming quest was the search for the elusive Holy Grail, the goblet used by Christ and his disciples at the Last Supper, and which later caught the blood that flowed from Christ's body as he hung on the cross.

Arthur lost many of his great knights on that long and futile search. More heartbreaking, he lost his wife, Guinevere, to his greatest knight, Sir Lancelot.

When at last Arthur lay dying, he threw Excalibur back into the mysterious waters where the Lady of the Lake dwelled. She caught the blade and waved it three times before vanishing with Excalibur beneath the waves.

That is the tale of King Arthur. Yet, as beloved as the story is, it is only a legend.

The true story of Arthur happened in a very different time and place. Even so, his life was every bit as adventurous and fantastic as anything claimed by the myths. His very existence has been debated for hundreds of years, but many historians now believe that Arthur truly walked the earth and that the romantic myth of "King Arthur" rose from the story of a real hero who lived and died a thousand years ago, in a period often called the Dark Ages. Recently discovered archeological evidence in Britain and historical reassessments have shed light on what may have been his true identity. This evidence suggests that Arthur was indeed the son of Uther Pendragon, a Sarmatian knight, and a Briton woman named Igraine of Cornwall.

By A.D. 183, the Roman Empire extended from Arabia to Britain. But the Romans wanted more— more land and more peoples loyal and subservient to them. Of all the people conquered by Rome, however, none was as important as the once-powerful, defeated Sarmatian cavalrymen. In exchange for their lives, and the lives of their families, these Sarmatian warriors were incorporated into the Roman military.

Many of them believed that it would have been better if they had died instead, for the second part of the bargain they struck indebted not only themselves, but also their sons, and their sons after, and so on, to serve the Empire as knights for fifteen years each in Britain.

For two hundred years this brutal practice continued. Each generation sent sons from their Sarmatian homeland to Britain to fight for the Empire.

Each of these Sarmatian knights reported to a Roman commander in Britain. And each of those commanders was named for the first: Artorius, or Arthur.

KING ARTHUR

✠

LANCELOT

THE VAST FIELDS AND ROLLING HILLS
seemed to have no end. As far as the eye could
see, the mighty plain flowed from the foot of the
snow-packed Caucasus Mountains all the way to the
Black Sea. There, a settlement of Sarmatian warriors
nestled on the shore.

It was an idyllic place and the nomadic
Sarmatians had hoped to find happiness in the fertile
valley. But their defeat at the hands of the Roman
army had turned the once-proud warriors into virtual
prisoners and slaves, each forced to serve the Empire
for a decade and a half—if he survived that long.

The few citizens of the little Sarmatian village
hoped that their remote location might keep them out
of harm's way, beyond the notice of the Roman army.
An entire generation of boys had grown to their teens

farming the land and shedding blood only when hunting for food. But the older men, who had served their time as Sarmatian knights, knew that it was only a matter of time until a battalion of Roman legionnaires rode into the valley, conscripting every boy over the age of ten into a life of hardship and brutality, and a future that almost certainly led directly to a violent end in battle or a lingering, agonizing death from disease or exposure.

When the legionnaires did one day appear on the horizon, Lansdowne, a limping little man with two sons, called out for the other Sarmatians to join him in the center of the village.

"Yonder!" he cried. "They approach! We know why they have come."

Riskin, once a deadly archer who now spent his days tending his garden and raising hogs for meat, nodded firmly. "They can come, but we can arrange it so that they will never leave," he cried. "Sarmatian men, get your weapons!"

"It is madness," came a voice from the small crowd. "There are too many of them. We will all be killed."

"And what if we are?" shouted Lansdowne. "Are we not Sarmatians? An honorable death in battle is better than meek surrender!"

"That's right!" Riskin yelled. "They will take our sons and rape our daughters. Sometimes they burn villages. We will lose everything anyway—let us fight to the last!"

"We cannot," said a quiet voice. All eyes turned to Henzil, a strapping old man of forty with bright red hair and a rough beard that hung to his chest. "Are we afraid that our sons will die in Roman captivity?" he said. "If we fight the Romans, our sons will surely die at their hands. So will our daughters, our wives . . . all of us." He looked around. "Every man of us became a knight when he was no older than our boys are."

"Not a Roman knight!" Riskin shouted.

Henzil shook his head. "That is true." He put his arm around the shoulder of his twelve-year-old son Lancelot. "Nor will our sons be Romans. They will fight in the army of the Empire, and the Empire's enemies will become their enemies. But they will always be Sarmatians, until the day they die."

Lancelot looked up at Henzil gravely. "Father," he said, "I want to go. It is my time." Another boy, barely eleven years old, stepped forward. "And mine," he said. All the other boys in the crowd began to gather beside Lancelot, shouting and cheering.

Their fathers looked stricken. Many of their mothers shrieked with grief and fear. But the boys, with the indomitability of youth, could not help grinning at each other, excited by the impending adventure. Great things lay ahead of them: battles, victories, parades, all the spoils and honors due to conquering warriors.

Henzil embraced his son tighter and said, "Our sons will be heroes. They will make us proud." He gazed down into Lancelot's face and said, "May the gods be with you, wherever you go." Henzil reached to his neck and removed a cloth and gemstone talisman, then carefully slipped it over Lancelot's head. The medal hung low on the boy's chest and he fingered it, looking closely at it. On the talisman was carved a crimson dragon. "It saw me through many battles," Henzil said quietly, "and it will protect you, too. I swear it."

The Roman legionnaires came into the village, tense and braced for trouble. They were surprised, and more than a little suspicious, to find none. They briskly rounded up the boys. The activity occurred without incident; most of the boys had already packed their belongings and were prepared to move out immediately.

So surprised were the Romans at the ease of the operation that they did not even bother to burn down any buildings or defile any of the women.

Within a few short hours, twenty young boys were slowly leaving their village. Ten of them rode on horseback and the other ten sat huddled in carts. They were flanked by mounted Roman legionnaires and led by a stern Roman officer. The boys were all between the ages of ten and thirteen. Their parents and relatives lined up to watch them leave home. Some were solemn, others wept openly. Still others, like Lansdowne, scowled, wishing they could attack the Romans and save their sons.

They all hoped for the best, but in their hearts

they knew that they were saying farewell to their boys forever. As he rode away, each of the boys, excited as he may have been earlier in the day, now looked back sadly for a last glimpse of their homes, their people.

But one of the boys on horseback did not look back. Lancelot looked straight ahead at the endless horizon, his face grave, emotionless.

Back in the village, Henzil, his face and torso marked with the scars of countless battles, stood tall, proudly watching his son's departure. A lean, powerful dog sat by his side, whimpering slightly as he watched his young master Lancelot disappear into the distance. Suddenly, Henzil cupped his hands to his mouth and let loose a mighty war cry. Other men around the village took it up as well. Soon, the air was filled with that chilling cacophony. The sound rumbled across the plain like thunder.

As the cry sounded from all around, Lancelot's dog broke away from his father's side and ran up alongside Lancelot's horse, tail wagging, face alert and eager. Lancelot refused to look down at his beloved pet, but he felt his presence. For the first time that day, a bitter tear began to roll down his cheek. Angrily, Lancelot dug in his heels and the horse's walk turned into a gallop. The dog began to run as well, faster and faster in a futile attempt to keep pace with the stallion. Eventually he was outdistanced. The dog sat on the plain, whimpering again, as his master rode determinedly out of his life.

GUINEVERE

A SHARP BLADE OF LIGHT SLICED THE
darkness. Brighter than a candle, it traveled like
a fiery arrow straight toward Guinevere's strained
eyes. Sunlight, unseen now for . . . how long?
Normally Fulcinia came in the night when no one
would notice her clandestine visits, when no one
would report her insubordination to Marius.

The shaft of light flashed brightly and painfully,
and then disappeared suddenly, replaced by the softer
flickering of a candle, seemingly floating down the
bleak passageway. Fulcinia arrived at the bars and
knelt down, close to Guinevere's pale, frightened face.
She set the candle on the floor beside her and lifted a
cloth from atop the small basket she bore in her left
hand. She passed a large crust of bread through the
bars. As Guinevere began devouring it greedily,

Fulcinia handed her a small shank of lamb, and a potato.

"Do not eat it all at once, child," Fulcinia whispered. "I cannot say when I will be able to come again." She wrinkled her nose with disgust and looked around in the darkness. From down the corridor came soft groans. Somewhere, a woman was weeping and a child was screaming with hunger or fright or pain—or all three.

"Oh, the smell!" Fulcinia said. "You poor girl—I cannot see how you stand it!"

Guinevere stared at her with nearly empty eyes. "I can stand anything," she said hoarsely, "until the day I get out of here—and kill him!"

Fulcinia looked around frantically, as though someone might have been eavesdropping. "You must not say such things," she said, "not even to me. Not even in secret."

Guinevere ate in silence for a moment. "Where is he?" she asked, finally.

Fulcinia seemed puzzled by the question.

"Marius," Guinevere said. "Your husband. He must be away or you would not have come during the day."

"He is in the village," Fulcinia said. "Some of the farmers have been late in paying their tribute to him. I am afraid he will punish them severely."

Guinevere smiled bitterly. "Ah," she said, "that means I will have some new friends before long. It is always so pleasant to meet new people."

Fulcinia's eyes filled with tears. "I have begged him to release you—begged him!"

Guinevere ate a bit of the potato, and then set it aside for later—or tomorrow. "He will never release me," she said, "not after the horrible crime I committed." She looked directly into Fulcinia's eyes. "I forget," she said. "Exactly what was that horrible crime?"

Fulcinia had no answer and stared back at the girl desperately. But Guinevere knew. When the mercenaries who served Marius, the great Roman land baron, first captured Guinevere along with others of her village in the forest, they put the prisoners to work around the estate. Guinevere had been luckier than some, assigned to household chores: washing clothes and dishes, building fires and preparing meals. The work was difficult and endless but not backbreaking.

Then Marius noticed the young woman at her work and immediately saw her potential for another kind of work, a kind that seemed to him to be much easier, far more pleasurable. With all the confidence of a master who was never refused anything, he approached Guinevere from behind and put his arms around her. His hands caressed the soft slopes of her breasts. "Yes," he whispered, "you are being wasted here. Your life is about to get much, much better."

Guinevere wrenched herself out of his arms and glared at him defiantly. "My life will never be better," she said angrily, "until I am free—until all my people are free—to return to my village."

Marius smiled complacently. "I like a wench with fire in her. Go clean yourself up, then come to my chambers."

Guinevere did not move, or say a word.

Marius frowned. "When I give an order to a slave, I expect immediate obedience!" he snarled.

"Burn in hell," Guinevere said quietly.

Marius slapped her hard across the face, knocking her backward. She steadied herself at the table. Suddenly, she lunged back at him, raking her fingernails down his face, leaving four bleeding lines stretching from his cheek to his chin.

Marius struck her once with his fist, then again, and again. She slipped to the floor, her eyes already bruising, blood bubbling from her lips and streaming from her nose. Through the ringing in her head, she heard Marius summon the guards. Then she felt herself being dragged from the house and into the dreaded stone building across the courtyard. Numbly, she saw the gallows that stood just outside the prison's doors, and she wondered if they were going to hang her or merely lock her in a sunless dungeon until she rotted away.

There had been many days since then that Guinevere wished they had taken her directly to the gallows. The darkness and deprivation, the putrid stench and the constant cacophony of agony that came from all around combined to make this place truly hellish.

Guinevere might have given up hope already, except that Marius's wife, Fulcinia, visited her whenever possible, bringing her food and fresh water, telling her stories of hope, both talking and listening to Guinevere. Fulcinia never said so outright, but Guinevere knew that she had also been on the receiving end of her husband's brutality. Perhaps that was why the woman, old before her years, had taken such pity on the unfortunate girl.

Fulcinia said, "I must go now. I have bribed the guard, but even so, these mercenaries can only be trusted to a degree. If Marius learned of this, I would soon be sharing the cell with you."

Guinevere reached her filthy hand through the bars and touched Fulcinia's face, still streaming with tears. "Thank you," Guinevere said. "Thank you for everything."

Fulcinia picked up her candle and stood. "I will come back, very soon." She turned and began walking away.

"Fulcinia," Guinevere said. The woman stopped and turned.

"Please," Guinevere continued, "get me out of here . . . "

Fulcinia choked back a sob and hurried down the passageway. When she reached the door, there was once again that blinding flash of precious sunlight, striking at Guinevere's eyes and heart like lightning. Then, once again, all was darkness.

ARTHUR

ARTHUR WAS BEING THE PERFECT soldier.

The ten-year-old boy marched down the street, an imperious look upon his face. Periodically, he stopped to bark out terse orders to passing dogs or any one of the many imaginary legionnaires who followed him slavishly through all of his adventures. Now and then, he drew the wooden sword from his belt and engaged in frantic combat with the vicious warriors who emerged from the darkness of the forest. Sometimes, when those warriors were not fierce enough, he fought bears or dragons. Each of these violent engagements ended in total victory for "Arthur the Great." And when they did, he often gave himself a lavish victory parade, striding down the street, gra-

ciously accepting the adoring cheers of the crowd,
who strew flower petals in his path. He bowed at his
make-believe admirers, always the modest Roman
victor.

His mother, Igraine, disapproved of such games.
They were not Romans, she insisted impatiently, they
were Sarmatians. "Your father served the Romans,"
she often said, "but he never pretended to be a Roman
himself. The Sarmatians were greater than anything
the Pope's empire ever produced!" Arthur did not
quite understand his mother at moments like that, but
he never tired of listening to her tell him about the
exploits of his father, the greatest of Sarmatian
knights, Uther Pendragon. She told him about his
incredible victories, his fantastic adventures, his
nearly miraculous skill with the huge sword Excalibur
that he carried every day of his life, and which he
held, its massive blade dripping blood, the day he died.

And she told him stories about the Sarmatians
themselves. They had lived in Britain for hundreds of
years, but they were not British. They were born of a
great tribe of nomadic warriors from the Black Sea
who had roamed the world for centuries, conquering
all who stood in their way. They fought from horseback, wielding mighty, highly decorated swords. It
sometimes seemed to young Arthur that they worshipped their swords as other people worshipped gods.
When a Sarmatian warrior died, his grave was marked
not by a Christian cross or a headstone or other monu-

ment. Instead, the warrior's sword—detailed with its own intricate and unique design—was plunged into the earth at the head of the burial mound. There it stayed forever, a standing tribute to the bravery and honor of the man who had once carried it.

Igraine never told her son about the Sarmatians' devastating and humiliating defeat at the hands of the Roman army—how the surviving knights had had to swear allegiance to Rome. How Arthur's father had struggled under the bitterness of that defeat and had served the Romans as a prisoner might serve his jailers.

And his mother never told Arthur the even more shameful story of how she and Uther had met and fallen in love—she, a married Briton with three daughters, he a dashing warrior who had actually faced Igraine's husband on the field of battle. Their love was immediate and devastating. She left her family, her village, everything she had ever known, to roam the British countryside with Uther Pendragon. Although her soul wrenched with regret for the pain she had caused to her husband and daughters, Igraine could not have imagined life without Uther. When their magical son Arthur was born, she began to feel that her sacrifices had been worthwhile, that she might yet find happiness and contentment.

But that fleeting hope disappeared the day that Uther fell on the battlefield. His body was pierced with a dozen arrows, and then beheaded by the battle

axe of one of the mysterious tattooed warriors sometimes known as the Picts, and more commonly known
as Woads, a nickname derived from the plant used to
make the dye for their tattoos.

Something vital in Igraine died that day. She
remained a caring, loving mother to Arthur; but as a
woman, she was little more than an empty shell. She
wore a heavy cloak of sadness and pain, where once
she had wrapped herself in the brilliance of passion
and love.

Arthur may have recognized some of this, but in
the self-absorbed way of children, he paid little heed
to it, instead preferring to occupy his mind with
thoughts of battle, of colorful banners and cheering
troops and towering victories. Most of the Roman
legionnaires who guarded his village were not battle-
hardened veterans, but some of them had seen action
and the others were more than willing to invent stories
to thrill the eager boy. He particularly loved passing
the time with a legionnaire named Ramus. Older than
most of the other recruits—he must have been as
ancient as thirty, Arthur thought—Ramus was a well
of great war stories that promised never to run dry.
Arthur did not realize that if Ramus had done even a
fraction of the deeds to which he laid claim, he would
have been acclaimed all over the Empire and com-
memorated with statues and coins instead of stationed
in a minor little town on the edge of nowhere.

As the sun sank low in the sky one evening,

Arthur marched up to Ramus, who was standing guard at a short palisade facing the forest. Ramus saluted the boy ceremoniously and Arthur gravely saluted back—peers.

"Have you come to relieve me, soldier?" Ramus asked.

Arthur smiled in spite of himself. "No, Ramus," he said, "you must stay at your post. But if you were attacked, you would need some help." Arthur drew himself up to his full height. "And here I am."

Ramus almost smiled but instead nodded gravely. "Well, I must admit to feeling quite nervous," he said. "But now that you are here, all will be well." Although Ramus allowed a bit of a playful lilt to enter his voice he was not, in truth, feeling very cheerful at the moment. The forest trees had begun swaying in an odd manner earlier in the day. The legionnaire had watched this strange phenomenon closely over the next few hours. The trees swayed, then stopped; swayed, then stopped. Ramus sensed that the wind was not causing the motion. And he wondered what was.

Arthur stood beside his friend, also peering intently in the direction of the woods. But the boy was too wrapped up in his childish games to notice anything out of the ordinary, especially anything as subtle and natural as the swaying of trees.

"Ramus," he said after a moment, "if you could—"

Suddenly a cry came from the other side of the village. "Woads!"

In an instant, the air was filled with an unearthly cry, high-pitched screams coming from the forest in every direction. Arthur looked up at Ramus in fear and then followed his gaze in the direction of the woods. Strange men, their skin painted the color of bark, leaves and earth, emerged as if by magic, running toward the village, screaming their cry of terror.

Ramus lifted his bow and hastily loaded an arrow. "Go home, Arthur!" he cried, firing the arrow. A Woad warrior fell backward, his feet kicking spasmodically, an arrow embedded in his neck. Arthur stared at the grisly sight, frozen to the spot. "Move!" Ramus said, giving him a shove. "Take care of your mother!"

The Woads were already in the village as Arthur darted among the small wooden huts with thatched roofs. The legionnaires tried to fight them back with sword and spear, but the Woads quickly overwhelmed them, one at a time.

Arthur ran toward his home and saw his mother standing in the doorway, a desperate, panicked look on her face. "Arthur!" she shouted when she saw him. "Thank the gods!"

He rushed into her arms, sobbing with terror, and she quickly pulled him inside. Night was falling as they collapsed on the floor in the middle of the room. "Stay down," Igraine said. "An arrow could come through the window."

For hours, Arthur cowered in his mother's arms as a battle raged outside of their small home. The sounds of war vibrated the thin walls of the hut and the acrid smell of smoke drifted in. So did another smell. It reminded Arthur of an awful time when he'd watched some of the village men slaughter four hogs for a feast day. Arthur longed to go to the window, to see what was happening, but his mother clutched at him, wailing with fear.

Suddenly, Arthur saw a torch at the window. Terrified, he leaped to his feet, but an instant later, he realized that it was Ramus holding the torch. "Are you all right, Arthur?" Ramus shouted. "Igraine, are you all right?" Arthur just looked at his friend in shock. Ramus was bleeding from a nasty gash across his forehead and he periodically had to wipe the blood from his eyes. Igraine cried, "Save us, Ramus!"

Hearing a sudden noise behind him, Ramus turned just as a Woad plunged a sword into his chest. Arthur screamed, "Ramus!" The legionnaire slipped backward as the Woad ran on. Ramus clutched at the wound in his chest then suddenly collapsed, like a flag in a dying wind. The torch dropped from his hand and fell through the window into the house. The flimsy structure, all straw and wood, immediately burst into flames.

Reacting to the holocaust, Igraine frantically pushed young Arthur out the door as flaming beams hurtled to the earth. Before she could get out herself, one of the beams fell into the doorway, trapping her inside. Arthur looked back to see his mother just beyond the flames. He rushed to the door but was driven back by the blaze. As his mother screamed in agony and fear, Arthur searched for something to clear the way.

Seized with an idea, Arthur ran from the house, raced through the forest and rushed downhill, headed for the knights' cemetery. In this dark and surreal place, Arthur ran through and around the swords which stood at the grave of each entombed knight. Some of the blades were old, and some were nearly disintegrated. But others were sparkling fresh and newly planted.

Arthur found the grave he sought and grabbed the hilt of a magnificent sword, its details hidden in shadow. The sword was Excalibur, the weapon of his father. Arthur yanked at it with all his strength—but it would not budge.

Arthur cried out, "Father! Please! Let loose your sword!"

With a mighty heave, he wrenched Excalibur out and fell backward flat onto the ground. The fall nearly knocked the breath from his chest, but immediately Arthur leaped to his feet and, Excalibur over his shoulder, struggled up the hill back toward the fight and his burning home.

If confronted by a savage Woad, Arthur was determined to wield Excalibur just as his father would have done—even if that would be physically impossible for the small boy. But at that moment, screeching a battle cry, the Woads disappeared into the forest.

Arthur approached the burning house, the Woads forgotten as he focused entirely on the task of saving his mother. But the blaze was like a furnace. There were no screams coming from within, nothing but the roar of the fire. He could see Ramus's legs sticking out from a pile of burning debris where the wall had collapsed on him.

"Mother!" Arthur shouted, his voice choked with tears. "MOTHER . . . !"

Finally, the intense heat of the raging flames forced him back. He dragged Excalibur with him, whimpering, "Mother . . . "

ONE

THE KNIGHTS WERE ALREADY AT THEIR places at the round table when Arthur strode into the room. As he looked around at their alert faces, Arthur thought that they always looked so much more formidable on the field of battle than they did in this room. Perhaps it was because here, they were relaxed, among friends—brothers, really. Men who laugh easily, who tease each other relentlessly, do not necessarily seem like fearsome killers.

But Arthur's perception, he thought, also had to do with the table itself. There were over one hundred chairs around it, each one dedicated to a knight whom Arthur had handpicked to sit there. But now most of the chairs stood empty; only seven knights took their places at the table. Arthur knew that the mission he brought to them today might mean that there would be even fewer than that tomorrow.

Arthur had decided at the very beginning that he would never replace one of his great knights. He had chosen each one so carefully that it seemed almost a sacrilege to treat them as mere working parts in a machine. They were all special, he decided. Irreplaceable. Their numbers would continue to dwindle until one day they would all be gone.

In the beginning, there was only Arthur. He joined the Roman army when he was only ten years old, just days after the death of his mother. And as soon as he was old enough to command, he was made an officer. Because his father, Uther Pendragon, had been the leader of the Sarmatian knights, tradition demanded that Arthur follow in his footsteps.

He quickly gained a reputation as a fearless fighter and an intelligent leader of men. He easily bested nearly every enemy, but he held a particularly bitter contempt for the Woads. The night of his mother's death continued to live in his heart, and he experienced it all again day after day, hearing her pitiful screams, smelling the horrible odor of burning flesh. If all the Woads were wiped off the face of the earth, Arthur believed, the world would instantly become a better place. On the occasions when he actually faced the Woads in combat, his logical military mind immediately dissolved into a hate-filled thirst for revenge, and Arthur took an almost inhuman pleasure in slaughtering as many of the tattooed warriors as possible.

He led Roman troops in victory after victory, but he became dissatisfied with the regimented way in which the Romans waged war. Then, he began planning something revolutionary. Arthur wanted to put together a handpicked Sarmatian cavalry, each man highly practiced in the art of battle, each man with his own unique skills. For instance, few of the enemies of Rome used horses in battle, and Arthur knew that men who could fight from the saddle would have more than one advantage over their adversaries.

When he began assembling this cavalry, Arthur knew exactly who had to be the very first recruit: Lancelot. Arthur believed that Lancelot was the greatest fighter he had ever seen, as well as the most loyal friend. The two had met when they were both fourteen and had trained together and fought side by side almost constantly since then. And as the friends began to learn of other aspects of life—like the beautiful women who always seemed to be available to brave knights in Rome—they experienced those pleasures together as well.

For over two years, Arthur and Lancelot worked their way through the Roman army, looking for Sarmatian warriors worthy of becoming Arthur's knights. Looking around at them now, Arthur remembered when he had first encountered the boisterous, two-fisted fighter Bors and the serene, almost delicate scout Tristran, one of the greatest archers Arthur had ever seen fire a bow and arrow. He met the brave Galahad in battle and extricated Dagonet—fierce in manner but surprisingly gentle of heart—from a Roman military prison where he was serving a term for insubordination. And Gawain had come to Arthur pleading to be a part of this extraordinary assemblage of great fighters. When Arthur saw what Gawain could do with both lance and sword, he immediately invited the young man to join their numbers.

The first time all of the knights gathered together, they were shocked to find the huge, round table in an otherwise bare room. Arthur stood at his chair and said, "Brothers, we sit at a round table, a table for which there is no head, no foot, no hierarchy, no place of greater or lesser importance." The knights looked around at each other uncertainly. None of them was accustomed to being addressed in such a manner by their commanding officers. Arthur continued, "I want it to be clear to every man in this room that we are all one, we are all equal at this table and in this company." He sat down again, just one knight among many. Lancelot stood up, his goblet of wine held high. "Hail Arthur!" he said. The other knights stood up, lifting their glasses and shouting in response, "Hail Arthur!" Despite Arthur's words, they all knew that there was a leader in their midst, and they knew who it was, and they were happy to acknowledge it.

Now, Arthur smiled to himself as he surveyed the

room. There were so many more memories, so many great and loyal knights. But their seats were empty now. Their bodies were lying under mounds of earth in the knights' cemetery on Badon Hill, just beyond the main gate of Hadrian's Wall. Or their bones still lay where they fell in battle, unrecoverable, unmarked but not forgotten. "All dead," Arthur thought bleakly, "because of me."

The six knights perked up when Arthur entered the room. They could tell from the expression on his face that something was up.

Arthur said, "My brothers, go get your battle gear and be ready to leave within the hour."

The men said nothing, but their eyes shone with eagerness. A mission—the reason that they existed.

Bors said, smiling, "Nothing dangerous, I hope, Arthur."

Arthur returned his smile. "And are you suddenly afraid of danger, Bors?"

"Never," Bors replied. "But our term of service is up tomorrow. We are about to be declared free men."

The knights beamed happily at each other. Free men, after fifteen long years.

Dagonet took a long pull from his wine goblet. "Bors is right," he said. "Be a terrible shame if we get ourselves killed just before we are granted our freedom. That would make for a lot of unhappy ladies who we have yet to encounter!"

The knights laughed. Tristran said, "Yes, I'm sure

many a beautiful maiden is praying for the moment when Dagonet and his huge belly will come tramping in."

More laughter. Dagonet patted his stomach proudly. "We can compare numbers when it's over, Tristran," he said. "I will be happy to give you a head start!"

Only Lancelot did not seem to be taking much pleasure in the badinage. "Where are we going, Arthur?" he said.

"There is an emissary from Rome coming here to Hadrian's Wall," Arthur said. "His name is Bishop Germanus."

The knights were not impressed. Of them all, only Arthur was a Christian. The rest either thought little of religion at all or clung to the pagan gods of their Sarmatian ancestors.

Gawain said, "And what is so important about this bishop?"

Arthur smiled, "Well, for one thing, he bears our papers of release."

The knights cheered.

Arthur continued, "And they are coming directly through Woad territory. The bishop is only guarded by a handful of Roman legionnaires, and you know how useless they can be if there's trouble. So, naturally, our job is to go out and make sure Bishop Germanus and his entourage arrive safely."

Bors stood up. "Well, I would hate for anything to happen to those papers . . . "

Dagonet added, "Although I do not care what happens to the bishop."

Arthur nodded. "Well, save the papers for all of us. And save the bishop, just for my sake."

Lancelot nodded. "Fair enough," he said. "Let's go get ready, men."

Laughing and jabbing at each other, the small band of knights got up from their round table and went to prepare their gear, delighted at the thought of action.

TWO

❧

THE ORNATE COACH MOVED LABORIOUSLY along a dirt road, its large wooden wheels struggling through ruts in the earth cut there by generations of rude carts, carriages and wagons. The rough-hewn vehicles that normally passed this way had little in common with this piece of rolling luxury. The coach was guarded by mounted Roman legionnaires—eight in the rear, eight at the front. Each legionnaire carefully scanned the plain that flanked the road on one side and the dark forest on the other.

Inside the coach, Bishop Germanus dictated official messages to his secretary, Horton, who scratched out the letters on sheets of parchment, little droplets of ink spraying from his goose's quill with each bone-rattling shake of the carriage. Horton was a small man with a nervous demeanor and a sharp, rodent-like face. He disgusted Germanus, but had somehow convinced himself that he was in a position of power, ready to ascend to the next level of importance, from secretary to aide to lieutenant. Someday, he might be a bishop himself. Germanus would have found Horton's desires to be as absurd as Horton himself. To the bishop, the little man was lucky to have gotten as far in life as he had. It was only his total obsequiousness that gave him any value at all.

A thin man enveloped in purple ecclesiastical robes was seated beside Horton, cramped and uncomfortable. He was the priest Hamus. Because of a series of infractions back in Rome, Hamus was punished by being forced to leave his comfortable quarters for this long, agonizing journey in the company of the feared Germanus and the contemptible Horton. Neither spoke to him, or even acknowledged his presence. That was fine with Hamus, who occupied himself by daydreaming about a series of very unpriestly activities.

The Romans' horses, more sensitive to their surroundings than were their masters, sensed the approaching pounding of hooves before the riders ever heard a sound. The pace of their gait never changed, but the mounts reared their heads and flared their nostrils, sensing instinctually that danger was coming their way.

A Roman guard noticed his horse's nervousness. He patted the steed consolingly on the side of its neck

and felt the chill of fear ripple through his own. The
legionnaire peered more closely into the blackness of
the deep forest beside the road. He saw nothing at
first. Then . . . a blur of movement in the purple shadows. Peeking out from behind the trees, and peering
down from them, were strange pale creatures, other-
worldly beings that appeared out of nowhere and then
vanished just as suddenly, like a hallucination.

Which, for an instant, was precisely what the
legionnaire believed he was experiencing. The creatures were more than simply pale . . . they were *blue*.
But a second later, when an arrow embedded itself in
his neck with a sickening thud, he knew that the creatures were real. It was his final realization as he tumbled from his horse, dead before his body hit the
ground.

Suddenly, a formation of seven knights charged
onto the plain toward the front of the Roman column,
galloping in tight single file. Even at a glance, it was
clear that these men were not standard cavalrymen,
indistinguishable from each other in matching uni-
forms. Each of the men was unique, clad in a variation
on the regular cavalry armor of the Roman army, sup-
plemented by Sarmatian gear. Some of their accou-
trements were of their own invention—scratched
metal, leather, and wool, dusted with a thick patina of
dirt from countless hard rides. Six of them wore helmets which were bullet-shaped, rising to a rounded
top. A few of the helmets were equipped with metal

chin guards; one or two of them also sported a metal nose guard, which hid most of the rider's face. One defiantly bared his head—topped by a stubble of closely cropped hair—to the dangers of battle. As they rode, the knights' broad swords sagged low at their horses' flanks. Drawing closer to the Roman caravan, they pulled their swords from their scabbards, holding the imposing blades straight ahead of them, almost at eye level.

At the head of the formation rode one who was tough, handsome and absolutely self-assured: Arthur, the leader of the Sarmatian knights. Just behind him and to the right was his friend and right-hand man, Lancelot. The same age as Arthur, and even more handsome, Lancelot had dark eyes that gleamed with eagerness at the impending fight. While Arthur bore the weight of his responsibility to his men and to Rome—in that order—Lancelot approached life as a grand adventure. Around his neck he wore, as he had for well over a decade, a cloth-and-metal talisman in the shape of a dragon.

Holding his legendary sword Excalibur in his right hand, Arthur circled it over his head. "Dragon formation!" he cried.

Instantly, his knights maneuvered into position. The "dragon" formation called for one rider to move out front as the head of the beast, while the rest of the knights fanned out in a *V* shape, protected at the flanks by the dragon's two "wings"—the tough and sardonic thug Bors and the confident, almost preternaturally calm archer Tristran. Bors was short and stocky, his body like one big muscle. Tristran was tall and thin, a natural aristocrat. Each of the "wings" carried composite bows, cocked and ready. While the knights aimed the powerful crossbows, fingering the triggers, they steered their steeds with their knees.

At the same instant, the mysterious blue creatures swarmed out of the forest, brandishing swords, spears and knives, and attacked the rear. The strange warriors were guerilla fighters who dyed and tattooed their skin for the purposes of camouflage. Today, they were blue. At other times, they adorned themselves in brown and green, the color of tree trunks, leaves and earth.

The largest of the Woads, clearly their leader, dashed from the forest to challenge the leading Roman officer, armed with a short sword. The officer spurred his horse forward, intending to run down the big Woad and trample him into the dust. The Woad stood calmly as the horse charged toward him. He held his sword aloft and when the horse got close enough, he swung the blade in an arc downward, chopping off the horse's front legs. The horse crashed to the ground, whinnying loudly and flinging the Roman officer off to the side of the road. Stunned, the legionnaire was attempting to raise himself up on all fours when the leader of the Woads walked over casually and brought the sword down on his neck. The head rolled three times before landing right side up, its unseeing eyes staring out at the battle, of which the officer was no longer a part.

While Arthur and his knights continued to race hard toward the Roman column, the Woads unleashed arrow after arrow on the column's rear. The arrows arbitrarily hit the wagons, the horses, Romans or nothing at all. The Woads were not sharpshooters, but their volleys were so relentless that they were highly effective nonetheless.

Within moments, the Roman guards were in immediate danger of being overwhelmed by the Woads. Bishop Germanus emerged from the safety of the carriage, his sword drawn. With fury contorting his face, the bishop began swinging the blade at the Woads with more ferocity than skill.

The leader of the Woads strolled over to the Roman officer's severed head, picked it up and held it aloft like a trophy, grinning proudly as his fellow Woads cheered, acknowledging his bravery. He heard hoofbeats coming up behind him and turned just in time to see Arthur swing Excalibur toward his neck. His head was severed from his body and went flying, still bearing the slightly curious expression with which he had glanced back at Arthur.

The Bishop continued to swipe and slash at the attacking Woads with his sword while Horton cowered inside the carriage, whimpering and trembling. Hamus sat slumped in his seat, a dazed expression on his face. An arrow passed through the curtain, just missing Horton's head and imbedding itself inches from

Hamus's nose. The priest tried to slump even lower while Horton flung himself to the floor with a shriek, covering his head with his shaking arms.

The Woads continued to emerge from the forest in what seemed to the Romans to be nearly endless numbers. They engaged the enemy in frenzied, savage hand-to-hand combat, a form of fighting at which the Woads were far more experienced than the conventionally trained legionnaires. One by one, the Roman guards dropped from their horses, felled by arrows or slashed by swords, and then were trampled or beaten to death by the blue demons.

Arthur's knights plowed through the Woads, knocking them to the ground. Two precision arrow shots from Tristran and Bors brought down a pair of Woads fighting side by side. The two knights shared a proud smile, and then reloaded and quickly fired again.

One Woad leaped on the carriage driver and swiped his rough knife blade across the driver's throat, opening up a ragged, gushing crimson gash. Lancelot galloped in, leaped off his horse and in a single, perfectly choreographed motion, pulled out two short swords and sliced into the Woad. Arthur charged past and chopped the Woad off the carriage with a perfect sword swipe.

Bors and Tristran arrived at the carriage. A surviving Roman guard, his short sword drawn, stood defiantly, glaring at the knights, ready to fight.

"Stand down!" Tristran demanded. "Put down your sword!"

The Roman guard raised his sword slightly and squinted his eyes suspiciously at Tristran and Bors. "Who are you?" he said.

"We are knights, you fool," sneered Bors.

"Your escorts," said Tristran.

Before the guard could respond, Bors and Tristran peeled off, looking to kill more Woads. In the midst of this confrontation another knight, Dagonet, powered past the guards on the opposite side of the carriage. He yanked back the canvas door and confronted a weeping man in ecclesiastic robes. A Woad arrow slammed forcefully into the side of the carriage. Hamus shrieked and pulled the canvas shut, as if the coarse material might stop an arrow or sword. Dagonet shrugged and backed away from the carriage. He charged back out to the battle.

A Woad jumped up into the seat of the carriage and prepared to commandeer the vehicle, but Arthur slid in beside the Woad and drove the long shaft of Excalibur's blade straight through him. Excalibur passed through the Woad and the wooden wall of the carriage, and came within inches of the nose of the terrified Hamus.

There was more than just the necessity of battle behind Arthur's thrust. The look of disgust on his face and the viciousness of the attack betrayed his consuming hatred of the Woads. Withdrawing the sword from the limp body, Arthur gazed at the Woad for a moment with a kind of satisfied revulsion he might have felt had he just dispatched a particularly loathsome breed of rodent.

At this point, Horton had had quite enough. His eyes wide with terror, his mouth opened in a silent scream, he jumped out of the carriage and ran aimlessly as the knights, Romans and blood-crazed Woads battled to their last breaths. Hamus would have followed Horton in flight, but was rooted to his bench in the coach by sheer terror. Looking back, Horton decided that there was more safety to be found under the carriage than by running away. He turned around and rat-scampered between the wheels, huddling close to the ground. All around, horses' legs tore up the earth. Horton could see the lower bodies of fighters dashing this way and that. A Roman legionnaire dropped dead beside him. His lifeless face seemed to gawk curiously at Horton, who could only stare back, whimpering in horror.

A Woad who had lost his sword in the battle ran toward Galahad and jumped up on his horse behind the knight, trying for a chokehold around Galahad's neck. Galahad wrenched his body to the left. The Woad, unbalanced, fell from the saddle, directly beneath Galahad's horse. He managed a short, agonized scream before his skull was crushed by the horse's massive front hooves. Two more Woads rushed him, but Galahad slashed at them with his sword. One fell to his knees, screaming, his hands covering his face in a futile attempt to stop the blood gushing from the wide gash that stretched from forehead to jawbone. The other angled close to Galahad in an attempt to thrust his sword into the knight's back, but Galahad was faster. With one wide swipe of his sword, he separated the Woad's head from his body, and it went flying off to the side of the road like a ball in play. The headless Woad continued to stand upright for an instant. Then the body crumpled to the ground like an empty sack.

As legionnaires continued to battle Woads on the back of the carriage, Tristran and Bors unleashed arrow after arrow into the fray. Tristran's first arrow struck directly between the eyes of one Woad, slamming him backward with savage force. Bors's arrow was delivered with such power that in an instant his Woad became nailed to the side of the carriage.

Out on the plain, Dagonet plowed his horse straight into the Woads, knocking them left and right. He held his sword at the ready, but for the time being was content to let his horse serve as his weapon. Dozens of Woads were left trampled in his wake. Nearby, Lancelot rode between two lines of Woads, slashing at them with his sword, first in his left hand, then in his right. The Woads fell before him like practice targets.

Tristran wheeled his horse around and spotted several Woads in the trees. He placed an arrow on the drawstring of his bow and unleashed it. The arrow struck a Woad in the throat and he dropped to the ground, where he writhed and choked for a moment before he lay still.

In the midst of the Woads, Bors found that he had run out of arrows. Quickly, he shouldered his bow and pulled out his battle axe, swinging it forcefully at the back of a Woad's head. The blow seemed to send the Woad flying through the air, but the flight was brief. It came to a stop when the Woad's lifeless body hit the ground facedown.

Other Woads were now simply trying to flee the chaos. Bors followed them, knocking them flat with his battle axe. One Woad tried to retreat into the river. Hearing hoofbeats approaching close behind him, the Woad turned and saw Bors's horse galloping forward, and Bors with his battle axe held high. The Woad held his arms high in the air, a pleading look on his face. Without hesitation, Bors brought his axe down on the Woad's forehead, neatly cleaving his skull in half. The Woad dropped backward into the river. His body began drifting lazily downstream, leaving a streak of deep red in its wake.

Tristran rode up the battle line casually, almost leisurely picking off Woads with his bow and arrows. With each hit Tristran smiled slightly, confident that he would be the high scorer on this day.

Dagonet was not content with killing at a distance. He rode into the midst of the Woads and leaped off his horse, slashing and slicing at them with his

sword. Too intimidated to fight back, they retreated
into the river. Dagonet simply followed them in,
killing so many he was soon wading waist deep
through what appeared to be a river of blood.

Galahad and Gawain used their horses to herd
Woads between them, trapping the Woads and ham-
mering at them with their swords. One furious Woad
ran toward Galahad's back, screaming, sword held
high. Before he could thrust the blade home, one of
Tristran's arrows struck him in the back of the neck.
The Woad dropped to the ground as Galahad kept
fighting, unaware of how close a call he had just had.

Arthur and Lancelot also were on horseback,
quickly overtaking the Woads and bringing them down
with their swords. It almost felt to the two friends as if
they were playing some sort of brutal game. Arthur
would drive a Woad within range of Lancelot, who
would kill the blue warrior and then chase down
another, forcing him over into deadly proximity of
Arthur's sword.

To Horton, crouched beneath the carriage, the
surrounding battle seemed like a nightmare, one terrible image after another, nothing quite rooted in reality.
He saw a Woad crouched and ready to pounce on
Dagonet. As he prepared to leap forward Tristran
killed him with an arrow to the back of the head. He
saw two Woads bring down a legionnaire, hacking at
him with their swords until they were both drenched in
his blood. To the right, Bors chased a group of Woads

into the river, killing one with a small metal weapon that slipped over the fingers like brass knuckles. Then he hopped onto the back of another and held his head underwater until the Woad drowned. To the left, Horton saw Lancelot charge a Woad who held both a knife and an axe. Without slowing his horse, Lancelot ran the Woad through with his sword, dragging the body behind for several feet until it finally slipped from the knight's wide blade.

At the edge of the water, Tristran killed a Woad with an arrow as he leaped for Bors. The force of the arrow changed the direction of the Woad's flight and he soared through the air and splashed dead in the water. Not to be outdone, Gawain sent another Woad flying, smashing him on the chest with his mace. One of the Woads on the carriage jumped off and knocked Galahad off his horse to the marshy ground by the lake. Infuriated and covered in mud, Galahad did not even bother to pick up his sword, but lunged for the Woad, clutching his hands around the blue warrior's throat, pressing his thumbs hard over his windpipe until the Woad stopped struggling and lay still, dead eyes staring at the sun.

As Galahad stood up, he saw Tristran almost taken from behind by a Woad. Before Galahad could get there, Tristran sensed the attack, wheeled his horse around suddenly and plunged his sword into the Woad's lower belly. Then he spurred his horse forward, trampling the Woad's body into the mud.

Lancelot saw that the Woad he had brought down was struggling to his feet again, blood spurting from the wound made by Lancelot's sword. Curious, Lancelot dismounted and walked over to him.

Blood flecked at the Woad's lips as he said in a hoarse voice, "For every one of us killed there will next be twenty and for every twenty, four hundred!" He coughed and sat down hard on the ground but never took his angry eyes from Lancelot's. "Spill my blood on this ground," he said, gasping, "and make it holy!"

Lancelot considered the request for a moment. "Gladly," he said, jabbing the man through the heart with his sword. He watched as the light of life slowly extinguished itself from the Woad's face. Then he pulled hard, disembedding the blade from the warrior's chest. Lancelot wiped the man's blood on the grass then stepped back into the fray.

The battle was nearly over. In the lake, Bors drowned another Woad, and on the bank Dagonet broke a Woad's back across his knee and hurled the corpse into the river. Just beyond him, Arthur pursued one of the last Woads into the water. As the Woad lieutenant turned to resist Arthur, the other knights surrounded him on their horses, swords poised. Arthur put his sword right at the Woad's throat and slowly forced him down. Although the Woad had dropped his weapon, he seemed ready to attack Arthur with his bare hands, given the slightest chance.

"What is your mission?" Arthur demanded. "Speak!"

The Woad lieutenant glared ferociously at Arthur, then said reluctantly, "There was word of precious cargo."

Arthur's eyes bore into the Woad, as if he wanted nothing more than to kill him as painfully as possible. But Arthur would not kill an unarmed man, even a Woad. He prodded the blue warrior out of the water, over to where a sword lay on the ground. With some effort, he managed to speak, though consumed with a warrior's vengeance. "Pick—up—your—weapon!" Arthur snarled.

The Woad did not expect this. Never taking his eyes from Arthur's, he bent slightly, moving cautiously for his sword. Though furious, the Woad shook with fear. His fingers closed around the sword's handle and he stood up straight, ready to die at the hands of Arthur.

But instead of killing him, Arthur lifted his sword high above his head. The Woad lieutenant did not understand at first that he was being released but when it became clear to him that Arthur did not intend to kill him, he scrambled across the river and ran into the forest, disappearing among the dark vegetation.

The other knights looked at Arthur, puzzled as to why he let the Woad go. They swapped looks with each other, acknowledging that there were often moments when they simply could not figure Arthur out. Without a word, Arthur replaced Excalibur in its sheath.

The largest, most imposing of the Woads stood silently at the edge of the forest, watching the knights as the Woad lieutenant ran to join him. A bear of a man in his late forties, he had not taken part in the battle, but had orchestrated every aspect of the Woad attack. He was Merlin, their commander. Flanked by four Woad warriors who were his personal guards, he stared impassively at the approaching lieutenant. The blue warrior bowed when he reached Merlin and said desperately, "I did not negotiate to live!"

Merlin said nothing, but touched the small cut on the Woad's throat left by the blade of Excalibur. He rubbed the blood between his finger tips.

"Artorius . . . " Merlin said quietly, staring across the field.

The Woad lieutenant followed Merlin's gaze, fixing his eyes on Arthur in the distance. The Woad's chest was heaving with a mixture of terror and relief—his life had been inexplicably spared twice: first by Arthur, now by Merlin.

Arthur felt, rather than saw, Merlin's stare. For one paralyzing instant, they seemed locked in a private communication across the immense space. Arthur was filled with bone-chilling dread. Shaking his head, Arthur broke the spell without quite understanding what had just happened. Regaining his composure, he turned his horse and rode away to join his knights, heading back toward the plain. As Arthur receded from sight, Merlin studied him, watching him and the knights as if they were an undeniable force of nature. After a time, he turned to the Woad lieutenant. "Gather up what is left of your men," he said. "We are leaving this place." By now the few Woad survivors of the battle had gathered by his side. Merlin looked at them sternly, yet sadly. Then he turned and led what was left of the Woad race back into the woods.

THREE

RIDING BACK OVER A FIELD LITTERED WITH the corpses of Woads and Roman legionnaires, Arthur and his knights turned their attention back to the coach. It was an unlikely image of beauty and splendor amid the gory horror of the battleground. Gawain and Bors were impressed by the rich and elegant design, and studied it carefully and a little jealously. "I am thinking of getting one of these for myself when all this is over," Bors said.

"Planning on becoming a man of means?" Gawain asked with a smile.

Bors nodded enthusiastically. "I have plans," he said. "Big plans. One day you will see me riding down the street in a coach like this, pulled by Dagonet and a couple of other dumb beasts, and I will be too grand to even acknowledge you."

Dagonet grinned broadly as he examined the sword of a dead Woad before slipping it into his belt.

Tristran steadied the carriage horses while Lancelot yanked aside the canvas that hung over the carriage openings in place of doors. Inside was the body of Hamus, an arrow protruding from his chest, his ecclesiastic robes soaked in blood.

"Here is a disgusting mess," Bors said, his nose crinkling in distaste. The others were not sure whether he was offended by the gory sight of the man's corpse or by the symbols of a hated religious faith that adorned his robes.

Bors caught sight of a slight movement at his feet. He bent over and saw Horton huddling beneath the carriage, praying, weeping and trembling. "Ah," he said, "and here's another."

Dagonet smiled and said, "Another disgusting mess?"

Gawain reached under the carriage and dragged Horton out, pulling him roughly to his feet. Horton began praying louder, his hands clasped tightly before his face. "No use praying to your God," Gawain said. "He does not live here!"

Bors and Dagonet laughed loudly. Insulted, Horton stood straighter, brushing himself off. He had stopped crying, but his eyes were still red and swollen and a long, silvery strand of mucus hung from one nostril. Bors thought that Horton looked like an over-grown, ugly three-year-old.

Arthur arrived at the carriage last. He had been

riding over the battlefield, surveying the carnage with a kind of sickened satisfaction. One by one the knights on horseback gathered around their leader. Arthur smiled as he looked around at them proudly. His men were bloodied and battered but victorious. Arthur was relieved to see that they had lost no one. Beyond the circle they formed around him, the field and riverbank was littered with the corpses of Roman legionnaires and Woads, and by varied body parts, roughly hewn from the bodies—but there were no Sarmatian corpses among them, and that made this victory particularly sweet to Arthur.

Horton looked around. The blue men were just as horrifying dead as they had been alive. "God help us!" he cried. "What are they?"

"Devils," Bors said with a mischievous gleam in his eye, "who eat Christians alive, I am afraid. You are not Christian, are you?"

Horton gasped and once again clasped his hands in prayer.

Bors asked, "Does that really work?" He clasped his hands in mockery but Horton clenched his closed eyes even tighter and did not respond to Bors's ridicule.

"Please," Horton said, his voice a hoarse, desperate whisper. "What are they . . . really?"

"They are called Woads," Bors said.

Horton looked confused.

With exaggerated patience, Bors explained, "Britons who hate Rome."

"What do they want?" Horton asked.

Lancelot stared at the quaking little man. "They want their country back," he said.

Arthur crossed over to Germanus, with his knights following on horseback and Horton following on foot. Only a few members of the Roman guard had survived the Woad attack. One of them stood before Germanus and faced the knights, sword drawn and at the ready. The legionnaire looked terrified, but was prepared to lay down his life for his master.

Germanus said sharply to the guard, "Stand down!"

The Roman reluctantly returned his sword to its sheath. Slowly the other legionnaires parted to make way for Arthur. Bishop Germanus was a man in his early forties, a ripe old age in this dangerous era. He smiled broadly as Arthur saluted him and, his voice filled with warmth, said, "Arthur Castus! Your father's image! I have not seen you since childhood."

Arthur bowed slightly and said, "Bishop Germanus. Welcome to Britain. Are you injured?"

Bishop Germanus shook his head no and held up his sword. "I was able to keep the demons away from me," he said. "And thank God I was not forced to shed any of their evil blood."

"Don't worry about that," said Bors with a barely disguised sneer. "We killed enough to take up your slack."

Arthur glared at him like an angry parent. Bors smiled and looked away.

Bishop Germanus did not bother responding to lesser beings such as Bors. Looking at Arthur he said, with just a touch of condescension, "And these are the great Sarmatian knights we have heard so much of in Rome."

Arthur bowed slightly. "At your service, Bishop."

Bishop Germanus gestured toward the corpse of a Woad. "I thought the Woads' control only extended *north* of Hadrian's Wall."

"Occasionally they venture south of the Wall," Arthur said. "They know that Rome is anticipating its withdrawal from Britain, and that has only increased their fervor to terrorize."

"Who leads them?" Bishop Germanus asked.

Lancelot replied, with a cynical edge to his voice, "He is called Merlin. A dark magician, some say."

Arthur gestured toward the carriage. "Your Eminence, if it pleases you," he said. "We have a long journey ahead of us, and we should get moving."

Bishop Germanus nodded and walked over to the carriage and stepped in just as Bors and Dagonet were dragging Hamus's body out the other side. They unceremoniously dropped him at the side of the road, just one more corpse among many. Horton started to follow Germanus into the carriage, but the bishop dropped the curtain in his face.

Horton looked around at the knights. "Are these . . . toads . . . apt to attack again?"

Galahad smiled. "Woads," he corrected. "Rest easy, brave sir. I believe we have shed enough of their blood for one day. I do not think we need fear any more trouble from them."

Dagonet snorted. "Toads," he said.

Arthur turned to Tristran and said, "Tristran, ride ahead and make sure the road is clear." Tristran nodded and rode away. Arthur then turned to the knights and gestured, making a circling motion with his hand. The men immediately responded to the order, moving into formation around the carriage. Germanus poked his head out of the coach's opening and said to Arthur, "I believe your men were only having fun with my secretary, but tell me true. Is there danger of another attack from the Woads?"

Arthur shook his head. "They run in packs, these Woads," he said. "A dozen here, two dozen there. Even if they return, they will be no match for my knights. You will be protected, Bishop. You may believe that."

Bishop Germanus nodded. "I have no doubt, Commander," he said. "No doubt."

Horton sullenly walked away from the ornate carriage to find a place in the rude wooden cart that followed it. He muttered to himself in a complaining voice, "Dozens do not worry me nearly as much as thousands!"

Lancelot, standing nearby, overheard Horton's words. His brow wrinkled with worry and he said softly to himself, "Thousands?"

FOUR

❧

IT WAS A RARE MOMENT FOR FUN FOR THE six British children. With dark clouds hanging low in the sky and a distinct chill in the air, the children knew they had to take full advantage of seaside opportunities like this. As their parents gathered stones and loaded them into two baskets slung across the back of a donkey, the children ran wildly up and down the rocky shore and in and around a large cave that stood at the edge of the beach. They squealed with delight as they jumped knee-deep into the surf, then sped breathlessly back to the cave, where the chase started all over again.

The work their parents were engaged in was difficult and tiring, but they, too, appreciated the coolness of the day. They smiled at each other occasionally, whenever they heard their children's delighted laughter. The stones were to be used in building a fireplace, hearth and chimney in their home. They all looked forward to passing long winter evenings there, singing songs and swapping tales, warm and dry as the gusty sea winds moaned outside.

One of the older boys noticed something in the distance and came to an abrupt halt. The other children, curious, gathered behind him and looked in the direction in which he was staring. Several dark ships seemed to materialize from the gloom like ghosts. They hung there in the fog, silently, as the children stared in fascination. Suddenly, a blazing missile shot from the deck of one of the ships, leaving a fiery trail in the sky. The children were delighted at this unexpected fireworks display, and oohed and ahhed. The smaller children jumped up and down with excitement.

Five more of the missiles appeared—flaming arrows aimed not at the sky but directly at the small party on the beach. The smallest girl, smiling at the sight, was struck in the chest by one of the arrows. She was dead in an instant, and as she fell backward into the sand, her ragged clothing burst into flames. The other children screamed in horror and turned to run back toward their parents.

Another flaming arrow hit a boy in the back and he went down hard, skidding across the sand before he lay still, his shirt smoldering beneath the blaze. His older brother stopped to help him and was slammed backward by an arrow shot into his forehead.

Their father shouted, "Run! Run . . . !" but none of the children would ever run again. Both parents dropped their bags of stones and rushed to their children. The ceaseless barrage of arrows rained down on them, thick and fast, and within seconds every member of the family lay dead on the beach.

On the Saxon ships, gray-clad swordsmen prepared to hit the beach. Close behind, crossbowmen dressed all in black formed on deck with fanatical, chilling precision. The crossbowmen were known by their fellow soldiers as "belly shooters." Along the edge of the deck, archers fired in more flaming arrows, clearing the beach in preparation for their landing. Some aimed at any living person in the distance, but other bowmen aimed for the little village beyond. Soon, the whole coastline seemed to be burning: every thatched roof, every sod barn, every rough wagon blazing into ash. From the ship, the archers could hear the faint sounds of screaming and shouting wafting gently toward them on the breeze.

Saxon soldiers left the ships by the hundreds and swept onto the north coast of Britain like a storm front. As they reached the first burning village, the few hapless Britons who had survived the firestorm of burning arrows fled from their approach as if from some natural disaster. A few villagers drew their broadswords and crossbows and stood bravely, attempting either to avenge the murders of their families or merely to stand their ground. But this handful of warriors had no chance; they were unceremoniously swept over by wave after wave of Saxons, who wielded their huge, vicious swords with relentless and efficient savagery. Where they passed, no living Briton was left behind and no building remained standing. The Saxons took whatever chickens, cows and pigs they needed to feed themselves, and then slaughtered the rest.

All up and down the angry and forbidding coast, the sea swarmed with Saxon ships, lined up at anchor, waiting their turn to unload supplies and even more troops, eager to lay waste to whatever land and people were unfortunate enough to stand in their path.

At the center of one platoon of troops, Cerdic, the Saxon commander, strode forward in the midst of his bodyguards. Cerdic projected quiet but absolute authority. He was known as a leader of great courage, and greater cruelty. His Saxons obeyed Cerdic's commands without question or hesitation, knowing that any insubordination would be met with the same savagery Cerdic dealt his enemies.

Just paces behind, Cynric, his burning-eyed son, followed at the head of his light infantry. Not quite eighteen, Cynric tried hard not to look like the untested warrior he was, but the fearsome quality he wished to project came across instead as nervousness. Cynric had inherited his father's cruelty but not his leadership qualities. His men did not fear him, but regarded him with veiled contempt. That their contempt remained veiled was due only to their fear of

Cerdic. For his part, Cynric was unaware of the absence of respect from his men; he believed that others saw him as a mighty warrior and a great general. But beneath his arrogance ran a painful streak of fear. It was not, however, battle and death that Cynric feared, but his commander—his father.

As Arthur, his knights and their caravan crested the hill, they were confronted by the massive Hadrian's Wall, dramatically backed by huge snowcapped mountains, the white of the snow dyed a deep crimson by the light of the setting sun. It was the biggest, most remarkable structure that any of them had ever seen, one of the great achievements of the Roman Empire. The wall stood fifteen feet high and measured eighty Roman miles from end to end, with small forts located at every mile along the way. Battlements, upright fortifications behind which soldiers stood, were perched atop the wall at regular intervals, adding another six feet to its height. Stretching from horizon to horizon, the monstrous structure dominated the landscape just as Rome dominated the world. Built to keep the "barbarians" out of Roman territory, Hadrian's Wall was more than a protective barrier: It was a symbol of the might and power of the Empire's ruling force.

Hadrian's Wall, in fact, was now a symbol of Rome's power over Britain in a more ironic sense. It was not the unbreachable obstruction that it once had been. At some places along the wall's great expanse, the brick and mortar had begun to crumble and some of the fortresses were either abandoned or manned only by a token force that could easily be overrun by almost any determined adversary. Some of them resembled villages more than fortresses, as Roman troops withdrew and local Britons came in to take over the buildings and fields for themselves. As Rome's total authority over the region slowly began to disintegrate, so was Hadrian's Wall chipped away, little by little.

The Roman fortress just behind the Wall at Badon Hill was one of the strongest and most fortified positions for miles in either direction. Because of its strategic importance as the gateway to Britain, Rome had concentrated on keeping Badon Hill's walls strong and its forces well manned. As had happened in so many other locations along Hadrian's Wall, a large village had grown up around this fortress. The farmers supplied the garrison with food and other kinds of assistance. The garrison, in return, protected the farmers from a variety of predators.

The first Roman soldier on the Wall who spotted the approaching caravan began to wave a large signal flag. Down the immense length of the structure, the first signal flag was answered by another, and then another, until flags signaled back to the main gate and the fort.

Just below the Wall, on the gentle slope of Badon Hill, the caravan passed by the knights' graveyard.

Arthur could never pass the place without thinking of his father, lying there all these years without a sword to mark his grave. And he thought of his brother knights who, one after the other, had taken their places there, after joining Arthur in his elite company. "Elite," Arthur thought bitterly. "I promised them glory and all I brought them was an early death. Now they lie alone and forgotten. They are remembered only by the seven of us who remain. And when we have joined them, there will be no one to remember us. All of our battles, our victories, our sacrifices . . . all for nothing."

If the other six knights shared Arthur's gloomy thoughts, they did not show it. For them, the papers of freedom borne by Bishop Germanus made the mood far too light to dwell on thoughts of death.

Now that they were within sight of the fortress and safety, their protective formation around Germanus's coach had slackened and they rode casually together in two groups. Galahad, Gawain and Bors rode together. Bors was almost always in a boisterous mood, but tonight he was in especially high spirits.

"Tonight, we are free men, lads!" Bors sang out. "We should drink until we cannot piss straight!"

Gawain smirked and replied, "You do that every night."

Bors said gravely, "Well, I have always had trouble pissing. There is too much of myself to handle down there. It is a problem." Bors's face broke into a proud smile.

Gawain laughed and glanced over at Galahad. But Galahad had a fretful, preoccupied look on his face. "I do not like him, that Roman," he said quietly, cocking his head toward the coach. "If he is here to discharge us, why doesn't he just give us the orders?"

Gawain shook his head and patted Galahad on the shoulder. "Is this your happy face?" he said. "Fool, do you still not know the Romans? They cannot scratch their asses without a ceremony."

"Why don't you just cut his throat first, Galahad," Bors said helpfully, "and discharge yourself after?"

Galahad's face remained serious, as if Bors were not joking. "I will, if it comes to that," he said.

Bors leaned back in the saddle. "You will miss the killing once you are back home, I think."

"I do not kill for pleasure," Galahad said. "Unlike some."

Tristran rode by at this moment and smiled at Galahad's comment. "You should try it," Tristran said. "You might get the hang of it."

"You have got a taste for it now, son," Bors said to Galahad, as if offering a friendly warning. "Killing is a part of you. It is not a thing a man just stops."

Galahad shook his head and closed his eyes for a moment. "As of tomorrow," he said, "all of this is just a bad memory."

Deep in disturbed thought, Galahad rode on ahead. Behind him, Gawain seemed to have been touched by the same sense of melancholy. After riding quietly for a while, he said, "I have often thought of what going home will mean, after all this. I do not know what I will do." He gazed reflectively upward, toward the graveyard.

Gawain continued, "I have been in this life more than the other. 'Home' is not as clear in my memory."

"Speak for yourself!" Bors said with a shudder. "Fucking cold back home. Me mother is dead and buried. Why would I go back there when I got my three wives and dozens of children right here? Now that we are free men, Dagonet and I will have the run of the place. I got plans! I will be governor, and Dagonet here will be my personal guard and royal arse kisser, won't you, Dag!"

Dagonet grinned and took out his dagger, jabbing it lightly at Bors's ass.

"Kiss it harder, ya dirty beast!" Bors yelled.

They all laughed loudly. It was a kind of play that they were all accustomed to. The rougher, the better. The more savage, the more fun.

Tristran held up his arm. A gray hawk swooped down and perched there. Reaching into his bag, Tristran pulled out a morsel to feed the bird. "Where have you been, now, old girl?" Tristran said in a low, soothing voice. Galahad glanced over, admiring the bird. Then, without a word, he rode on.

"When I get home," Gawain said, "the first thing I will do as a free man is to find a beautiful Sarmatian woman to wed before I get too old."

Bors looked at him incredulously. "A beautiful

Sarmatian woman?" he said sarcastically. "That in itself could take years. And what of you, Lancelot? What are your plans for home?"

"Well, if this woman of Gawain's is as beautiful as he claims," Lancelot said, "I expect to be spending a lot of time at Gawain's house. His wife will welcome the company."

"And where will I be?" Gawain said in mock outrage.

"Wondering at your good fortune that all your children look like me!" Lancelot said with a grin.

As the others laughed uproariously, Lancelot spurred his horse to a trot, and rode ahead to Arthur's side. Hearing the raucous laughter of his men, Arthur laughed as well. "It is good to hear them so full of plans," he said to Lancelot. "There has been too little of that these last few years."

"Did you hear?" Lancelot said. "Bors is governor now! The governor of shit."

Arthur laughed.

Lancelot said, "For myself, I start for home as soon as the sun's up. I may not even sleep. I doubt I can, thinking about it. What about you, Arthur? I was beginning to imagine you actually like it here."

"Well, control your imagination," Arthur said. "Come tomorrow, I make my own plans for Rome."

"Rome!" Lancelot nearly spat out the word in disgust. "And what will you do, Arthur, when you return to your 'beloved' Rome?"

Arthur answered in a jokingly reverent tone,

"Give thanks to God, Lancelot, that I survived to see it."

"Ugh! You and your God!" Lancelot said. "You disturb me!"

Arthur laughed again. For the moment, his dark mood had passed, and for the first time in a long while he felt optimistic, almost happy. He smiled and said, "Peace, Lancelot. I want peace. I have had enough of killing."

They rode on in silence for a moment, and then Arthur said with affection in his voice, "You should visit me. It is a magnificent place, Rome. Ordered. Civilized. Advanced."

"A breeding ground for pompous fools," Lancelot said.

Arthur shook his head. "The greatest minds in all the lands have come together in this one sacred place to help make mankind free," he said.

Lancelot glanced at his friend with a mischievous gleam in his eye. He said, "Ah, but what of the women?"

Arthur did not answer, but gave Lancelot a glance that only two best friends who have shared many women would understand. Lancelot chuckled. "Well, maybe Rome isn't quite as bad as I thought," he said.

The two men rode on, laughing together.

As the knights escorted the carriage through the entrance of the fortress at Hadrian's Wall, they passed several children playing knights with wooden swords.

Servants rushed forward to take the knights' gear. Leading the pack was Jols, the knights' squire, who gathered the reins of their horses together and started to lead them toward the stable.

"I am Arthur!" shouted one of the children, a bucket sitting on his head like a helmet.

"No!" shouted another small boy. "You are a Woad! I am Arthur!"

Arthur shook his head bemusedly as he passed. The children recognized him and began following him, shouting his name in glee. Several young women, admirers of the knights, joined the entourage. One of them handed a flagon of mead to Arthur, giving him a smile filled with erotic meaning. He accepted the fermented honey drink without looking at her and passed it directly on to Bors. Bors took a long, healthy swig, smiling lustily at the young woman all the while, and then passed the flagon on to Lancelot.

As Bishop Germanus stepped down from the carriage he watched the display of adulation toward the knights with a slight air of disgust. Then he eyed everything he saw in these meager surroundings with equal disgust. Only the important business of the Pope could have made him leave the comforts and beauty of Rome for this frontier squalor.

Arthur motioned the squire to his side. "Jols," he said, "give the bishop my quarters. Please make certain that he is comfortable and well cared for."

"I will, Arthur," Jols said. He walked over to

Bishop Germanus and bowed. "If his Eminence would care to rest," he said, "Arthur has made his room available."

The bishop nodded a not-so-humble thanks before he walked away, closely shadowed by Horton. Then, he stopped and turned. "Oh," Germanus said to Arthur, "shall we convene later to deal with the business at hand?"

Arthur nodded and said, "As you wish, Your Eminence."

The knights, hearing this, exchanged smiles. At last, freedom was so close they could taste it. The flagons of mead were refilled and some of the knights drew giggling young women into their arms, trying to decide which ones deserved a very special farewell.

Jols opened the door to Arthur's room and bowed, allowing Bishop Germanus and Horton to enter. Then he left without another word, hurrying back to Arthur's side.

Germanus took off his traveling clothes, thick with the dust of the road and battle. Horton retrieved a stunning red robe from the bishop's bag and helped Germanus put it on.

"Very kind of Arthur to give up his room," Horton said.

The bishop gave Horton a look that made him reconsider the sentiment. "But, of course," he stammered hastily, "it is no more than should have been expected."

Germanus just kept staring at Horton as if he had not said a word. "Finish unpacking my things," he said, "and then get out."

Horton looked puzzled and hurt. "Surely, sire . . . " he began.

Bishop Germanus looked at Horton sharply, silencing the secretary. "I dislike having to repeat myself, Horton," he said. Horton bowed and began emptying the bishop's bag of its contents.

While Horton did so, Bishop Germanus walked around Arthur's room pensively, carefully observing everything, lightly touching things as if he could get a sense of Arthur's nature from the objects. He ran his hands over the bindings of a collection of books.

Then he came to a small ceramic portrait of Pelagius. Germanus's face grew pale and grim with outrage at the sight of this likeness of the heretic monk, this heathen who pretended to be a Christian priest but who in reality grounded his blasphemous ideas in the monstrous beliefs of the pagans. Worse, Germanus knew that Arthur had studied with Pelagius back in Rome. It made him sick to think of young, impressionable Arthur sitting at the foot of this evil-doer, absorbing all of Pelagius's dangerous ideas about free will, all that nonsense that man could save himself through the strength of his own goodness instead of by the grace of God. Germanus scowled at the plaque and suddenly heaved it into the corner, where it shattered into a dozen pieces. Horton pretended not to notice the outburst and continued unpacking the bishop's bag.

There was a sharp rapping and Bishop Germanus and Horton turned to the open doorway. Squire Jols stood there smiling politely. "Your Eminence," Jols said, "I am here to escort you to the fortress hall." He had clearly witnessed Germanus's act of fury, but his face remained impassively friendly, that of a good worker eager to help.

The bishop nodded gruffly and moved toward the door, pushing past Jols. Horton followed him from the room, and then he and Jols walked behind Germanus down the corridor at a respectful distance.

As they walked, Horton said, quietly but haughtily, "When my master meets with your knights he must be seated last and he must be seated at the head of the table."

Jols grinned broadly at the idea. He said, "Your master may sit wherever he chooses."

FIVE

❧

I N THE MAIN HALL OF THE FORTRESS,
Lancelot, Gawain, Galahad, Bors, Dagonet and
Tristran stood behind chairs at the thick-plank circular
table, waiting. There were still many unoccupied seats,
but now the room did not feel so empty—it was filled
with hope for the bright future that would begin with
their freedom, any moment now. Before them, spread
across the table, were goblets, bottles of wine and
flasks of ale. The knights were in an upbeat—even
rowdy—mood.

Arthur was the last to enter the hall. His knights
looked up to see that he was wearing full Roman military attire with short skirt, leather-thonged boots and
cape. As usual, when they saw him like this, Arthur's
knights were impressed by his splendor and suffused

with a great pride of their leader and friend. Still, the warriors could not resist giving him a little teasing tweak. Lancelot bowed mockingly and said, "Hail, Arthur!" The others followed suit, bowing as low as possible. While he was face down at the floor, there erupted from Bors a thunderous fart.

They all laughed—even Arthur, who took such kidding in good spirit. He took his place and picked up his goblet of wine. At the gesture, a calm came over the room. It was just beginning to sink in that each of them was going to be leaving and splitting up from the others. As eager as they were for freedom, the knights had been such a close-knit group for such a long time that they felt a jolt of melancholy at the thought of saying good-bye forever.

Arthur raised his goblet and said, "Let us raise our wine to Gawain's brother and to all those gallant and extraordinary men and brethren we have lost, but who will be remembered for eternity." He took a long look around the table, at each vacant chair. The empty seats took on a special character now. Before drinking, each knight poured a bit of wine onto the floor for those who had been lost in battles that had been forgotten by everyone except the seven men present. They were lost in the sadness of the moment, until Bors once again decided to change the atmosphere.

"To freedom!" he shouted, raising his goblet high.

Galahad also raised his glass. "To home!" he said.

Dagonet and Gawain said at once, "To Arthur!"

The knights drank deep and cheered and broke into happy talk of the future. Suddenly, the rusty creak of the chamber's door demanded their attention. The group went silent as they faced the door expectantly.

Two Roman guards ushered in Bishop Germanus, followed at a respectful distance by Horton and Squire Jols.

Gawain nodded at Galahad with an "I told you so" expression on his face. "See?" he said. "Ceremony."

Both knights looked straight ahead but Galahad gripped his sword, ready to kill Germanus "if it comes to that," making Gawain laugh to himself and shake his head.

Although everyone in the room knew who the bishop was, Horton took it upon himself to announce his superior. "His Eminence," Horton said importantly. Suddenly, he noticed the unorthodox table and became flustered. Stuttering, he managed to conclude his announcement as a kind of afterthought: "Bishop . . . Gnaeus . . . Germanus."

Horton slipped aside to allow the bishop to approach the table. As Germanus stopped and stared at it, Horton gasped at Jols, "A round table? What sort of evil is this?"

Jols smiled and replied, "Arthur says that for men to be men, they must first be equal."

Arthur gestured expansively and said to Bishop Germanus, "Welcome to our table and our home." He nodded for the bishop to choose a seat. Germanus weighed his options—or lack thereof—and as he moved forward, all the knights sat. Germanus tried to disguise his disapproval, and was only partially successful. He looked to Arthur, smiled without humor and sat, noticing the many empty places at the table.

"I was given to understand there would be more of you," Bishop Germanus said.

Arthur was surprised to hear Germanus say such a thing. "We have been fighting here for fifteen years, Bishop," he said gently. "There once were many more of us."

The expressions of the knights, grim, sad and defiant, portrayed those fifteen years and the many brave and beloved knights who had been lost. Germanus realized his gaffe. "Ah. Of course," he said. "My apologies. Arthur and his knights have served with courage and with great losses to their own to maintain the honor of Rome's empire on this last outpost of our glory. Rome is most indebted."

Since they were indentured—some would say kidnapped—the knights, with great effort, resisted laughing in Bishop Germanus's face. But Lancelot retorted, "What brings a bishop all this way to deliver freedom to 'servants' of Rome?"

Germanus glared at Lancelot, insulted to be addressed so familiarly by a common knight. But seeing Arthur's expression and knowing his ridiculous ideas about equality, Germanus smiled a steely smile and answered.

"I volunteered," Bishop Germanus said. "I considered it a rare and welcome chance to meet all of these great legends in person and to serve my Pope. The mission is a blessing to me, I assure you."

Lancelot did not believe a word of this, but said nothing. Arthur saw the suspicious look in his friend's eyes and nodded his agreement. The rest of the knights continued to stare at Germanus with polite but impatient expressions, eager for the "ceremony" to be over with so that they could get to the main point of the meeting.

The bishop nodded to Horton, who stepped quickly over to the door to invite in the Bishop's Roman guards. The two legionnaires entered, carrying a large wine cask. They set it on the table and tapped it. Horton and Jols began filling the glasses as the knights eyed this rarity with enormous anticipation.

When the wine was poured, Germanus stood up and raised his glass.

"To you noble knights," he intoned. "To your final days as servants to the Empire."

Lancelot whispered to Bors, "Shouldn't that be *day* . . . not *days*?"

Bors looked back at him, suspicion on his face. Nearly all the knights shared it. They realized that the bishop had something up his sleeve.

While the knights enjoyed their wine, Lancelot and Arthur exchanged wary glances about Germanus. The bishop indicated his glass and said, "From the

Pope's vineyard." He looked at Arthur and continued, "His Holiness has taken a personal interest in you. He inquires after each of you."

Smiling, Arthur asked, "And what does his Holiness inquire?"

Bishop Germanus took a sip of wine and said, "Well, naturally, he is most curious to know if your knights have converted to the word of our savior, or . . . ?"

Before he could complete the sentence, or Arthur could answer, Gawain slammed his wine goblet on the table and said defiantly, "I'll pray to any god, goddess or devil if it means our freedom!"

The knights cheered as Germanus looked distinctly uncomfortable.

Bors said, "I don't mind Christianity, really . . . I saw a statue of your Virgin Mary once. Good-looking woman."

The knights all nodded genially. "Yes," Tristran said, "she was very nice and pretty." Dagonet agreed. "Absolutely," he exclaimed. "A real beauty!" They all raised their glasses for refills of wine.

Horton was appalled by the knights' unintentional blasphemy, but Germanus made a great show of smiling tolerantly. Arthur offered an apology like a loving but embarrassed parent.

Arthur said, "You must forgive my men, your Eminence. They retain the religion of their forefathers. I have never questioned that."

"Of course, of course," Bishop Germanus said,

waving his hand as if to dismiss any unintended insult. "They are pagans—as was Rome once. And some would say Rome was once better for it. For our part, the church has deemed such beliefs 'innocence.'" None of the knights could miss the condescension in his voice. "But you, Arthur," Germanus said, "your path to God is through Pelagius. I saw his image in your room."

Arthur nodded and spoke with deep affection in his voice. "He took my father's place for me," he said. "His teachings on free will, equality and the faith have been a great influence on me. I look forward to our reunion in Rome."

Horton shot a nervous glance toward Germanus but, as usual, his master ignored him, making every sign of being totally engrossed in each word that Arthur uttered. "Yes," he said impassively, "Rome awaits your arrival with great anticipation. You are a hero. In Rome, you will live out your days in honor and wealth." He turned to the knights and said, "And you, Sarmatian knights, will return to your homeland, having served faithfully and kept the covenant first struck with Rome."

Germanus brought out a set of scrolls and calmly set them on the table. The knights looked at the scrolls eagerly and impatiently. They knew that these were the papers that would release them from their indenture, making them free men at last, after years of fighting for Rome.

Germanus did not notice—or pretended not to

notice—their eagerness, but continued speaking casually and matter-of-factly as he organized the scrolls.

"Alas," he said, "we are all but players in an ever-changing world. Barbarians from every corner are almost at Rome's door. Because of this, Rome and the Holy Father have decided to remove ourselves from indefensible outposts such as Britain. What will become of Britain is not our concern anymore." He shrugged casually. "I suppose the Saxons will claim it soon."

Lancelot instantly sensed an ambush. This alarming turn in the conversation perked up the interest of all of the knights.

Arthur said, "Saxons?"

"Yes," Germanus said. "In the north a massive Saxon incursion has begun."

"You say that the Saxons will claim Britain," Lancelot said. "Saxons only 'claim' what they kill."

Gawain nodded emphatically and added, "And they only kill everything that crosses their path. It would take an entire legion to defeat them."

Galahad shook his head sadly. "So many years of war," he said, "and now the Woads will not be able to regain their land after all."

Bors looked even sadder than Galahad. "And I doubt that the Saxons will want me for governor," he said. "Damn them!"

There was an uneasy silence among the knights —not about the Woads, but about something unjust, in principle.

"Indeed," Bishop Germanus said, standing up

suddenly. "Gentlemen, here are your discharge papers. With these you are guaranteed safe conduct throughout Europe." The knights leaned forward, ready to be handed the precious scrolls. Germanus picked them up from the table. "But first," he said, "I must have a word with your commander."

The knights leaned back in their seats, exasperated. They made no protest, but they also made no move to leave the room.

"In private," Germanus said firmly.

"We have no secrets," said Arthur.

Germanus waited expectantly. The knights realized that he expected them to leave and that he and Arthur would stay. Arthur gave them a reassuring nod. Lancelot was the first to stand, although his expression was one of deep suspicion.

"Come," Lancelot said lightly to the others. "It is better that we leave Roman business to the Romans." He walked toward the door.

Bors stood up and began to follow Lancelot from the room when he thought of something. Stepping back to the round table, he hoisted the wine cask onto his shoulder, gave a small apologetic shrug to Germanus and left the room. The others stepped out behind him, each giving Arthur a penetrating look. Once all the knights were gone, Germanus swept up the discharge papers and handed them to Horton, nodding his head in dismissal. Horton took the scrolls and bowed, walking out with Squire Jols by his side.

The great hall was now empty except for Arthur,

Bishop Germanus and two Roman guards. Arthur and Germanus faced each other across the table but said nothing for a long moment. Arthur felt a prickling of dread in his stomach, knowing that what Germanus was about to say to him was bound to be unpleasant at best and tragic at worst.

Finally, Bishop Germanus took a deep breath and said, "Rome has issued a final order for you and your men."

Arthur looked confused. "Final order?" he said. "Their term is up. You came here with the papers that would free them. What do you mean, 'final order'?"

Germanus smiled consolingly. "I am devastated to be the bearer of sad tidings. But please understand, Arthur, this request comes directly from the Pope himself."

Arthur smiled sardonically. "Request?" he said.

Bishop Germanus returned the smile. "His Holiness makes this request of you," he said, "very earnestly."

Arthur continued to stare at Germanus suspiciously, but for the moment he was prepared to listen to what Germanus had to say. An order from the Pope could not be taken lightly, even if it was inherently unjust. Germanus recognized Arthur's look of suspicion and impatience, and realized that he had better start talking. Looking down at the table and aimlessly shuffling some papers, he said, "You are to travel north to rescue the family of Marius Honorius . . . "

The words hit Arthur like a slap in the face.

Germanus continued, " . . . and return—in particular—with Marius's son, Alecto. He is of paramount importance. For that, there were those in Rome who would kill him. So he was sent to Britain for safety. We had hopes of protecting the family with a small legion, but they would be no match for the Saxon army. I believe that Marius has his own company of mercenaries, and you may find them useful should trouble arise on the way back."

Bishop Germanus paused, wondering how Arthur was taking this. Arthur simply stared back at him without expression.

"Alecto is the Pope's favorite godchild and pupil," Germanus continued. "Like you, he is a young man of immense promise. It is his destiny to become a bishop. It is not inconceivable that he might even become Pope one day. And I am to be his teacher, patron—guide, if you will—on his path to the papal seat."

Arthur felt as if the breath had been knocked from his chest. He had never trusted Germanus, but had never realized until now how deep the bishop's ambition ran. Worse, he now knew that this ambition had led him to deceive Arthur's knights. His men were so close to freedom, and now . . . this. Arthur said quietly, but with steel in his voice, "How do I go to those brave men and tell them that now instead of freedom I offer death? They who have risked their lives fighting for a cause that was never their own?"

"Do not make things more difficult than they are, Arthur," Bishop Germanus said. "If your men are truly the knights of legend, this should be no more than a final adventure for them before the tedium of freedom." He shrugged. "And if the worst were to come to pass . . . well, perhaps some of them will survive. If it is God's will."

Arthur seethed with anger, all the more bitterly because he recognized how much Germanus was enjoying this.

"Your men want to go home," Bishop Germanus said. "And to get home they need to cross the entire breadth of the Roman Empire. Deserters would be hunted down like dogs. In the name of God, of course."

Arthur muttered in disgust, "In the name of God . . . "

"Will you defy the Pope, Arthur?" Germanus said, smiling kindly. "Rome . . . ? God himself . . . ?"

Arthur said bitterly, "You question my faith? I would not defy my God." He glared at Germanus. "Do not mistake a loyal soldier for a fool," Arthur said. "It is a common mistake of politicians."

Germanus stiffened at the title "politician" and girded himself to remain in control. He stood and pointed at Arthur. "Would you leave a defenseless Roman boy, destined to lead our church, in the hands of the Saxons?" he said.

This point hit Arthur hard.

Arthur said, "Where do these orders come from?"

Bishop Germanus replied, "As I told you before, they come from the Holy Father himself."

"Am I to believe that the Holy Father would betray my men, turn his back on his own promises?" Arthur said.

Bishop Germanus looked at him sternly. "Beware, Artorius Castus," he said, "that you do not add blasphemy to insubordination."

Arthur said quietly, "It is not I who blaspheme."

"Do this, Arthur," Germanus said, earnestly. "It will please the Pope. You will save a valuable young man." He smiled grimly. " . . . and you have no other choice."

Arthur looked away, filled with fury and despair.

Bishop Germanus said, "Fulfill this mission and your men will receive their discharge. Their papers will be waiting here the moment they return. You have my word."

Arthur stood and looked hard into Germanus's eyes. "Keep your word," he said in a low voice, "or I will have your head."

Germanus wheeled around and left the room, followed by the two Roman guards. Arthur, alone at the round table, looked around him at the empty seats. The wine that had been spilled on the floor for the lost knights now looked to Arthur like blood. Arthur gazed around the wall at the old battle standards—ragged and stained, the flags clearly showed the history of the horrendous fighting they had survived.

Arthur closed his eyes and prayed, "Are you here tonight, God of my father? Or have you deserted this island just as Rome has?"

The wind moaned through the drafty hall as if it were the voice of an angered God.

"Fill me with your strength, my God," Arthur said desperately. "In battle, be it Your hand and mine on Excalibur—help me to vanquish all who stand in the way of that freedom my knights so justly deserve."

Outside the fortress, near the hall, there was one, besides God, who heard Arthur's prayer. Dagonet sat unnoticed on the ground, legs stretched out before him, leaning up against a tree, like a loyal guard dog on watch. Dagonet was a simple man who could not understand exactly why Arthur was praying, but for some reason unknown even to him, he was comforted by the fact that Arthur prayed. Indeed, if Dagonet had known how, he would have begun praying himself.

SIX

❧

THE KNIGHTS HAD GATHERED IN A WIDE open yard of the fortress, around a bonfire that blazed furiously in the center. Blocks of stones had been strewn about in an irregular pattern and were being used as seats. All the knights were present, but Arthur was nowhere to be seen. For the moment, no one noticed his absence. A number of women moved around the bonfire, serving the men wine and food.

By unspoken agreement, no one talked of Bishop Germanus or the precious papers he carried—or the sense of foreboding they had all felt as they left him alone with Arthur. Until they heard differently, it was a night like any other night, to be spent drinking, gambling and frolicking with willing ladies—of which there was always an ample supply.

Just beyond the circle of light a small mob of children mingled, looking at the knights expectantly and jabbering with excitement. Several of them bore a distinct resemblance to Bors. Taking notice of them, Bors grabbed an armful of bread and stepped up to the little group of children, who immediately fell silent upon his approach. He studied them genially. One of the older children, a boy named Augustus, pushed his way to the front of the crowd.

"Father," Augustus said, "let's have some of that bread!"

Bors seemed to consider the request. "Have you been good?" he asked.

"Yes!" Augustus replied enthusiastically.

Galahad passed by and said to Bors, "Don't just feed your own bastards."

Bors smiled and said, "And how would I know which ones are mine?" He turned back to the children and shouted, "Have all you bastards been good?"

The children cried, "Yes! Yes!"

Bors tossed the loaves into the crowd as if they were game balls. A couple of the children immediately took huge bites out of the crusts and chewed enthusiastically. But most of the children who caught the loaves clutched the bread to their chests and ran home. This night, unlike many others, there would be supper for the family.

Pleased with his own generosity, Bors sat down next to Vanora, the woman who currently served him as something like a wife. She was tall and handsome, her breasts still heavy with milk for her new son. Bors had met her in another village about a year and a half earlier when he and the knights were on a mission. He found it impossible to resist her flirtatious manner, and she his, and they consummated their courtship about an hour after meeting. It did not escape Bors's notice that Vanora was similarly flirtatious with most of the other knights, and he had no idea how many other courtships she consummated during their brief time in her village.

But when she returned to the Hadrian's Wall fortress with Bors and later gave birth to a son she insisted was his, he chose to be philosophical and accept the child as his own. Now the baby sat happily on Vanora's lap, cooing and drooling. When Bors arrived, he reached over, pulled the laughing child to his own knee and began bouncing him enthusiastically —if a bit roughly. Vanora gave Bors a heavy, lingering kiss and a penetrating look filled with erotic promise, then got up and began to meander languidly across the yard.

Nearby, Lancelot was throwing dice with a pair of Roman guards. As Vanora passed, she gave Lancelot a flirtatious look similar to the one she had just given to Bors. Lancelot immediately responded with a knowing smile. Bors saw the exchange and suspiciously began checking the baby for any resemblance to Lancelot.

Gawain and Galahad sat on top of a table, taking

turns hurling knives at a target stuck to the top of another, overturned, table. Galahad hit within inches of center.

Tristran was carving an intricate arrowhead. His hand ran with thin streams of blood from the sharp edges. Just beyond, Jols happily watched the knights' fun from a respectful distance while Horton stood against the wall, moping over the fact that he was not in the inner chamber, beside Bishop Germanus.

The knights were drunk and happy, celebrating their impending freedom. Gawain threw his knife with such force and precision that he hit the center of the target and knocked it off the table.

"How on earth do you do that, Gawain?" Tristran asked, impressed.

Gawain replied, "I simply use the gifts the gods gave me."

Bors spoke to the baby, making fun of Gawain. "See him? Never changes. Stark raving mad, he is." He bounced the baby a little more, then admitted, "Great warrior, though, huh?"

Galahad looked sideways at his friend with mock suspicion and said, "He doesn't drink." He hurled his knife again, completely missing the target. "I don't trust men who don't drink."

Gawain laughed. "You don't trust men who do drink," he said. "You don't trust anyone."

Suddenly, their attention was drawn to Lancelot's game across the yard. One of the Roman guards threw down the dice in disgust. "You cheating Sarmatian scum!" he growled to Lancelot.

The two Romans reached for their daggers but Lancelot's twin swords instantly cleared leather and were pressed to the Romans' throats. A third Roman started to step forward in support of his friends. Galahad deftly took hold of his sword and cornered him. The look in his eyes told the Roman that Galahad was ready to kill at the slightest provocation. Lancelot pressed the tip of one of his blades to the throat of the guard who had accused him. "Speak . . . I beg you," he said, smiling an icy smile. "Speak . . . so I can cut your heart out and eat it."

Galahad, drunk and dangerous, slurred, "I . . . I would love to kill a Roman before leaving this stinking hell."

Looking on, as if enjoying a theatrical performance, Bors casually poured himself another drink, careful not to spill any of the precious wine on the child. "Ah, I wouldn't tangle with them," he said to the Romans. "Those are irritated free men who point those blades now. Nothing quite as dangerous as a free man."

Dagonet walked past the Roman who trembled at the point of Galahad's sword. With barely a glance in his direction, Dagonet punched the Roman to the ground. He turned to Galahad with an apologetic shrug. "Didn't want to spoil your fun," he said. "The Roman dog was just in my way." Galahad began sputtering with laughter and was immediately joined by the other knights. Aware that the dangerous tension in the air had been dissipated by the act, the other two Romans dragged their unconscious friend away from the bonfire.

Dagonet took a seat beside Bors and the baby. As Dagonet poured a drink, Bors punched him in the head affectionately but painfully hard. "Where have you been?" Bors said. "We have details and plans to work out for the new life tomorrow!"

As he talked to Dagonet, Bors held a small dagger in his right hand, jabbing at him at the same time that he slapped at him with his left hand. Dagonet poured some wine and leaned back and drank, acting like a horse that barely notices the annoying fly.

Bors leaned in close to Dagonet's ear and said loudly, "Can you hear me?"

With a long, sloppy swallow, Dagonet finished his drink and wiped his mouth with the back of his arm. "Not much of a choice, is there?" he said.

Dagonet stood up and, leaving behind his bothersome friend, walked over to Lancelot, who was surveying the scene with great amusement. His face darkened, however, when he saw the knight coming toward him; Dagonet looked as though something was troubling him. "Dagonet," Lancelot said. "Is all well?"

Dagonet sidled up beside Lancelot and whispered to him seriously, "Arthur comes."

After so many years together, the knights could read each other expertly. Dagonet had to say no more to let Lancelot know that when Arthur arrived, the news he brought would not be good. Lancelot looked past Dagonet to see Arthur approaching the clearing and immediately signaled his men with a clap and a whistle. The revelry of the evening ended instantly as the knights sprang up in immediate response to Lancelot's signal. Bors gestured to Vanora, who rushed up to him to take the baby from his arm. Jols went about ridding the clearing of women, children and anyone who was not in the inner circle. Each of the knights, as well as their faithful squire, acted as one on their leader's signal, without hesitation.

The knights gathered around Arthur, listening intently. Bors and Gawain exchanged grins, gleefully anticipating receiving their discharge papers.

Arthur gazed somberly at the faces of his friends, but his own expression betrayed no emotion. After a pause he said, "We leave at first light."

The men looked at each other in confusion.

Lancelot said, "Leave?"

Arthur nodded. "Our final mission for Rome will take us far above the wall, where there is a Roman family in need of rescue," he said.

At first, the knights thought they had heard wrong and continued to gape at Arthur as if he had been speaking French. But as Arthur remained silent, his statement began to sink in.

"Sorry. Must be drunk," Bors said. "I thought you said we leave for a mission tomorrow."

"That's right," Arthur said. "You had better get some sleep while you can."

Gawain took a step closer to Arthur. "Above the wall?" he said. "That is Woad territory!"

"Roman bastards!" Bors snarled loudly.

Lancelot cautioned him with a menacing tone in his voice, "Bors!"

Bors scowled, his good-natured demeanor lost for the moment. He threw his wine mug as hard as he could, smashing it against a stone wall.

"Bors is right! We are free men now," Galahad said. "We are done with our duty here . . . if it ever was a duty. A pact we made with Rome against our will—solemn and sacred and a load of shit!"

Bors said angrily, pointing to Arthur, "Round table! Equality! I don't see a round table—I see a long table with him at the head of it." He stood nose to nose with Arthur, who looked back at him calmly. "How many of us have died for your bloody Rome?" Bors said. "Every knight in this place has laid his life down for you. And now instead of our freedom, all you give us is more death—because Roman blood means more to you than ours!"

"We have our orders," Arthur said, quietly but firmly. "We are knights. And when we return, your discharges of freedom will be here for you."

"But why?" said Gawain.

Arthur patiently explained, "There are innocent people, a family, trapped in the north. They need to be brought out or they will die."

Bors spat on the ground and said, "Let the Romans protect their own against the Saxons!"

Tristran turned to Bors and said, "We are all going to die someday. If it is death at the hands of a Saxon that frightens you—stay here."

Bors pointed at Arthur. "He frightens me!"

"If you are so eager to die," Galahad said to Tristran with a snarl, "you can die right here! Some of us have something worth living for."

"A noble death in battle," Tristran said quietly. "That is worth living for."

Galahad seemed on the verge of lunging at Tristran, but Gawain restrained him with a touch on his arm. All around, the knights seemed about to explode, as if they were ready to take out their anger and frustration on each other since they could not punish the entire Roman Empire.

"Enough!" Lancelot shouted. The knights stood in a circle around Arthur, glaring at each other.

Dagonet, whose stare had never left Arthur, walked directly up to him. Face to face, he was an imposing figure, even to Arthur. He zeroed in on Arthur's eyes. "The Romans have broken their word," Dagonet said. "Do we have the word of Arthur?"

Everyone waited for his response. Arthur returned Dagonet's look with respect and honesty. "Yes," Arthur said. "You have my word."

That was enough for Dagonet. "I will prepare," he said.

As Dagonet crossed the yard to return to his

quarters, he passed Bors and stopped. "Are you coming . . . ?" he asked.

Bors, frustrated that he just could not keep himself from following Arthur, shouted angrily, "Of course I am bloody coming!" Slightly embarrassed, he looked to the other knights to explain his outburst. "Just speaking my mind, is all," Bors said. "It is a round table, is not it?"

Arthur said, "Anyone else?"

No one responded.

Arthur nodded. "All right then," he said. "We leave at dawn." He turned and left the yard. Lancelot watched him go, then turned to the knights and said, "Now, you heard your commander. Finish your wine and report to the armory."

Lancelot followed Arthur. As Bors and Dagonet made their way to the armory, they passed the Roman soldier who was semiconscious from Dagonet's blow. Bors's frustration and fury at the situation erupted at the sight of him and he began to pound the Roman back into oblivion.

Dagonet stood behind Bors and held onto his upper arms, pulling him gently away. "I know how you feel, friend," he said as he led Bors toward the armory, "but it ain't his fault." They walked away to gather weapons for the new mission, leaving the legionnaire stunned and hurt, his blood pouring onto the ground.

SEVEN

❦

ARTHUR WAS DEEP IN THOUGHT, GROOMING his war horse when Lancelot walked into the stable and stood near the door. For a moment the two friends remained silent.

Finally, Lancelot said, "Pray—to whomever you pray—that we do not cross the Saxons."

"My faith is my strength, Lancelot," Arthur said. "Why do you challenge this?"

Lancelot said, "I do not like anything that puts a man on his knees."

Arthur stopped brushing his horse and looked hard at Lancelot. "A man does not fear to kneel before the god he trusts," he said. "Without faith, without belief in something, what are we?"

Lancelot preferred not to get into a theological

discussion, so he tried again to get back to the practical matter at hand. "To try and get past the Woads in the north is insanity," he said.

"We've fought before," Arthur said quietly. "We've beat them before." He stopped brushing. "In this situation," he said, "the Woads are not the biggest problem we have."

Realization dawned in Lancelot's eyes. "The Saxons?" he asked in a whisper. Arthur merely looked at him. "How many Saxons will there be?"

Arthur's silence was his answer. Lancelot's shoulders fell as the enormity of the mission began to sink in. He put a hand on Arthur's shoulder and looked him straight in the eye.

"Answer one question," Lancelot said. "Do you believe in this mission?"

Arthur said in an even, noncommittal voice, "These people need our help. It is our duty as soldiers to bring them out."

"I don't care about your charge," Lancelot said angrily, "and I don't give a damn about Romans, Britons or this island." He waved his arm at the land outside and continued, "If you desire to spend eternity in this place, so be it, Arthur. But suicide cannot be chosen for another!"

Arthur said, his voice rising in anger, "And yet you choose death for this family!"

"Damn this family!" Lancelot said.

Arthur's face softened. "They are more important than you know."

Lancelot looked at him questioningly.

"If this family is not saved," Arthur said, "Germanus will deny your freedom. You will not be released. No one will be released!"

Lancelot looked stunned at the magnitude of this news. He turned and walked to the door of the stable and looked out at the night. Arthur walked over to him and spoke again with a tone in his voice that was close to pleading; he was desperate to make his friend understand. "Lancelot, tell me . . . , " Arthur said, " . . . what other purpose do we serve?"

Cynric's army was cast in the deep orange glow of the British village they had just set ablaze. All around the chaotic scene, amid the dreadful moans of the dying and the frantic screams of women and children whose men were being dragged away in chains, Saxon soldiers and engineers swarmed, going about their grim business. Supplies were being landed—rations, swords, racks of crossbows. Cynric's lieutenant Raewald and six of his officers flanked Cerdic as gray-clad swordsmen marched past. Cerdic strode forcefully ahead, always making sure that he kept the officers on his flanks. Raewald was very conscious of this arrangement.

In the center of the village, Cerdic sat on a stone, surrounded by his bodyguards. No matter how many times he experienced the conquering of a village, he never tired of the many fascinating aspects exhibited there. He watched with great interest as the men of fighting age were separated from their families. He loved seeing the women and children herded, screaming and kicking, into a cattle pen as Saxon warriors stood guard around the wooden palisade to make certain none escaped. And the sight of all those burning buildings, the roaring flames reaching up to the sky, seemed the perfect illustration of total victory. Others might prefer a theatrical performance or to make love to a beautiful woman. But this, to Cerdic, was the greatest show on earth, the keenest pleasure he could imagine.

Even over the din of a myriad of violent activities, Cerdic was startled to hear horrified screams coming from nearby. Curious, he motioned for one of his officers to come forward. Leaning over, the officer whispered in Cerdic's ear. Livid, Cerdic immediately jumped to his feet and stalked over past the cattle pen. Four Saxon infantrymen were huddled there, bent over, apparently watching something of great interest. From the nature of their goading and cheering, Cerdic had no problem guessing what it was they were enjoying. As soon as the soldiers noticed their commander's approach, they parted. Just in front of them on the muddy ground, a bodyguard was lying atop a screaming village girl, holding her tiny wrists together with one strong hand while ripping off the bodice of her dress with the other.

Furious, Cerdic grabbed the back of the guard's

tunic and pulled him off the girl, flinging the guard to the ground.

Cynric rushed to the scene, flanked by his own pair of tough-looking bodyguards. The man who had been trying to rape the village girl stood up, angry at having been interrupted in his pleasure. The girl, cut and bleeding, hugged Cerdic's leg and wept in grateful supplication.

Angrily, Cerdic shouted to the guards, "We do not touch their women!"

The village girl, weeping, said, "God's thanks, my lord . . . "

Cerdic looked down upon her with repulsion and shook her off his leg. "To mix with these people would be like a plague upon our own," he said. "Unlike Rome, we must remain immune. That is why Rome falls. It is why we will not."

The would-be rapist stormed up behind Cerdic. He was heated by passion and not very steady on his feet, due to an excess of wine that he had liberated from one of the village's casks. The man was nearly a giant and had only recently joined Cerdic's army. But he had been a soldier for much of his life and he knew the rules that the conquering army lived by. "According to our laws," he said to Cerdic in a slightly slurred voice, "no man may deny me the spoils . . . "

Cerdic slowly turned around, focusing a fierce and terrifying gaze upon the Saxon soldier. The effect of that stare immediately sobered him.

"No man may deny you?" Cerdic said quietly. "I am no *man*." With a single rapid, fluid movement, Cerdic pulled out his sword and ran the soldier through. He fell to the ground with a crash, writhing and spitting blood, looking up at Cerdic in total confusion. In a moment, the expression left his eyes and he lay still.

Cerdic said nothing else but he scanned the faces of the other men. His own expression clearly asked, "Anyone else?" Cynric, Raewald and their men watched their commander in silent respect and fear.

"Are there any more of you," Cerdic said, "not strong enough to forego a moment's temptation for the future of our kind?"

Cynric stepped forward and said, "Yet you kill our own kind?"

Cerdic looked around at his men, then back to his son. He smiled darkly and then said, "The tongue of a child." He pulled his son close in a parody of a fatherly embrace. The tension was released and the men laughed.

Patting Cynric on the shoulder, Cerdic said to his son, "Walk with me . . . "

As soon as they were out of earshot of the army, Cerdic said, "If you question my tactics ever again, I will kill you. I will gut you like a pig."

Cynric said desperately, "I am your own son —your own blood."

Cerdic replied evenly, "I will spill your blood—

the blood of my own, as I spilled the blood of my own father."

Cynric just stared at his father in shock.

Cerdic said, "Hear me well," and then walked away and sat down again, alone. Cynric was so incensed, embarrassed and frightened that he could not manage to move a muscle. For a long time he stood on the spot like a statue, glaring at his father with hate-filled eyes.

The next day, the army moved on to another small British village. Some of the Saxon soldiers unloaded equipment while others went about the work of kidnapping village men to serve in their ranks. Cynric had reluctantly joined his father again, still angry at the way he had been treated the day before but still eager to make his father respect him. While halfheartedly supervising the troops, Cynric looked up to see a British scout moving slowly toward Cerdic, being pushed along by Raewald.

The scout made his report to the commander: "We are two days from the Roman estate if we camp one night."

Cerdic shook his head and said, "Then we do not camp. As Roman royalty, their ransom will pay for our southern invasion." He turned to his son. "Where is your tracking dog?"

Cynric called out, "Come, Briton!" He gestured and a muscular, weathered British scout named Geoffrey trotted over to stand beside Cynric. Cerdic said, "What can we expect between here and the estate —besides the Woads?"

Geoffrey pointed to a drawing of Hadrian's Wall on a map drawn in the dirt and said, "I would expect trouble from this direction."

"The wall?" Raewald said to Geoffrey. "What troops are stationed there?"

Geoffrey replied, "Well, mostly inexperienced Roman infantry." He hesitated. "And possibly . . . "

"Speak up, beast!" snarled Cynric.

"Sarmatian knights," Geoffrey said reluctantly. "Arthur Castus is their leader."

Cerdic looked up sharply at the mention of Arthur's name.

Cynric noticed his father's reaction and asked, "And who is this Arthur?"

"A warrior of great fame. It is said he and his knights have never been defeated in battle," Geoffrey said. "It is said . . . "

This comment was lost on Cynric but immediately piqued Cerdic's interest. He obliterated the map in the dirt with a swipe of his boot and said with satisfaction, "Arthur Castus." Cerdic nodded. "When I kill him, my fame on this island will rise."

Cynric pointed to a group of young women as they were being herded through the filthy village street. "Are we taking all those girls with us?" he asked his father.

"Yes," Cerdic said, "we are taking them with us.

But the others . . . kill them. All. Make ashes of every village along the way."

"But they seem utterly unable to field an army against us . . . " Cynric began.

Cerdic said, "We must bring a war down upon them so terrible, so horrible, they will flee and hide rather than fight. To conquer this land, our victory here must not last a day—it must last for centuries . . . "

"But what of the Romans?" Cynric asked.

"Our enemy is the land and the people of the land, whoever they may be," Cerdic replied. "Take their hope, and this land is ours. The Romans will fall, in time."

By dusk, the Saxon army was prepared to evacuate the village. In their midst were Cerdic and Cynric, flanked by bodyguards and led by the British scout. "I had a vision," Cerdic said, "in a dream, that he who would rule this land would bring his enemies death by the sword and by fire." Cynric turned to his father and raised a short sword in salute.

Cerdic leaned into Cynric and spoke, his voice a snarl. "Now cleanse this earth!" he said.

At Cynric's command, dozens of torches were heaved into the huts by Saxon soldiers. Swordsmen went about finishing off any remaining villagers. Amid the flames and the screams of the dying women and children, the Saxon army double-timed away from the holocaust. Behind them, in the deepening dusk of this bloody day, the raging fire of the village turned white hot.

EIGHT

IN THE FORTRESS AT HADRIAN'S WALL, THE
stable doubled as an armory. The knights had
already seen to their horses and now had set about the
task of packing and cleaning their weapons. A dark
cloud of unspoken words hung over the room. The
overriding air was not one of despair, precisely, but the
giddiness the knights had felt earlier in the day had
given way to a bitter pessimism. The danger of the
bishop's order was not lost on any of them. To be so
close to freedom and then to have it snatched away and
replaced by a mission that would certainly kill some of
them was the most serious of betrayals.

Each of the men clearly showed his disgruntle-
ment. But more important, they were disciplined and
brave, dedicated to shouldering responsibility and
completing the tasks that had been laid before them,

even at the cost of their own safety. If the men felt fear or sorrow at the thought that their lives might soon be ending, it was not acceptable for them to exhibit it. For the moment, their expressions were impassively grim. No one spoke; they just did their jobs with efficient thoroughness. Soon enough, they would work their way back to their normal state of raucous, good-natured roughhousing.

Arthur walked into the armory/stable. Because he had turned over his quarters to Bishop Germanus, his weapons, bedding and other belongings still lay in the corner of his horse's stall where Jols had laid them upon the knights' return earlier that day. He saw at a glance that Jols had already repacked everything neatly. The young squire noticed that Arthur's horse was already groomed. He knew that Arthur always saw to that chore himself. Arthur believed that there was a special bond between a warrior and his steed. If the man expected loyalty and bravery from the animal, then he himself must serve that animal, feeding it, brushing it, nursing it when sick or wounded.

Arthur had brought in a handful of small carrots and fed them to his large, black charger, one by one, all the while gently patting the long, wide flank of its neck and murmuring softly. The magnificent horse reared and snorted, eager for action.

None of the knights acknowledged Arthur, and he was content to allow each of them time to come to terms with the inequity of Bishop Germanus's mission in his own way.

Arthur watched with curiosity as Lancelot pulled back the canvas on an old crate and passed his hand over the ornate face of a huge body shield. Arthur had never seen a shield like it—it was completely unlike any gear the knights normally carried, and Arthur wondered where Lancelot had found it.

Out of the corner of his eye, Arthur saw Dagonet suddenly heft his huge war axe and stride across the room toward him with purpose. Arthur braced himself; his first instinct was to reach for Excalibur in the fleeting belief that Dagonet had turned on him and was about to attack. But Dagonet simply walked past, without even glancing at Arthur. Feeling strangely breathless, Arthur leaned up against the cool wall of the stable, wondering how he could have suspected his friend, even for a split second.

Arthur stepped out into the middle of the stable and called his men to his side. "Keep it simple," he said, as they gathered around him. "We will have no need for Sarmatian battle gear—it would only slow us down. We will be traveling light and fast. Through the forest and fast up this pass. We will outdistance our Woad friends and head straight to the estate."

Tristran said, "That should take three or four days, I think."

Arthur nodded. "Three days of hard riding. With good luck, we will grab these people, keep out of the Saxons' way and ride straight back to the Wall."

Lancelot said with a grim smile, "And with our

usual luck . . . " Arthur and Lancelot locked eyes with each other for a moment. There was anger in both of their expressions, but Arthur realized that the anger had different colorings for each of them. There was something like betrayal in Lancelot's eyes. Arthur's own expression was tinged with sadness; he was heartbroken that his friend seemed to hate him, though he knew it was only temporary. They had never split before, even on trivial matters. It made Arthur terribly uncomfortable to think of them going on a mission together while feeling this kind of animosity. Even so, Arthur knew—prayed—that it would not last long. Their bond had been forged with blood. It ran so deep and wide through both of their hearts that Arthur considered it unbreakable. The alternative did not even seem like a realistic opportunity. He knew they would heal this rift sooner or later, that their friendship would soon be totally restored.

After a long moment, they broke their gaze and Lancelot turned away, covering the shield back up as if it were more precious than gold.

Silently, Dagonet walked back across the stables and continued to pack his gear. Then, the rest of the knights followed suit, sharpening blades, checking the strings on their bows, loading small bags with loaves of bread and round cheeses wrapped in cloth.

Squire Jols wrapped up huge bundles of arrows to load on a packhorse. He also made sure he packed extra knives and swords, in case one of his knights had a sudden need in the midst of battle.

Suddenly, Bishop Germanus entered the stable, closely followed by Horton. Germanus could not keep the expression of distaste from his face. It was clear that he considered Arthur and his knights to be a gang of ruffians, without breeding, without honor—and certainly without the proper religious beliefs. He looked around at them with a kind of disgusted foreboding, as if he had stepped into the midst of some club of thugs and killers.

Arthur stepped out of his horse's stall to greet the bishop. Germanus gestured dismissively toward Horton and said, "To represent the holy court, my trusted secretary will accompany you on your quest." Horton had a queasy look on his face, clearly dismayed to be forced into this highly undesirable situation.

For their part, the knights simply stared at Horton with a mixture of suspicion and amusement. There was no doubt in any of their minds that Horton was coming along for one reason only: to serve as Germanus's spy.

Arthur's face expressed nothing to suggest to Germanus that he thought Horton was a fool—as was the bishop. Instead, he smiled politely and then said, "Jols, find him a horse."

In the stall behind him, Arthur's charger gave a sudden ferocious snort and Horton leaped backward, startled.

Jols smiled and shook his head. "Oh, no, no, no,"

he said, "this is Arthur's battle horse. You can't have him." Jols took Horton by the arm. "Now this one over here, on the other hand . . . "

He led Horton to a dark stall in a corner. At first it looked as if the stall was empty. But suddenly, a huge, brown monster materialized out of the gloom. The horse was as still as death, his black eyes portholes to oblivion. If he had been a human, Horton thought with a shiver of dread, he would be in a madhouse.

Horton looked at the horse with open terror. "Uh . . . lovely!" he squeaked.

Galahad strolled over and said heartily, "You should be honored. This great horse was once the mount of a famous and courageous knight."

Horton nodded enthusiastically, trying his hardest to appear to be as brave as the knights themselves. "I am . . . I am honored!" Horton stammered.

Arthur turned back to his knights and said, "Now that we all have suitable mounts, we had better be on our way, my friends." Each of the knights finished packing their saddlebags, flung them over the backs of their horses, then mounted.

Arthur looked over at Lancelot. Now, as always, he wanted them to move and work as a unit. Lancelot returned Arthur's gaze with a sardonic look that said, *Well . . . ?* Arthur considered for a moment, and then snapped his reins, moving his huge black steed forward.

As the knights rode past him and left the stable, Bishop Germanus raised his arm in blessing. "Godspeed as you fulfill your duty to Rome," he said.

Arthur replied without looking at him, "My duty is to my men."

Bishop Germanus smiled and nodded, every inch the caring clergyman. As the knights disappeared into the predawn darkness, he called after them, "Then get them home!"

Miles away, a Woad scout stepped slowly through the still-smoldering British village, straining his ears for any sign that the monsters who had done this horrible thing were still in the area, or that any of the poor Britons who faced those monsters were still alive. Everywhere he turned, he saw nothing but devastation, the horrible aftermath of a Saxon attack. Every human and animal in sight was dead. Every building was burned. The fields beyond were scorched. Sickened, the scout knelt beside a mutilated victim. It was a young woman, her face frozen forever in an agonized scream. Her arm was outstretched to the side. Just inches from her bloody fingers was a baby, the side of its skull still bearing the indentation made by the boot heel that had crushed it. The scout pulled a dagger out of the lifeless body and looked at it closely, his eyes stinging with tears and with fury. The dagger was adorned with Saxon symbols. The scout sat down in the dirt beside the dead British woman and held the blade. His hands shook violently with anger, with horror and with a burning lust for revenge.

In a somber single file, the knights rode out the fortress gates. At the base of Badon Hill, above the fortress and Hadrian's Wall, they passed by hundreds of graves, each a large mound with a sword buried in it to the hilt—two hundred years' worth of monuments to the Sarmatians who had given their lives for the Roman Empire.

Jols and Horton brought up the rear of the column, riding side by side. As they passed the graveyard, Jols bowed his head in silent respect. Horton watched him curiously and said, "What is this place?"

"Badon Hill," Jols explained. "It is the holy resting place of all Sarmatian knights who died in Britain." Horton glanced over at the cemetery, not quite understanding why Jols seemed to be so impressed with the place. He wondered how holy could it be, if there were no Roman soldiers buried there.

As the knights passed the gloomy place, just becoming lit by the first weak rays of the sun, each man gazed silently at the cemetery. The same thought was in each of their minds, as it was nearly every time they came by Badon Hill. Each knight was wondering if he, too, was doomed to spend eternity in Britain, lying forever among this multitude of forgotten warriors.

They approached the mighty gate of Hadrian's Wall. No longer in single file, the knights rode seven across, with Horton and Jols still bringing up the rear. Over the distant hills, lightning flashed and the low growl of thunder rumbled over the plain. It was, Horton thought, an ominous start for the day—and for their journey.

After riding silently for a while, Arthur looked over at the glowering Lancelot and said, "Out with it."

Lancelot continued to look straight ahead as he said, "You know where I stand." Arthur looked at him without expression. Lancelot continued, "It will not affect my loyalty."

At the back of the group, Horton asked no one in particular, "What are the chances of encountering more blue men?"

Galahad said, "Are you a wagering man?"

Horton hesitated, worried lest such information should make its way back to Germanus. "On occasion," he admitted.

Galahad nodded. "Bet all you own; all you can steal," he said.

Bors, seeing that there was fun to be had in spooking Horton, said in an eerie voice, "In the north, in those mountains, trees speak. Beasts converse with men. Mountains become monsters by night. And the dead walk."

It worked. Horton shook with fright, but desperately tried to maintain his composure. "Your swords seem to work well enough," he said hopefully.

Jols replied, "That is because Arthur's sword has pagan magic. Excalibur. He tore it from a stone."

"A stone?" Horton said, his eyebrows raised in astonishment.

Jols nodded. "Stabbed into the rock by the gods," he said. "It was the sword of his ancestor, a mighty and powerful king. Many tried to pull the sword from the stone, but each great warrior who tried it was struck dead immediately!"

Horton stared at Jols, his mouth open.

"When Arthur pulled it loose," Jols said, happy to have such a gullible listener, "fire and lightning bolts were flung all around."

The knights heard this and chuckled to themselves, careful not to let Horton hear their ridicule.

Lancelot said to Arthur, smiling in spite of himself, "Pulled Excalibur from a stone?"

Arthur said nothing.

"Did you fill the boy's head with that nonsense?" Lancelot asked.

Arthur said, "I pulled it from my father's burial mound when I was a boy. That is the Sarmatian tradition."

Lancelot had heard the story before. They rode along for a few moments, then Lancelot said, "You may have learned to love from the Christ, but you learned to fight from us. Which do you suppose will be most useful on this quest?"

Arthur did not reply. His attention was focused on the huge gates of Hadrian's Wall, the gates which were about to be opened to allow the knights to pass beyond. It was a massive task—Roman guards had to swab the gargantuan hinges and bolts with large brushes dipped in animal fat. Once they were completely lubricated, one by one, the thick bolts were hammered back. Finally, four troopers urged forward two oxen, one yoked to each door and—inch by inch—they opened. Many of the villagers stopped their work to watch the great gates in motion.

Atop the Wall, Bishop Germanus stood with the fortress commander and watched the knights exit.

The commander said, "It seems with our diminishing strength, those Romans will not be much safer here than back at their estate."

Germanus said, "They will not be here for long. As soon as Arthur brings them back, we will leave immediately for Rome."

"*If* Arthur brings them back," the commander said.

Bishop Germanus smiled. "Arthur serves Rome with all his might. And I have more faith in his might than in that of any Roman 'warrior.'" He glanced at the commander, whose face flushed at the insult.

"We have been promised a relief column," the commander said. "What of them?"

"No word," Germanus said, looking straight ahead.

The commander knew that he was lying. He wondered if he and his men were the next sacrifices on the insatiable altar of Rome. Germanus's face betrayed not a hint of emotion as he crossed himself piously and then walked away.

NINE

✦

THE INSTANT THE KNIGHTS PASSED THROUGH the imposing gates of Hadrian's Wall, they immediately spurred their horses, which exploded out of the north side of the gate, galloping off across the field and into another world. Bors hung back long enough to swat Horton's maniacal horse on its flank with great force. The animal let out a terrible cry, reared, and then took off after the knights, a terrified Horton clinging desperately to its neck for his life.

They rode their steeds as hard and long as they dared before stopping briefly at a spring, where they rested and watered the horses before taking off again. They continued the pattern all day and into the night, and through the dark hours into the next morning— never stopping for camp. They rode their horses to the edge of exhaustion and paused only long enough for the steeds to regain their strength.

The horses actually seemed to thrive on the furious pace. So did the knights. As angry as they still were at having the mission thrust upon them so unfairly, the truth was that they were exhilarated by the action. With each mile they rode, they grew happier. Only the unfortunate Horton, unused to such a grueling schedule, seemed to be suffering. Each time he bumped up and down in the saddle, he moaned piteously, praying desperately for the next break, no matter how brief it might be.

Toward the end of the second day, the knights reached a forest. It was already dark within and they peered in vain, trying to see what might lie ahead of them. They pulled up to the edge as their horses panted from exertion.

Tristran looked up and down the wall of trees carefully and then said, "There!" He pointed to a barely perceptible opening about a hundred yards away. "I knew the path was close by," the scout said. "It is narrow and dark, but it will lead us through the forest."

Even the bravest of the knights looked into the forbidding tunnel with a shudder of fear, but one by one, they clucked and lightly jabbed their horses forward. Once they were inside, the forest looked even gloomier, although there was more light sifting through the trees than they had expected. The forest actually seemed to possess its own life force, to contract around the knights like a hand closing around the hilt of a dagger. Horton was openly terrified, shivering uncontrollably in his saddle. The overriding sensation was claustrophobia as the trees continued to close in around them.

Because he knew the trail, Tristran rode at the head of the company, with Lancelot and Arthur nearly side by side behind him. He turned his head slightly and said, "This would be a very good place for an ambush."

"I hope so," Lancelot replied, with forced casualness. "I'm bored already."

Bors snorted at Lancelot's bravado. "When they jump us," said Bors, "you can have my share."

Soon, the trail took a hard right and seemed to sink deeper into shadow. Tristran checked to see that his bow was loose in its holster. Behind him, each knight tensed in anticipation of whatever might emerge from the shadows. Arthur gripped the hilt of Excalibur. Lancelot drew his sword and held it near his lap, the razor-sharp tip pointing directly at the sky. Bors and Dagonet loaded darts into their crossbows. They were ready for anything.

Even this close to dusk, hazy shafts of sunlight continued to slice through the thick mist that hung in the air. The deeper the knights rode into the gloomy forest, the more eerily quiet it became. There was no sound but hoofbeats and the wind in the treetops. The

knights had their arms at the ready; nevertheless, even
the bravest of them were unnerved by the spooky surroundings. Horton rode with his eyes tightly shut,
trusting his fearsome horse to continue walking in the
right direction; indeed, the trail was so narrow and the
trees so thick on either side, he could hardly have done
otherwise.

They rounded a bend and the trail widened. In the
middle of the road ahead, strolling in their direction,
was a hunched-over old man leaning heavily on a walking stick. He wore a long cloak with a hood that hung
so low over his face that only his mouth was visible.

A thrill of nervous excitement ran up the spine of
every knight as they first spotted the stranger. Bors
said brightly, "It is nothing more than a harmless old
man." The others laughed with relief—all but Horton.

"Harmless he may be," Arthur thought to himself,
"but this is still a strange path for an old man to be
walking alone." He turned to Lancelot and said, "We
had better meet this 'harmless old man.'" The knights
stopped their horses across the path, forcing the old
man to halt as well. Galahad said loudly, "Hey, old
bear. Seen any Woads?"

The old man looked up at them and smiled, showing a mouthful of blackened, ragged teeth. He shook
his head amiably and said, "No sir, I have not. Not a
single one." He laughed a little and then he began to
continue on his way.

But the old man's response was not quite good

enough for Arthur. He drew Excalibur and held it in front of the man's face, stopping him again. "Even if you have not seen any," Arthur said, "surely they are here."

The old man shrugged.

"Where are all the Woads?" Arthur asked.

The old man looked up at Arthur and smiled again, even wider this time. "Everywhere," he said. He began to laugh even louder and repeated, choking with his guffaws, "Everywhere!" The laughter affected Arthur in an unexpected way. As the chortles continued with a glee that was somehow sinister and frightful, Arthur was filled with the sensation that the old man was looking deep inside him, learning his secrets and freezing his heart with fear. Reluctant to betray these emotions to his knights, he lifted his sword and allowed the old man to continue down the road. Without a word, Arthur continued riding in the direction they had been headed, and the knights followed.

When he was nearly out of sight, the old man straightened. Suddenly he was not nearly as ancient as he had seemed moments ago. Merlin smiled to himself and tossed his walking stick away. Farther down the path, Arthur turned his head for another look at the strange old man, but there was no one on the road, as far as the eye could see.

A cold drizzle began to fall. The knights trudged forward up a muddy slope, miserable, wet and freezing, always keeping a sharp eye on the forest around them. Lancelot felt particularly nervous for reasons he could not quite fathom. Like an angry wasp, he wove his skittish horse in and out of the line of knights. He pulled up alongside Arthur, who was eyeing the forest. Every movement caused a gut-wrenching surge—was it a deer or another old man . . . or a Woad? Arthur and Lancelot glanced at each other, aware that the other was feeling on edge. The drizzle turned into a downpour of rain. The knights lowered their heads, draped their capes over their helmets and continued to trudge forward through the ever-darkening forest.

It rained for over an hour, drenching the knights to the skin, causing each to tremble with cold. Even when the rain suddenly stopped, it did little to brighten the knights' moods. Their horses had slowed to a walk. All around, the trees swayed ominously. Or perhaps it was more than just the wind; perhaps it was something far more dangerous. The rain dripping off the leaves began to sound like nothing so much as the stealthy footsteps of a savage and unstoppable predator. The men were spooked but remained stalwart and on guard.

"If they are out there, why don't they attack?" Galahad said, aware that he was speaking in a whisper.

Gawain put a finger to his lips. "Ssshh . . . " He turned his head left and right, trying to discern shapes in the murky depths of the forest.

Dagonet's horse staggered sideways, and with some effort Dagonet steered her back to the road.

Arthur and the others looked at him with concern.

Dagonet said, "She's tired. That is all."

"Look at the load of shit she's got to lug around!" Bors said.

"As long as she stays on her feet," said Arthur.

Dagonet nodded emphatically and patted the horse on her neck. "That she will," he said.

Horton, riding among Gawain, Bors and Galahad, asked quietly, "What became of the renowned knight who owned this magnificent beast?"

"He was killed," Gawain said.

Galahad added, "Most horribly."

"I am desperate with grief," Horton said. "What great terror killed this wondrous knight?"

Bors pointed and said, "That damn horse."

Once again, Horton was terrified by Bors's words. The others somehow managed to keep a straight face.

Arthur had once again taken the lead. There was no way to get off the path, so Tristran's skills as a scout were not, for the moment, necessary. He dropped back to ride beside Gawain. Arthur led the knights into a clearing. He saw that about a hundred yards ahead the woods converged sharply, giving the clearing a funnel shape.

Arthur watched carefully. The trees swayed slightly, as if gently bandied back and forth by a soft breeze. But Arthur was suspicious. There was something about the movement that struck him as more than slightly unnatural. All the branches seemed to move in unison, rocking back and forth together, as if they were all act-ing on one command. The movement was subtle, but soon all of the knights noticed it. They stared at the trees in tense apprehension. Horton, believing that he was already as terror-stricken as was humanly possi-ble, found that there was yet another level of fear to which he could descend.

Arthur said, very quietly, "The trees."

Bors glanced at him, relieved. So it wasn't his imagination after all.

Tristran rode forward and said to Arthur in a low voice, "Woads."

Unseen by the knights, the forest was indeed occupied by dozens of Woads. Some of them were on foot, while others watched carefully from places high in the trees. All of them had been hidden from view as they traveled silently alongside the knights. As they moved forward, they tugged and pulled on strands of sinewy vine that traced up and through the trees. It was like a long, winding thread that had been sewn through branches, connecting one tree to the next.

Up ahead, more Woads tugged lightly on the vines. Like puppeteers, they made the trees do an eerie dance. They tugged and moved forward, tugged and moved forward, passing each other again and again as they tracked the knights, always moving in parallel with them, always hidden in the darkness.

Midway down the line, Merlin stood watching with his lieutenant. "When do we let loose?" the lieu-tenant asked.

Merlin answered in Gaelic and the lieutenant nodded.

The trail widened into another clearing. It looked like a safe place to the knights, but they approached with caution. If the Woads had been tracking them, as Tristran said, here was a good place to make a stand. The knights broke into the clearing and Arthur immediately whipped his horse around, facing back down the path. The others followed his lead, turning to face the enemy they were certain was about to attack.

"Dragon formation!" Arthur called out.

Galahad moved ahead to the "eyes" of the formation. Tristran and Bors dropped back to the "tail" of the dragon. The other knights fell into place, as the dragon's "body." Jols and Horton took the safest possible position, in the midst of the formation, surrounded by knights.

Suddenly, the forest became absolutely calm, with no sound but a soft wind wafting through the trees. The knights listened as closely as they could, peering into the distance, desperate for any sign of Woads. But there was nothing. After a few moments, Arthur relaxed and returned Excalibur to its sheath.

Abruptly, with a cacophony of shrill screams and blood-curdling shouts, the Woads emerged from the forest, shooting arrows from every direction. Arthur pulled Excalibur out again. He and the knights charged forward, arrows whizzing by. Woads rushed toward them on foot brandishing broadswords, crossbows and short spears.

Tristran and the others rode hard, steering their horses with their knees, firing arrows into the mass of attacking Woads as quickly as they could load and shoot. All around them, the interconnected vines shot up with precision and speed, creating a webbed blockade that prevented the knights from exiting the forest in several directions. With the army of Woads before them and the web all around them, the knights were forced back into the forest clearing, where the Woads could tightly surround them.

Deeper in the forest, as the battle sounds wafted faintly in, the wet and ragged Woad scout who had been riding for days appeared at Merlin's base camp. Merlin sat with his war council advisers, as the battle with Arthur continued a few hundred yards away in another part of the forest. The Woad dismounted and carried the Saxon dagger to Merlin. He spoke in Gaelic, telling Merlin of everything that he had seen in the ravaged British village.

Merlin closely examined the dagger. When he saw the symbols carved into it, he understood that it was a Saxon weapon. Abruptly, his expression changed.

Merlin said to his war council, "Saxon."

Immediately, his worried advisers began speaking to one another, aware that this information made a substantial change in the war they thought they were engaged in.

One of the Woad advisers said, "Romans leave and new invaders appear! What can this mean?"

The others were silent. Each of them turned to

look at Merlin, waiting for him to tell them what to do, to guide them. Merlin looked back at them without expression. "It is time," he said.

The advisers said nothing, not quite understanding what Merlin was saying.

Merlin continued, "I believe there might be a purpose for this Artorius and his knights."

To the shock of the war council, Merlin suddenly called an aide to his side. "Sound a ceasefire," he said. "End the attack now." The aide bowed, then rushed away to carry out his commander's order.

Back in the clearing, the knights killed Woads left and right, but they were clearly outnumbered. Arthur knew it was only a matter of time before their situation became dire. Then, from deep in the forest, Arthur and his men heard a distant horn sounding. Just as suddenly as it began, the attack stopped. The Woads instantly disappeared into the forest as if they had somehow become trees and leaves and vines themselves. The din of battle ceased abruptly. An eerie silence replaced it. The rain began again, first as a drizzle, then building to a torrent.

The exhausted knights simply looked at one another in shock. All the blood had drained from Horton's face; he looked as if he were about to faint. "Let's get away from this place," Arthur said. No one said a word—no one wanted to argue the point. They left the clearing and galloped forward along the path as fast as their horses could carry them.

They rode through the night and all the next day,

eating and even sleeping in the saddle. At sunset on the
second day, the knights crossed a stream and saw
before them the rugged outlines of tall, craggy mountains in the distance. The rain, which had been falling
since the Woad attack, stopped. The knights emerged
from the forest and paused on a stone-strewn beach of
a lake to allow their horses to drink. Arthur took a long
look up and down the shoreline. Before them, the
glimmering water took on the pink and orange hues of
the sunset. Behind them, the forest lay dark, silent and
foreboding. Arthur dismounted. "This looks like as
good a place as any to camp for the night," he said.

Lancelot said, "Yes. As long as we sleep with one
eye open—facing the woods."

The others got off their horses and began to prepare to camp. Jols immediately scurried to the edge of
the forest to find enough dry wood to start a fire.

Almost as a response to the gray, rainy day, the
night became brilliantly clear, the sky illuminated by
thousands of twinkling stars. The knights, often boisterous around a campfire, were subdued this night,
each deep in his own thoughts. Tristran carefully and
reverently carved simple images of personal deities
into the side of a great tree. Dagonet sat against a large
boulder, sipping water from his cup, periodically sharing it with his horse, who was clearly accustomed to
drinking with his master in this way. Bors sat close to
the fire, leaning back, aiming his bow at the stars.

Horton, used to more comfort than this stony

beach provided, occupied himself with gathering arm-
fuls of pine needles and making a nice soft bed for
himself. It had been a stressful day, and now he desired
nothing as passionately as a good night's sleep. He
spread a blanket over the pine needles and lay down,
almost groaning with pleasure as he lowered himself
onto the luxuriously soft bed. His fearsome horse stood
nearby, staring at Horton with deep, black, unflinching
eyes. As soon as Horton appeared to be drifting off to
sleep, the horse deliberately set his hoof down on a
twig. *Snap!* Horton's eyes opened in a panic. After a
moment, timing it perfectly, the horse stepped down
hard on a rotten branch. *Crunch!* Now Horton was
wide awake, trembling and staring out into the darkness, hoping to identify the next unsettling sound. He
realized, with a sinking feeling, that there would be no
sleep this night.

Lancelot lay on his back, staring at the moon.
Arthur walked over and sat beside his friend. Lancelot
pointed upward. "What is that thing?" he asked. "Is it
the afterworld? Death?"

Arthur looked at the moon, contemplating
Lancelot's questions but saying nothing.

Lancelot continued, "Is death a place? Is it a
god?"

Arthur smiled. "You won't find that out for a long
time," he said.

"I wasn't concerned for myself," Lancelot said.
He gestured toward the other knights. "I've known

these men since we took our first steps. We played together, learned to ride together." Lancelot looked at Arthur. "They've always looked to me . . . I don't know why."

"They look to you for courage, Lancelot," Arthur said.

Lancelot replied, "And to you, Arthur, they look for wisdom and righteousness. These knights will follow you anywhere, take up any cause on your whim. Die for you."

Arthur looked troubled. What Lancelot was saying was indeed true, but Arthur did not like hearing it.

"So I must ask again," Lancelot said, "is this Roman errand wise? Is it righteous?"

Arthur looked back up at the moon. "It is duty," he said.

"Arthur," Lancelot said after a moment, "you fight for a world that will never be. Never. There will always be a battlefield . . . I will die in battle. Of that I am sure. And, I dearly hope, a battle of my choosing. But if it be this one, will you grant me a favor?"

Arthur looked over at his friend.

Lancelot continued, "Do not bury me in our sad little cemetery back on Badon Hill. Burn me. Burn me and cast my ashes to a strong east wind."

Bors loaded an arrow into his composite bow. Leaning far back against a rock, he aimed carefully at the moon and fired. The eyes of the others followed the path of the arrow into the air. As it zipped off into the void, a bright shooting star illuminated the sky. Bors looked around at his fellow knights, smiling proudly at having "brought down a star" with a single shot.

The next morning, the knights continued on their journey. On this side of the forest, the countryside gradually became more harsh. Frost spread a cold, white carpet across the fields and decorated the trees with silvery shards of ice. Leaves shredded from branches in the bitter wind. Overhead, low-lying gray clouds swirled as if in caught in a tornado in the sky. It seemed to the knights that the very world itself was changing, turning into something else, an alien landscape utterly unlike the place they had left behind.

In fact, the geography *was* changing, from the flatlands behind them to the craggy hills ahead. Each day's ride became more difficult than the one before. The horses struggled up the increasingly steep slopes, sweating and gasping for air in the thinning atmosphere. Dagonet's horse particularly seemed to be straining under the weight of his master, but all of the horses struggled through the laborious ascent in a state of near exhaustion.

Finally, Arthur recognized that the horses were in danger of collapse. He ordered the men to dismount. "Walk them to rest," he said. "We are going to ride hard tonight." The knights got off their mounts and began leading them over the steep, rock-strewn slopes. Hour after hour, they struggled up the mountain until, late in the day, they arrived at the crest. Arthur reached the top first. As the others approached, he raised his hand. The exhausted knights and horses stopped, side by side, and looked down onto the expansive lowlands spread before them. Miles ahead they could see a vast estate surrounded by a wall and an outer village.

Dagonet, too tired to speak, brought up the rear on foot, his horse walking beside him.

"Is that it?" Lancelot asked.

Arthur nodded. "It is the estate of Marius and his family," he said. "The people we are sent to rescue."

Bors made a sour face and patted his tired horse. "I hope they appreciate it."

Tristran stepped up alongside Arthur. "No Woads following us," he said. "They must be worried about Saxons."

Arthur nodded gravely and said, "So are we. We have to know how close they are."

The knights remounted and crested the hill, heading down into the valley toward the estate.

TEN

✦

THE KNIGHTS APPROACHED THE OPEN gate of Marius's estate, passing men and women working the land. Sod huts dotted the forest's edge. As they passed, the startled farmers took refuge in their crude homes. In the distance came the metallic sound of an alarm, and the knights saw mercenaries rushing to man the walls. The iron gate slammed shut. The knights came to a halt. From above, they heard the shout of a captain of the guard.

"Who are you?" the mercenary called out.

Lancelot replied in a loud voice, "Roman knights!"

The mercenary captain vanished immediately. In a moment, another man appeared at the gate—corpulent and self-important. Arthur knew at a glance that he was the master of the estate, Marius Honorius.

Marius shouted, "Who are you?"

Lancelot turned to Arthur, smiling. "At least they ask easy questions," he said.

Arthur said, "I am Arthur Castus, commander of the Sarmatian knights, sent by Bishop Germanus of Rome. My men are hungry and need rest. Open the gate!"

It was as if Arthur had said the magic words. Marius's round face lit up with delight and he signaled the guards to crank up the gate at once. As the knights rode into the estate, the awestruck villagers crowded around to gawk at them.

Once inside, the knights dismounted, and Galahad and Gawain handed their reins to Jols. Jols, in turn, attempted to hand a pair to Horton, but the secretary turned up his nose haughtily at such common labor.

The knights looked around the estate. The main house was lavish, built of stone and timber in the Roman style, and spacious enough for five large families to coexist comfortably. At some distance behind was another stone building, but this one struck no one as lavish. Cold and windowless, the building looked forbidding, an impression that was amplified by the ominous presence of a gallows just outside its single door.

The children of the village crowded around the knights, grinning happily in their excitement, but it was not only the young who seemed thrilled to greet Arthur and his men. A monk grabbed Arthur's hand from his reins and kissed it, murmuring ecstatically. Arthur pulled his hand free and looked at the man in concerned astonishment, thinking the monk might be a lunatic. The other knights gathered around.

In moments, a different kind of entourage surged around them. These were servants, soldiers and, leading the pack, the master and mistress of the estate, followed by a keen-eyed boy of about twelve years of age. Marius's wife Fulcinia had clearly once been a great beauty. Now she had the bruised and frightened look of a battered woman. She stood slightly behind her husband and kept her eyes cast resolutely to the ground.

People continued to mob the knights. A few reached out to touch them as if trying to convince themselves that they were actually real. One of the monks began tugging on Bors's sleeve. "Are you from Rome?" the monk asked.

"No," Bors said. "I'm from hell. And I am taking you back with me."

The monk stared at him in alarm, wondering if Bors's words were true.

Marius clapped Arthur on the back. "It is a wonder and a miracle you have come," he said. "Did you have to fight the Woads?"

The knights merely looked at Marius until who they really were finally sank in. "Good Jesus!" he exclaimed. "Arthur and his knights!"

Arthur said, "Our orders are to evacuate you immediately."

Marius looked puzzled and shook his head. "Impossible," he said.

Arthur looked around at the crowd. "Which is Alecto?" he asked.

The handsome twelve-year-old boy pushed through the crowd and faced the knights. He bowed respectfully. "I am Alecto," he said.

Marius ignored the presence of his son; he had still not gotten past what Arthur had said about evacuation. "Everything we have is here," Marius insisted. "This land was given to us by the Pope of Rome."

Lancelot shrugged and said, "Well, you are about to give it to the Saxons, with the holy father's compliments."

Alecto looked at Lancelot sharply. It was immediately clear that he was much quicker than his father. "Saxons?" he asked.

"They have invaded from the north," Arthur said to the boy.

Marius, with a desperate edge to his voice, said, "Then Rome will send us an army!"

"They have already done so," Arthur said. "And we are it. Now, you should start to prepare immediately. We must leave as soon as you are packed."

Marius shook his head vigorously, still looking bewildered. "I refuse to leave!" he said, his voice descending into a whine. "This is my sacred commission!"

Arthur said calmly, "Let us be clear: if I fail to

bring you and your son back, my men and I can never leave this land. You are coming with me if I have to tie you behind my horse and drag you all the way to Hadrian's Wall." He bowed with mock respect. "My lord."

Bors and Dagonet were grinning widely. They always enjoyed seeing noblemen being made unhappy.

Arthur turned to Fulcinia and said, "Lady, my knights are hungry."

Fulcinia glanced at her husband, in a mute request for permission to feed the knights. Even though Marius was badly rattled by the news brought by Arthur, it was still clear that he called the shots. He glowered at the knights for a long moment, and then nodded curtly to Fulcinia and stormed away.

Fulcinia bowed to the men and said, "If you gentlemen will follow me . . ."

She turned and started walking toward the main house. The knights followed her. As they walked, an eager young villager dogged Arthur's heels. He looked to be about sixteen years old.

"You, sir, are the knight Arthur, yes?" the boy said. "I am Ganis."

Arthur ignored him and kept walking.

"I am a good fighter, and smart," Ganis said. "I would serve you proudly!"

Arthur stopped and looked at him. "You wish to serve me?" he said.

Ganis nodded eagerly, "Oh yes, sir. Oh yes!"

"Then gather the villagers together," Arthur said. "When I have eaten, I must speak with them. All of them."

Then, without another word, Arthur continued on toward the house, leaving Ganis to his task.

Deep in the forest, the Saxon soldiers under Cerdic and Cynric's command arrived at a fork in the broad trail. Geoffrey, the British scout, waited for them and the troops halted as Cerdic and his bodyguard approached the intersection. Behind them was another sacked, burning village.

Geoffrey looked up into the sky. There he saw a hawk drifting lazily above on the air currents. He had the oddest feeling that the hawk was looking at him, watching the movements of the troops. He had heard of such enchanted animals and it did not particularly surprise him that some great wizard in the area had ordered one to act as a lookout. Geoffrey resolved to be very, very careful. Finally, he pointed straight ahead. "This way is longer," Geoffrey said to Cerdic, "but easier travel."

"Ease doesn't concern me," Cerdic said. "Time concerns me."

Again, Geoffrey sensed something. This time he looked up into the trees, listening carefully. Over his head, the branches swayed in the wind. Light filtered down in a confusing array.

Tristran, Arthur's scout, hid in the trees and watched. As his hawk descended and lit on his master's arm, Tristran parted a branch for a better look below. When he did, the British scout paused, straining to hear any suspicious sound, no matter how soft. Tristran hid himself again, quickly and silently. He was very impressed at Geoffrey's keen senses. The scout was good at his job—perhaps even as good as Tristran himself.

Arthur surveyed the village outside the main gate of Marius's estate. Fulcinia had spread a lavish, if impromptu, meal for the knights, but Arthur was too keyed up to enjoy it. He took the leg of a chicken and left his knights at the table. He leaned in one of the parapets on the crenellated wall and watched as the villagers who lived on the outskirts of the estate brought in baskets of vegetables, eggs and grain. Sensing someone nearby, Arthur turned to find Alecto leaning on the wall beside him.

"I for one will be glad to see Rome again," Alecto said.

Arthur pointed toward the people in the huts. "You shut these people outside the gates every night?" Arthur said. "Where there is danger from Woad attacks?"

Alecto said, "My father assured me it is the way of our God and our mother church."

"But under which of God's laws do you treat people so?" Arthur asked.

"They are serfs," Alecto said with a shrug.

Arthur said, "I am unfamiliar with the word."

Alecto said patiently, as if talking to a child, "Serfs are people who, because of God's plan, must work their master's land. Until death."

"God's plan?" Arthur asked. "You mean, predestination?"

"Yes," Alecto said. "It is why my family came to Britain, to help put an end to this subversive ideal of free will. I am honored to believe we have had some small effect."

Arthur fought off the impulse to toss the smug little bastard off the wall. His voice grew angry. "This vile idea has now become an excuse to torment and exploit innocents?"

Arthur paused. Alecto looked shocked and confused. Arthur could see that the boy had no idea what he was talking about.

"Forgive me," Arthur said. "These are dark days, for all of us."

Without another word, Alecto ran back toward the house. Arthur turned his attention back to the village. He noted that Ganis had done his job well and had gathered most of the villagers together in the field just beyond the gates of the estate.

Arthur stepped down from the wall. Young Ganis had been watching him from a distance and immediately ran to follow Arthur as soon as he saw that he was on the move. Arthur walked through the gates and positioned himself among the villagers. Most of the peasants looked at him but dared not approach. Marius had taught them well what they could expect by failing to give the proper obeisance to their betters.

Arthur shouted, "A large and terrible army is coming this way." He paused while a frightened murmur made its way through the small crowd. "They will spare no one," he continued. "No thing. Those of you who are able should pack up and begin to move south," he pointed, "toward Hadrian's Wall."

Now the murmurs became louder and more agitated.

"Those of you who are unable to travel on your own," Arthur said, "shall come with us when we leave this place." He tried to muster an encouraging half smile. Ganis tugged at his sleeve and Arthur reluctantly turned to him.

"There is much evil here," Ganis said. "More than you may imagine. These people are plagued and cursed!"

Arthur ignored him and began to walk away. Almost immediately, he was stopped in his tracks by the sight of a craggy man in his fifties. The man's arm was stuck through a hole drilled into the trunk of a dead tree, his wrist chained on the opposite side. It was clear by his haggard, filthy appearance that he had been there for quite a while.

Arthur demanded, "Who is this man?"

"Our village elder," Ganis replied.

"Your elder?" Arthur said, outraged. "What is this punishment for?" He tugged at the chain. "Answer me!" he said.

Ganis pointed up at Marius's mansion, gathering his courage. Finally, he spoke.

"He defied our master, Marius," Ganis said.

Arthur stared at him.

Ganis said, "You are from Rome. You know the truth. Marius has told us that he is of the church and a spokesman for God. He has told us that it is a sin to defy him."

In answer, Arthur angrily whipped out Excalibur and split the trunk of the tree, freeing the elder.

Arthur turned to Ganis and said in a low, angry voice, "Marius is not of God, and you—you were free from your first breath." He stormed away, leaving a dumbstruck Ganis staring after him.

As Arthur strode back to the estate, Tristran fell into step beside him. "The Saxons have flanked us to the east," Tristran said, "and are coming from the south, cutting off our escape."

"How many?" Arthur asked. "How long until they are here?"

Lancelot stepped up to listen to Tristran's report.

Tristran said, "An entire army. They will be here before nightfall. Perhaps even sooner." He looked at Arthur with an expression of urgency. "We have to leave now," he said.

Arthur nodded grimly and said, "We must find an alternate route."

Tristran pointed into the distance. He said, "I located the start of a trail heading east. We will have to cross the path the Saxons took."

"What if there are more of them heading this way?" asked Lancelot.

"We don't have another choice," Tristran said. "It is the only way out of here."

Arthur nodded. "Then let's go."

Under an hour later, in the courtyard of the estate, Lancelot acted as an overseer, helping to get Marius's family loaded and ready to flee. Marius still protested loudly every step of the way. The knights ignored him. His wife watched him warily, knowing all too well that he might eventually turn his frustrations on her. Two mercenaries stepped carefully out of the mansion carrying a heavy crate, which they started to lift into a cart.

"Get rid of that," Lancelot demanded. "This isn't a baggage train. It will slow us down."

One of the mercenaries protested, "This is my lord's bedding."

Lancelot said, "He will sleep on the ground like the rest of us." He kicked the crate onto the ground.

Arthur was staring at the massive stone building with the gallows, lost in thought. When he heard Lancelot upbraiding the mercenaries, he turned and walked over to him. "Make sure we have all their horses," he said. "There are some villagers who will never make it out of here if they have to walk."

"Villagers?" Lancelot said, incredulous. "Those people will slow us down. Our obligation is to transport the family—that is our 'duty' to Rome!"

Arthur said, "We are honor bound to save them all if we can."

Lancelot shook his head in disgust. "Honor," he said. "A very fancy idea." He stormed away to the corral, to see if the horses were ready to go.

As the knights hurriedly organized a column of civilians, light snow flurries began to dust the ground around them. Arthur stared again at the stone building. The evacuation effort had acquired a more desperate edge as Saxon signal drums began to echo from the far distance. Everyone knew what the sound meant: They were running out of time. If they had been hurrying before, now the knights were almost frantic, shouting and herding everyone into carts and onto horses.

Arthur looked back at the stone building behind the mansion one more time, as if it were nagging at his soul. He did not know why, but the ominous structure seemed to be speaking to him in some way. Suddenly, he leaped off his horse and started running toward its massive door. Two mercenaries saw him crossing the yard and attempted to get in his way. Without slowing down, Arthur pulled Excalibur from its sheath and brandished it menacingly.

"Move!" he said to them.

The mercenaries reluctantly backed off. At the sound of Excalibur clearing leather, all of the other knights were instantly there to back Arthur up. Lancelot was first on the scene, his sword drawn as well.

Arriving at the building, Arthur saw suspicious shadings in the surface. At first he could not decide what was different about the wall. Then he realized. The door had been sealed up. He put his hand on the stone and then drew it back, wet with fresh mortar. He turned to Dagonet. "Open it up," he said. Dagonet stepped forward and heaved back with his huge battle club. He brought it down with a bone-shaking crash and blasted aside huge chunks of the new-laid stones.

Monks and mercenaries gathered to watch, disturbed looks on their faces. They glanced at one another with concern, knowing what Arthur was about to find. Dagonet continued to pound away at the stones until the wall was shattered, revealing a heavy wooden door.

Marius and his entourage stormed up to the group. The estate owner's face was red with fury. Arthur tried the door but it was locked. Lancelot put his sword to a mercenary's throat and said, "Key."

"It is locked!" the mercenary said.

Lancelot pushed the tip harder into the man's Adam's apple, causing him to wince in pain. The knight repeated, with a distinctly menacing tone in his voice, "Key!"

The mercenary sounded desperate as he said, "It is locked from the inside! There is no key!"

Dagonet smiled at the challenge. "As it happens," he said, "I have the key right here." Once again, he wielded his club and crashed through the door. With two more blows, the door splintered apart. As soon as the barrier had been knocked away, several mercenaries rushed forward, but the knights immediately swung around, swords leveled at the soldiers' chests.

Arthur immediately stepped through the door, tightly gripping Excalibur. Inside the stone building, beyond the light that came from the open door, it was so dark that Arthur could not initially tell if his eyes were open or closed. He continued to step forward carefully, allowing himself time for his eyes to become accustomed to the dark. One by one, horrifying shapes began to appear in the murk. Cells lined one side of the building, vanishing into the dark. Instruments of torture lurked in the shadows like monsters. Arthur realized that he had indeed stepped into a prison. Worse, it was a torture chamber. He was shaken by it, but continued to make his way along the corridor, slowly and carefully. Lancelot stood back reluctantly in the doorway with the others, ready to rush to Arthur's aid when needed. The stench from inside was overwhelming.

Arthur turned and called out, "Bring me a torch." Without a second's hesitation, Jols grabbed a torch and dipped into a nearby cook fire, then ran into the building and up to Arthur's side. Taking a deep breath, Lancelot followed him.

In the sudden flickering light, Arthur was shocked

to see an elderly monk with eyes like a madman rise from prayer at a tiny altar. In a hoarse voice the monk demanded, "Who are these defilers of the Lord's temple?"

Arthur took the torch from Jols and held it at arm's length, getting a better look at the terrifying reality surrounding him. In the cells were starving, dying men. The one or two who could still manage to move reached out through the bars, moaning piteously. They seemed to be unable to speak. Or perhaps there simply were not words to describe what they had been through. One of the monks from the outside grabbed Lancelot by the arm. "How dare you set foot in this holy place?"

Furious, Lancelot drew his sword and impaled the monk. In shock, the other monks fell to their knees and began weeping and praying.

The insane monk stared in horror at the corpse. "That was a man of God!" he cried.

Lancelot said bitterly, "Not *my* god."

Lancelot planted his boot in the dead monk's face and scraped his remains off the blade. Outside, a couple of mercenaries moved toward the door. Gawain pointed his sword at them at eye level. "Touch a knight, you die," he said calmly. The mercenaries backed away.

Gawain with his mace and Galahad with his battle axe moved from cell to cell, breaking prison locks. Peering inside one cell, Galahad said, "This one is dead."

"Gods," Gawain said. "From the stink, they must all be dead!"

Lancelot took the torch from Arthur and led the way as they moved farther into the prison. Stepping from one ghastly sight to another, he turned to Arthur and said, "Is this the work of your God?"

Arthur did not have a ready answer—he was revolted by the scene. He grabbed the torch from Lancelot's hand and said, "Whoever's work this is, we end it now!" Arthur and Lancelot descended a sloping stone ramp into the bowels of the dungeon. Left and right were cells inhabited by rotting corpses. It was a charnel house—a virtual hell of horrors.

Arthur called out, "Is anyone down here?" In the gloom, he saw something, a movement. A faint voice sounded from one of the cells. He lifted the torch higher and stepped forward.

Moments later, Lancelot emerged from the prison depths, closely followed by Arthur, who carried a young woman in his arms. With one skeletal hand, she covered her eyes against the light; she was filthy and brutalized. Gawain spread a blanket and Arthur carefully laid her on it. Nearby, four other prisoners were laid out on the ground. One was a small boy, about ten years old, named Lucan. Dagonet ran to the boy's side and knelt down. Gently, he helped Lucan into a sitting position. Enraged, Lancelot kicked a mercenary into action.

"Get water to these people!" he demanded.

Dagonet was infuriated by the sight of the boy, so

brutalized and lying among the dead. His expression hardened as he reached for Lucan. The boy flinched with fear and Dagonet softened a bit.

"No," Dagonet said. "You will not fear me."

He tried to pick the boy up, but Lucan grabbed hold of the arm of a woman next to him. From the looks of her, she had been dead for several days. "Mother," Lucan said in a low, whimpering voice. "Mother . . . " Dagonet sadly pried loose the boy's weak grip and picked him up in his arms.

Lancelot, impatient for his order to be carried out, stormed over to the well, filled a cup, and rushed back over to hand it to Arthur. Turning to the woman he had carried out, Arthur lifted it to her lips and she sipped tentatively, all the while staring into his eyes. She looked like a terrified wild animal who did not know if these new faces brought with them salvation or slaughter.

"I am a Roman officer," Arthur said, his tone calm and soothing. "You are safe now. Safe." She said nothing in return, but continued to look at her savior without expression. Arthur noticed that her eyes were beautiful behind the dirt.

Bors and Gawain dragged Marius over to Arthur and shoved him to his knees. Furious, Arthur grabbed his collar and brought Marius's face close, so that the two men's noses were nearly touching. At that proximity, Marius desperately tried to look anywhere but directly into Arthur's eyes—but he couldn't escape the knight's angry gaze.

Arthur snarled, "What is this madness, animal?"

Marius was flabbergasted at Arthur's fury. "They are pagans!" he said, as if that explained everything.

Galahad put his sword to Marius's throat. "So are we," he said.

Marius was now completely confused. "These pagans refuse to accept the place God set for them at the table of life. They must die! As an example to others!" He repeated, desperately, "As an example!"

"Refused to accept their place?" Arthur said. "You mean, they refused to be your serfs?"

Marius nodded eagerly, relieved that he was getting through. "Yes, yes! You understand!" he said. Arthur pulled Marius's collar tighter around his throat, reducing his voice to a gravelly squeak. Marius knew he had to talk fast. "Of course, as a Roman knight you would understand," Marius said. "As a Christian . . . "

Arthur suddenly released his grip on Marius, sending him flailing backward. Sitting on the ground, Marius shouted bitterly, "We don't need your escort! My mercenaries are force enough!" He pointed at the prisoners lying on the ground. "And these people you have taken from my prison have been condemned to death—and that is God's law! *His will shall be done!*"

Fulcinia rushed to the girl's side. The battered young woman seemed to recognize her. Marius, catching the look that passed between them, crawled to his feet and grabbed Fulcinia around the neck.

"You!" he shouted. "You kept her alive! You fed her!"

Marius slapped Fulcinia and she fell to the ground weeping. Suddenly, Arthur brought his fist to Marius's chin with a force that lifted him off his feet. For a moment, Marius and Fulcinia lay almost side by side on the ground.

"She tempted me . . . " Marius said to Arthur, a steady stream of blood flowing from the cut on his chin. " . . . as she will tempt you!" Arthur saw that the girl was glaring at Marius with open hatred.

Mercenaries and monks rushed forward to help right Marius, but none of them moved to assist Fulcinia. Lancelot gently lifted her to her feet.

Marius's face was red with fury. Flecks of spittle bubbled at the corners of his mouth. "When we get to the wall and your superior from the church," he spat out, pointing at Arthur, "you will suffer horribly for your heresy."

Arthur pulled Excalibur from its sheath and said, "Perhaps I should kill you now and seal my fate."

The monk from the altar ran forward and grasped Arthur's sleeve. "I was willing to die with them," he said, "to lead them to their rightful place."

Arthur stopped suddenly and looked at the monk, his eyes filled with menace.

"Wall them back up," he said quietly. Arthur turned to the knights, who looked back at him closely, as if trying to decide whether he was serious. Arthur looked directly at Dagonet and repeated, "I said, wall them up!"

Dagonet smiled broadly. He had absolutely no

problem with an order such as this. As he stepped forward to get to work, the other knights herded and pushed the monks into the prison. Once they were inside, wailing pitiably, Dagonet immediately started piling up stones and mortar.

As the knights worked, Arthur looked at Marius, then at the mercenaries who surrounded him. He did not say a word. He did not need to.

ELEVEN

THE DRUMMING OF THE ONCOMING SAXON armies grew steadily louder. The knights, led by Dagonet and Gawain, rode away from Marius's estate. Behind them, the villagers streamed out into the open plain, some on horseback, others on foot. But not all the serfs had joined the exodus. Some believed that they were safer near the walls of the estate. Others felt that, with Marius gone, they could at last live a happy life. If the Saxons were coming, what of that? They, too, would leave eventually, and the estate would then belong to those who stayed behind to claim it. Arthur had pled with the stubborn villagers, but they merely smiled at him smugly and bade him farewell. With a shrug, he rode away to join the caravan, leaving them to their fates.

One wooden cart, pulled by two horses, held the wounded and the sick. A cloth cover was rigged over the cart to keep the prone figures dry in the deepening snowstorm. Dagonet sat inside, his back resting against the side wall of the cart. He held a sleeping Lucan in his arms, gently caressing his forehead, alert for any signs that the boy was in pain or needed water.

A few feet away, the girl was passed out on the floor of the cart, a blanket covering her, and a bag of flour serving as a makeshift pillow. Fulcinia sat beside her, comforting her and cleaning and wrapping her wounds. The girl's hands were heavily bruised and distended. It looked to Fulcinia as if every one of her fingers had been broken.

Arthur rode up alongside the cart and looked at the girl. Then he spoke to Fulcinia. "Why was she in that prison?" he said.

Fulcinia looked at Arthur with eyes that suggested she was in full sympathy with his sense of injustice. She replied, "Why, indeed?"

The words were enough to create an understanding between them. At that moment, Marius trotted up on foot and tried to keep pace with Arthur's horse. Fulcinia quickly moved her glance away from Arthur, fearing her husband's anger would flare up again. She had had a painful lifetime of learning how to avoid the outbreak of his wrath.

Marius was breathless from having to walk so quickly, but he tried to invest his voice with as much authority as he could summon. "I want my wife returned to my care immediately," he demanded, rushing up alongside Arthur. "We can make our own way to the wall!"

Arthur did not look down at him, but continued to scan the horizon. "Divide our forces and whichever half the Saxons find will be slaughtered." He glanced down at the puffing Marius and said, "Who do you think is more fortunate: you or we?"

Marius was about to reply when he tripped over a rock and went sprawling. As he lay in the dirt cursing, the cart, accompanied by Arthur, continued to roll onward.

Arthur noticed Ganis, bearing a farm axe, veering off from the group and heading toward the woods. "Boy!" Arthur called out as he rode toward the young man. "Where are you going?"

Ganis replied, "I am going to pick off Saxons and clear your path."

Arthur almost laughed, but struggled to keep a stern look on his face. "Not likely," he said. "Turn around. You are coming with us. Rejoin the caravan."

Ganis looked at him with pleading eyes. This was going to be his chance to show his potential to become a heroic knight.

"Now!" Arthur ordered firmly. He wheeled his horse around and rode away. With a dejected sigh, Ganis shouldered his axe and began walking back toward the group.

The girl opened her eyes and saw that Arthur was once again riding beside the cart. She noticed that his boot was in his stirrup and, even in her dazed condition, the girl was fascinated by the device. Her eyes moved up to Excalibur's ornate hilt, with its intricate pagan carvings. And then she looked at Arthur's face, ready to close her eyes and pretend to be asleep if he should notice that she was watching him.

Arthur did not look at the girl, but spurred ahead to ride at the front of the column. Lancelot rode up fast behind him, catching up so that they could ride side by side.

As Arthur and Lancelot took point, carefully scouring the landscape ahead for any signs of impending attack, Lancelot said, "She is not going to make it." Arthur did not reply and Lancelot continued, "Neither is the small boy. We are wasting our time on all these people. They are going to get us killed. You know that, don't you?"

Arthur replied evenly, "If we have to, we will put them on the backs of our horses. Whether they are with us or not, if this trail ends we will have to fight." He glanced over at Lancelot. "Save your anger for that," he said.

Without another word, Lancelot turned and rode off. Arthur paused to look back. In the distance, he saw smoke rising from the direction of Marius's estate. Up ahead was a snowcapped mountain. Arthur looked at the imposing peak with dread. He knew it would be no easy task getting up and over it. And he knew that his pathetic caravan had no other choice if they were to save their lives and complete their mission.

It was dusk. At the prison building, Cerdic and Cynric looked over the landscape with Geoffrey, the scout. They also had noticed the fresh mortar on the wall, and that meant that, for the second time that day, the stone wall had been shattered and the doorway opened.

Two soldiers found the crazy monk and dragged him, squealing and pleading, toward Cynric. In no mood to deal with this blithering idiot, Cynric grabbed him roughly by the throat. "Shut your mouth!" he shouted.

One of the soldiers reported, "He says they walled him up in a building and took the family. Someone named Arthur . . . "

Geoffrey nodded. "The one I spoke of," he said. "Arthur Castus, commander of the Sarmatian knights."

The news excited Cynric. He said, "The mortar was not even dry—they cannot have been gone long."

Geoffrey said to Cerdic, "They will almost certainly go south to Hadrian's Wall." He pointed to the foothills in the distance. "They should be heading in that direction, unless they have come up with an alternate plan."

Cynric stepped forward and said to his father eagerly, "My men and I can overtake them if we move swiftly."

Before Cerdic could respond, Cynric quickly

turned around and strode toward his men of the light infantry. There, he huddled with them, planning. Cerdic watched the conference and did not like it. It smelled of challenge and ambition. Then something occurred to him. He turned to Geoffrey and asked, "Wait. Do they know we are after them?"

"I see tracks coming from the Wall," Geoffrey said, "but none leading back. My guess is that they are being evasive."

"Then where is the family?" Cerdic asked.

The British scout pointed toward a tiny trail in the distance, nearly hidden. He said, "If they have not headed south in the straightest route to the Wall, they have probably gone east." Geoffrey paused and looked at Cerdic. "That is the way I would play it, if it were I."

Cerdic looked off in the distance, pondering his choice.

Cynric came back to his father's side, full of purpose and ego. "We are ready!" he said

Cerdic nodded, and then turned to Cynric. "Take your light infantry and run them to the ground." Cynric hesitated a moment and Cerdic shouted, "Go!"

Cynric was too surprised to move. "East?" he said. "To face the knights alone?"

Cerdic said, a small smile playing about his lips, "Yes." He glared at his son. Cynric knew that this was either a test or a death sentence. After a moment, he bowed and said, "Yes sir."

Cerdic said, "I will take the army south, directly

to the wall. Between us, we will take one prize . . . if not both."

Raewald bounded over to his commander. He shoved the lunatic monk forward. Raewald said, "What shall we do with this monk?"

Cerdic looked to Cynric, with a challenging light in his eyes. He said nothing, but the answer was obvious: *What would* you *do with him?* A cold look came over Cynric's face. He turned to Raewald and said, "Put him back where you found him."

The monk began to scream as Raewald dragged him back to his tomb, to be walled up alive for the third—and final—time. Cynric looked at his father and smiled with satisfaction. They were equals in this moment. To Cynric, it felt like power. To Cerdic, it just felt dangerous.

Arthur and Lancelot rode side by side on the trail, joined soon by Tristran, who had been scouting ahead. It was snowing heavily, making objects in the distance dance and appear distorted in the dense, white flurries. The caravan moved slowly up the ever-steepening slopes and the knights instinctively rode close to Arthur, both to benefit from his strength and to protect him. Ahead, the trail narrowed.

Fulcinia lay beside the girl, asleep in the wagon. She covered herself with a heavy cloak, but still she shivered in the cold. Arthur slid from his horse into the wagon and sat there for a moment, watching the sleeping girl. Then he climbed up into the driver's seat and sat beside Dagonet. Lucan slept in Dagonet's lap, wrapped tightly in one of the knight's capes. Dagonet wore his heaviest cloak, with the collar pulled up high around his neck.

Behind them, the girl awoke suddenly. She stared at Arthur, wondering for a moment if she were still asleep and he was merely some strange, fascinating creature from her dreams.

Dagonet acknowledged Arthur's presence with a nod. Arthur looked down at the sick boy and said, "How is he doing?"

Dagonet shook his head. "He burns, Arthur," he said. He smiled a little. "Maybe he's lucky. It's the only thing that keeps him from freezing to death in this weather."

The girl responded with a start when she heard Arthur's name; her father had spoken often of this knight with something like respect. Others in her village had talked of him as if he were an angel or devil, capable of amazing and superhuman feats. Arthur lifted the cape covering the boy and studied a deep, festering cut on the child's arm. He gently put his hand on Lucan's face and neck, checking for fever. When Lucan began trembling from the cold, Arthur replaced the cape, drawing it tightly up around the boy's chin.

Fulcinia pulled a bulb of garlic out of her jacket. She broke off half and handed it to Dagonet. "Crush this and rub it into his wound," she said. "He has a chance if you keep him covered." Immediately, Dagonet removed his own heavy cloak and covered Lucan with it as well, leaving his own muscular arms exposed to the bitter cold. The boy was only semiconscious, but somehow Lucan seemed to acknowledge Dagonet and his generous deed. As Dagonet applied the garlic, Lucan reached up with his other hand to touch Dagonet's scarred face. Dagonet instinctively recoiled. But then a look of compassion broke over his face, and he allowed the boy to trace his facial scars with his small fingers. "If you aren't afraid of me," Dagonet said in a whisper, "I suppose I cannot be afraid of you."

Arthur climbed back into the cart and knelt at the girl's side. He saw that Fulcinia had wrapped the girl's misshapen fingers with torn strips of cloth. Arthur reached for one of her hands. Immediately, she winced with pain and pulled back. Arthur persisted carefully and slowly, and the wild child allowed him to take her hands and unwrap the bandages. Arthur was shocked by her ravaged condition and with great effort did his best to hide his feelings from her. The girl kept her eyes fixed on him. Still, she did not speak.

Arthur said in a low, kind voice, "They dislocated your fingers. If your fingers stay like this you will never be able to use them again. I must push them back into place."

She kept staring into Arthur's eyes as if searching for something that would allow her to trust him.

"It will hurt," Arthur said. "It will hurt terribly." The girl said nothing, but he saw that something like defiance had begun to steel her face. Arthur turned her hand so that the back rested against his chest. He tightened his grip on her index finger, looked her in the eye and . . . *Snap!* He expected her to shriek with pain— he figured he would have, under the same circumstances—but the girl only stared harder at him, as if he had laid down a challenge and she was accepting it, daring herself to break.

Arthur took the next finger, pulled hard and snapped it back into place. The pain, he thought, must have been incredible, but the girl remained resolutely mute. As he moved to the next finger, the pain finally became too much for her and the girl laid her head against Arthur's chest, her eyes clenched tight. Her free arm pulled him close as she fought the pain. Finally, after being so stoic for so long, she cried out in anguish. As if to take her mind off the matter at hand, she began talking for the first time.

"They tortured me . . . " she said in a hoarse whisper. Arthur looked at her sharply, surprised that she was talking at all. She said, "They tortured me with . . . machines."

Arthur relocated another finger. The girl groaned and said, " . . . They made me tell them things I never knew to begin with."

Another finger. Indescribable pain. Nevertheless, she managed an angry, ironic smile. At the sound of her voice, all the knights began to ride closer, listening. Arthur set another finger back into its socket.

"Each finger," she said, "I swallowed back my voice. If I do not have a voice, I cannot talk." Arthur snapped another finger. Somehow bearing the agony, she continued her own train of thought. " . . . Then I heard your voice in the dark," she said. "Saw you, holding a light."

The last finger was the worst of all. She suppressed a scream and tears ran from her eyes. But all that broke through her lips was a soft squeak. "You brought me back," she said. "All the way from death."

Arthur gently caressed her forehead. She closed her eyes under his cool touch and then said, "I am Guinevere." She moved her face closer to his. Arthur was not sure if she intended to kiss him—or bite him.

"You are Arthur," she said.

Arthur nodded

"Of the knights from the Great Wall?" she asked

Arthur had never heard it put in quite this way.

Arthur nodded again and said, "I am . . . We are."

Guinevere reached up and weakly brushed Arthur's cheek. Although the touch was soft, her look remained tough. She lowered her hand and studied Arthur a bit longer.

Guinevere said, "My father spoke of you." She looked at him with a slightly sharper gaze. "You are the famous Briton who kills his own people."

Arthur was stunned. He tried to think of some

way to respond to her extraordinary statement, but
Guinevere, exhausted from her ordeal, rolled back,
passing out. Arthur sat beside her for a long moment,
then arose, stepped off the cart, and remounted his
horse. Silently, he rode ahead into the deepening snow.

TWELVE

❧

CYNRIC AND HIS LIGHT INFANTRY ARRIVED at the beginning of the highlands. Geoffrey, the British scout, rode ahead, alert to any tricky maneuvering by Arthur and his knights. He scanned the ground carefully, but all he saw were tracks moving off in a single direction. He thought with some satisfaction that the snowfall was making his job easier than usual. Geoffrey dismounted, kneeled low and carefully pushed the snow aside with his finger. He said almost to himself, "Less than one day's snow on this track." He looked back at Cynric, who remained on horseback. "We have almost caught them," he said.

Cynric nodded with satisfaction. Suddenly energized, he furiously waved his men forward. The light infantry moved out ahead of Cynric and the scout, who hurriedly leaped back onto his horse to join the gallop.

• • •

Merlin walked somberly through the burned-out ruins of Marius's estate. All around the grounds, between the remains of the huts and the smoldering main buildings, the charred bodies of humans and animals lay, their corpses twisted and grotesque. Some of the victims were ashen monuments to the horror of their deaths, their faces grim masks of anguish and pain. The villagers who had stayed behind to claim the estate as their own had, in a way, gotten their wish. Now they would never leave.

The Woads who accompanied Merlin to this place of death were powerfully affected by the gruesome sights and smells. These were people accustomed to violence and horror, but this was almost more than they could bear. One Woad bent convulsively and vomited. Others looked as if they were about to start weeping.

Merlin bent down over the burned, almost unrecognizable body of a young boy. A Woad lieutenant exited from the stone prison, looked at Merlin and shook his head. Everyone inside was already dead. In despair, the monks had committed suicide only moments after the last stone had been set in place by Raewald's men. The monks were not bred to appreciate irony, so perhaps they would have seen none in the fact that the walled-up doorway to the big stone building had actually been knocked down a third time in a single day. Had they only held on, they would have been freed once again.

Or perhaps not. To the lieutenant, it was unclear whether Merlin was relieved or distressed at the discovery of the corpses. His expression revealed little, but the lieutenant understood immediately that Merlin knew more than he was saying.

The knights and their caravan inched forward across the highlands as the blizzard steadily worsened, effectively blinding them in an endless landscape of white. The sick and wounded in the cart huddled together for warmth. The rest simply put one foot or hoof before the other, enduring this bright, frigid hell with a stoicism born of the fact that they had no other choice. There was no point in stopping to rest or prepare meals. About the only way the people and horses could avoid freezing to death was to keep moving.

Arthur rode over to the supply wagon and picked up a large bag filled with loaves of bread. Then he rode alongside the cart and handed bread to Dagonet for Lucan, then to Guinevere. She received it at once grateful and resentful.

Arthur looked down at her and said with a sympathetic smile, "Feeling better?"

She was stronger now . . . more herself. More defiant. Guinevere said, "I can walk just as well as the next."

Arthur was surprised and pleased to see her acting so lucid. "And you shall," he said, "when I see that you are entirely healed."

Petulantly, Guinevere said, "And will you dare give me a horse to ride or will you keep me a prisoner as well?"

"When you are strong enough," Arthur said, "you are as free as anyone to ride into the arms of the Saxons."

"No man needs do anything for me," Guinevere said angrily.

The smile was now gone from his face. Arthur said, his voice carrying a clearly irritated tone, "No man is doing anything just for you. It is for the benefit of all. We move faster if the wounded ride."

"If you consider me wounded, then," she said with a sneer, "let me ride—a horse!"

He glared at her. Then suddenly, Arthur spurred his horse and rode on ahead. Guinevere bit into the bread, watching him go.

Moments later, he returned to the cart, another horse in tow. "You want to ride a horse?" he said. "Here is a horse." He commanded the driver of the cart to stop and extended his hand to Guinevere to help her step out. She ignored his hand and eagerly—if shakily —climbed to the ground. She was still weak, and swayed slightly, but she was too proud to betray her feelings to Arthur, and Arthur was too annoyed to acknowledge her condition.

He led her a few yards away from the caravan and helped her onto the horse, setting her feet in the stirrups. Arthur saw that she had no shoes. Her feet were wrapped in heavy cloth.

The instant one foot was in a stirrup, Guinevere immediately pulled it out again. She said, "Is this a Roman invention to drag you to your death?"

Arthur was getting fed up with her constant griping. He snapped, "Sarmatian, actually."

Arthur forced her feet in. As he mounted his own horse, Guinevere watched him. She was immediately comfortable on horseback, and Arthur could see at a glance that she was an experienced rider. He began riding away and she kicked lightly at her horse's flanks, urging him forward. In a moment, Arthur and Guinevere were riding side by side.

"It would be a lie to say I have not heard of you," Guinevere said.

"Yes, you said that your father had told you lies about me," Arthur said.

She said heatedly, "My father does not lie. Besides, I heard about you from many others in addition to my father."

Arthur looked straight ahead. "Oh yes?" he said. "And what did you hear?"

"Fairy tales," Guinevere said. "The kind you hear about people who never exist. People so brave and selfless they cannot be real. Arthur and his knights. A leader both Briton and Roman. Yet you gave your allegiance to Rome—to those who take what does not belong to them. The same Rome that tore your men from their homeland."

Arthur snapped at her, his voice filled with pique, "Do not pretend to know anything about me or my men!"

Calmly, Guinevere asked, "And how many Britons have you killed?"

"As many as tried to kill me," Arthur said. "It is the natural state of any man, to want to live."

Guinevere said, "Animals live! It is the natural state of man to live free in his own country! I belong to this land. Where do you belong?"

Arthur softened and turned to her. "Is that why they tortured you," he asked gently, "because you were free?"

"Far too free," she said. She pointed at Lucan and said bitterly, "And do you know why they tortured the boy? He spat on one of *your monks*. He needs to be saved to bring up more children who will spit on monks."

"Those monks are not my people," Arthur said.

Guinevere shook her head. "Arthur," she said, "you don't have a people."

They rode in silence for a while. Then Arthur asked, with sympathy in his voice, "Why did they torture you?"

Guinevere was confused by Arthur's surprising tone of concern. She said, "Why does it make any difference to you why I was tortured?"

Arthur said simply, "It does. How are your hands?"

Guinevere did not know what to make of this man, whether to respond to his personal warmth or to despise his affiliations with Rome. She said to him, still defiant but with a playful tone in her voice, "I will live. I promise you."

Arthur smiled.

Guinevere said, "Is there nothing about my land that appeals to your heart?"

Arthur was taken off guard by the question and by Guinevere's decidedly more flirtatious tone. She continued, "Your own father married a Briton. Even he must have found something to his liking."

Arthur did not know how to respond to her remark. "You seem to know a great deal about my background," he said. "But there are things you do not know. Things that you should know before you judge me so harshly from the heights of your own superiority."

He reached into his coat, took out a plant bulb and placed it in her hand. Now it was Guinevere who did not know how to respond to this caring act. They exchanged a moment in silence, and then Arthur rode ahead, leaving her. She slowed down for a moment.

Lancelot, riding nearby, kept his eye on her. As Arthur rode away, Lancelot approached Guinevere and rode alongside her. She glanced over to him and said, "It is a beautiful country, is it not?"

Lancelot looked around. It looked like nothing more than snow-covered desolation to him. "You are joking," he said.

Guinevere was insulted. "And where do you hail from that compares?" she demanded. "The Black Sea! This is heaven for me."

Lancelot smiled at her outburst. "I do not believe in heaven," he said. "I have been living in hell." Lancelot could never be this close to a pretty woman without flirting a little and now was no exception. " . . . but if you represent what heaven is," he said with a breathy voice, " . . . then take me there." He smiled his brightest smile.

Guinevere was insulted, but she could not help also being just a little flattered. Lancelot was, after all, one of the famous knights—and a handsome one at that.

Smirking, she said, "I pray that you are far more deft with your sword than with your flattery."

Lancelot laughed loudly. "Many victims have fallen before both, I assure you!"

Suddenly the flurries of snow were mixed with rain. Lancelot looked up at the sky and held his hand out to catch the drops. He shook his head darkly. "Rain and snow at once," he said. "A bad omen." He turned to Guinevere. "You should get back in the wagon," he said.

Guinevere looked as if he had insulted her again. Lancelot smiled kindly. "You are not fully recovered yet. Take good care of yourself. Heal."

She was exhausted by her short ride and, even though she rebelled against taking even a good suggestion from one of the haughty knights, she had to admit to herself that the relative warmth and dryness of the wagon now seemed far more appealing than more miles on horseback in a combination rain- and snowstorm. She nodded and rode over to the cart, stepped off the horse and got inside. Then she tied her horse to the back so that it could saunter along comfortably until she needed it again.

An hour later, the weather getting worse by the minute, Arthur heard laughing and singing coming from the cart. Curious, he rode over to see what was happening. Peeking inside, careful to remain unseen himself, Arthur saw Guinevere and Lucan. She was singing a funny song to him, doing hand gestures that made him laugh. She tickled his face and chin with each different verse. Lucan was clearly in heaven. Dagonet looked back now and then from the driver's seat, clearly delighted at even a little sign of peace and happiness on Lucan's face.

Arthur rode on, intrigued to have seen yet another side to Guinevere.

Driving the wagon, Dagonet hummed along contentedly with Guinevere's song. As he did so, he slammed his fist down onto the face of his shield, shattering a glasslike layer of ice. He reached back into the cart, holding up a large piece for Lucan. The boy was weak from his few moments of play with Guinevere and looked as though he could barely summon the energy to smile. Dagonet thought, with a sinking feeling, that the boy's health still seemed to be uncertain. With Guinevere's help, he covered Lucan with his shield while the boy gratefully sucked on the ice.

As dusk fell over the miserable winter day, high in the mountains, the knights arrived at a giant snow-covered plateau, thick with conifers. Arthur reined in and the knights collected around him.

"We will sleep here and take shelter in the trees," Arthur said. "We move out at dawn."

Lancelot protested, "We should keep moving."

"And spend tomorrow burying bodies?" said Arthur. "No, we will give them rest."

Lancelot clearly disagreed, but said nothing more. Guinevere, watching from the wagon, witnessed their exchange, wondering if it was emblematic of some deeper difference in strategic philosophy.

Arthur said, "Tristran, I need you to go out again."

Tristran nodded. "Gladly," he said. "Better than freezing to death in my sleep."

Ganis heard Arthur's order and perked up. Tristran turned his horse back down the slope, moving fast back down in the direction of the Saxons. Arthur and the others moved off to prepare their campsite. Ganis watched longingly as Tristran disappeared toward the darkening horizon, off to have the kind of adventures that Ganis himself so deeply desired.

Inside the canvas tentlike cover on the wagon,

Fulcinia methodically washed the filth from Guinevere's hair using a rag and bucket. As she did so, Guinevere slowly shed her torn, dirty clothing. Outside, Lancelot was returning with his gear when he saw the silhouette of Guinevere naked in the wagon. The door flap was open and as he continued to walk by it, toward his horse, Lancelot and Guinevere locked eyes. He was entranced by the sight. Guinevere merely looked curious, as though wondering why he was staring at her so. Fulcinia slowly pulled down the flap, breaking the spell.

Still haunted by his glimpse of Guinevere, Lancelot settled down on sentry duty and built a large fire. From where he sat he could see Arthur sleeping by his horse, another fire warming them. The other knights alternately slept or pulled sentry duty around the camp. Suddenly, soundlessly, Guinevere was by Lancelot's side. Her hair was still wet and her face flushed with the hard scrubbing administered by Fulcinia. She was wrapped in a heavy cloak with a hood. Lancelot looked at her as if hypnotized. Until now, she had been nothing more than a filthy refugee, one of the villagers he would happily have left behind to be taken care of by the Saxons. But suddenly she was transformed, and he was surprised by how inadequately his imagination had prepared him for her beauty. At her approach, Lancelot stood up abruptly and clumsily.

Guinevere sat down beside Lancelot's fire without

saying anything. He stood there awkwardly for a few
seconds and then, after a moment, sat down beside her.
"What is it like?" she asked, staring into the flames.
"Your homeland?"

Lancelot said, "Oh, like most places. We sacrificed goats, drank their blood, danced naked around
fires . . . " He smiled at her annoyed expression, then
his face softened as he decided to answer her seriously.

"Sarmatia," he said. "Home. What do I remember
of it? An ocean of grass, the sky bigger than you can
see, from horizon to horizon, further than you can ride
—no boundaries."

Guinevere nodded. She inched a little closer to
the fire and pulled her knees close to her chin. She
said, "Some would call that freedom. That is what we
fight for. Our land, our people, the right to choose our
destiny. Yet you yourself know freedom comes with a
heavy price. So you see, Lancelot, you and I are much
alike."

Lancelot said nothing.

After a moment, Guinevere said, careful not to
look at Lancelot, "When you are home, will you take a
wife, have sons?"

Lancelot shook his head. "I have killed too many
sons," he said. "What right do I have to my own?"

Guinevere was touched by the honesty and sadness of his reply. "No family, no religion," she said. "Is
there anything you believe in?"

Lancelot looked over at Arthur, alone by his fire.

He then peered straight into Guinevere's eyes. "For myself, I would have left you and the boy to die." Guinevere was shocked by the response and said nothing. After letting the statement sink in, Lancelot stood up and walked away to check the perimeter of the camp.

Deep in the night, nearly all of the villagers were asleep. So were the members of Marius's family and entourage—except for Marius. Sitting by a small fire, he talked in a low voice to several mercenaries. Dagonet watched them, wary but unable to hear their whispers. Then he took a shivering Lucan in his arms, wrapped a blanket around both of them and lay down on the ground.

At various points around the camp, each of the knights watched the forest for any sign of the enemy. Only Bors seemed unconcerned about any imminent danger. He sat on a rock beside his steed, braiding the horse's mane. Both man and horse were totally serene.

Across the way, Arthur nodded beside his fire, willing himself to stay awake but unable to. His chin dropped slowly to his chest and then, suddenly, he woke with a start, staring about the camp suspiciously. Somewhere, quite nearby, he heard a voice, silky and indistinct. His first thought was that it was Guinevere, singing again as she had sung to Lucan in the wagon. Then abruptly, it stopped. Arthur stood up and looked around the camp. The air was suffused with an eerie silence. The camp was completely empty—there were no knights, no villagers, no horses . . . no Guinevere. A shiver of fear bolted up Arthur's spine. He drew Excalibur and spun in all directions, confused and disoriented.

Then the singing started again, closer than before. He could tell that it was a woman's voice . . . lovely . . . haunting . . . frightening. And the most frightening thing of all was that Arthur recognized it.

He returned Excalibur to its scabbard and moved warily into the darkness, following the enticing sound of the spectral voice. As he stepped toward a tree, a path suddenly appeared where there had been none only an instant before. Arthur was puzzled but not exactly frightened. He felt strangely confident, as if he knew where he was going, knew precisely whom he was about to meet. As he walked cautiously up the path, there was a rise in the terrain, hiding what was on the opposite side. With slow, measured steps, Arthur ascended the rise.

Somehow, from somewhere, a strange, diffused light illuminated the path. Arthur looked around, but the light seemingly had no source. His hand dropped again to Excalibur, and at that moment the singing voice rose clearer, more beautiful than ever.

The path opened on a stream and a forest pool that seemed to be the source of the unearthly glow. On the opposite side of the pool a beautiful young woman moved languidly, as if drifting across the water. She turned to face him. With a feeling of shock, Arthur recognized the woman as his own mother, as young and beautiful as when Arthur was a child. Smiling ethereally, she moved off, deeper into the forest. Walking faster, Arthur pursued the figure. He heard splashing at each step and saw that the path was now a tiny stream. The stream itself glowed, seemingly producing its own light.

Arthur tried to keep up with the retreating figure. The branches and briars tore at his clothes. The darkness seemed almost impenetrable, except for the shimmer of light that cleared a path before him. Suddenly, he broke through the branches and found himself in a huge grotto. The very walls of the grotto sparkled as if studded with diamonds. With a glance, Arthur realized that the sparkling actually came from "fire ore," the iron pyrite which had been exposed at the surface. It was the ore in the water that created the eerie glow. Arthur was momentarily comforted by this discovery, as if everything else about this weird experience might also have a similarly logical and rational explanation.

His mother's singing had stopped again. He looked all around and found she had completely disappeared. But now Arthur heard another voice.

"Peace between us this night, Arthur Castus," the voice said.

Merlin stood directly in front of Arthur, who was thoroughly puzzled as to why he had not seen the Woad commander before now. Behind Merlin, spaced around the grotto on ledges, were more Woads. But instead of wild-eyed warriors filled with hate, they appeared to be ordinary people: women holding children, young boys and girls, unarmed men. Arthur regarded them suspiciously, wondering if they were real people, or part of some strange dream . . . or ghosts.

Arthur instinctively drew Excalibur again, brandishing it threateningly before him.

Merlin smiled sadly. Pointing at the mighty sword, he said, "Is that what we must do, finally meeting after all these years?"

Arthur lowered his sword, then grabbed the collar of Merlin's cloak. For a moment, the two were locked together as if in a test of strength, but Merlin did not struggle. Instead, he just looked at Arthur with a kindly, slightly disappointed smile on his face.

"Find your sword, Merlin," Arthur demanded, "so that we can have a fair fight!"

Battle-hardened warriors moved in on Arthur, but Merlin's smile widened as he pulled free from Arthur's grasp. He nodded toward the veterans.

"My best fighters were determined I challenge you when you entered our woods," Merlin said. "But my younger men . . . feel differently. Look at them. Can you see it in their eyes?"

Almost against his will, Arthur did look at the people, scanning their faces. He turned back to Merlin and said, "I am sorry the new generation will not get to practice their skills on us."

Merlin was disappointed by the response, but not

surprised that Arthur remained unmoved. Merlin nodded to a Woad, who tossed a crossbow at Arthur's feet. "Our young men will have plenty to challenge their talents," Merlin said.

Arthur picked up the crossbow and studied it. "Saxon?" he asked. "They have many?"

Merlin nodded. "My spies say one eighth of their whole army marches within a few miles of where you and I stand," he said.

Arthur was disturbed by this news.

Merlin continued, "And at the same time, Rome leaves, its tail tucked between its legs." He looked closer into Arthur's eyes. "But what of Arthur and his knights?"

Arthur tossed the crossbow back to the ground. "We won't be staying for the farewell party," he said.

A young Woad approached Arthur. With a shock, Arthur recognized him as the Woad he had spared in their battle to rescue the bishop's coach. The Woad warily reached out to touch Excalibur. Arthur almost pulled back, but then saw that the young man meant no harm. The Woad passed his hands carefully over the reliefs of the carvings of pagan gods on the hilt. He asked in Celtic, "These are our gods?"

Merlin answered, "*Fianna bátar . . .* "

Arthur hesitated, his eyes straying back up to the Woads arrayed all around the glowing grotto.

Merlin asked, in Celtic, "Do you understand our language?"

Arthur nodded, and replied in the same tongue, "I speak your language."

The Woads gasped to hear their mortal enemy speaking their own words. They now seemed even more human to Arthur. "Yes, look," Merlin said, "do you now see yourself in their eyes?" He moved closer to Arthur. "Four hundred years of blood has drenched this land!" Merlin said. "It cries out for a true king. My time is past! It is now the time of you—and your knights."

Arthur said, "My knights are foreigners to this land—and I am Roman!"

"Do you think it was chance that brought your knights to this island?" said Merlin. "As for your Roman lineage, those are our gods on your sword!"

Arthur held Excalibur aloft. "This is my father's sword, and his father's before . . . "

"Yet like you," Merlin said, "it is of *this* land. These are your people."

Arthur looked around at the Woads, no longer able to deny their kinship.

Merlin said, "This new generation believes as a Roman you have the ability to stop the Saxons. As a Briton you have the will."

Arthur said, "You are their leader. Think of it, Merlin. If you beat the Saxons, one day you can be king."

Merlin looked deep into Arthur's eyes and said, "Not I. That is a place reserved for you!"

All at once, as if a curtain had been lifted, Arthur knew the truth of Merlin's words. But true or not, they flew in the face of everything that Arthur believed. He could not help but continue to resist. "You are mad," he said.

Merlin said, "Listen to me . . . it is no longer my time. The world is crumbling all around us, Arthur. Death, fear, hate . . . it is the days of men. The time for a spiritual leader has passed. Our land needs a righteous warrior. It is the time of you, your knights and these people."

With sudden passion, Merlin stepped closer and said to Arthur, "The people united! United! My own young men believe you can do anything. You and your knights have a fearsome reputation!"

Arthur replied, "And to my knights goes my allegiance. They trust me not to betray them to their enemy."

Arthur turned away from Merlin. For an instant, the spell was broken. Then Merlin leaned close to Arthur's ear and said, nearly in a whisper, "And who is your enemy, Arthur?" Arthur turned to face the Woad commander once more. His eyes were still defiant, but were now tinged with dread, as if he knew exactly what Merlin was about to say.

"Who is your enemy?" Merlin said again. "Your mother . . . ?"

Arthur instinctively raised Excalibur in attack position. His left hand clenched tight into a fist. Arthur shouted in Celtic, "My mother was a Briton killed by her own people!" He slumped, as though the words had exhausted him. Arthur lowered Excalibur until the tip of its blade was buried in the dirt of the grotto. In a tired voice, in English, he continued. "What was her sin, Merlin?" Arthur said. "That she fell in love with *your* enemy?"

Merlin shrugged. "It was what happens . . . " he said.

Arthur scoffed.

Merlin said, "How many mothers have your knights left childless or without a husband?"

"I don't choose my enemies," Arthur said.

Now angry, Merlin stepped forward and swept the world with his hand. "*Everyone* is your enemy!" he shouted. "Are you going to take that sword to Rome with you, Arthur? And when the Romans do not agree with you will you cut their heads off? All their heads?"

"I am not going to Rome to fight," Arthur said. "I go to follow the steps of my father's beloved teacher."

"For what?" Merlin said. "To escape Britain?"

"For the freedom of all," Arthur said.

Merlin said with quiet authority, "You will never find in Rome the freedom you seek—and not ten thousand Arthurs with ten times ten thousand knights could change that. In Rome, in the end, you will die a meaningless death. Here . . . " he swept his hand to the Woads behind him " . . . there is a need, a hope . . . a people you can save. Here, Arthur, you can build a new world!"

As Arthur turned away again, Merlin could see the frustration and confusion on his face.

Merlin said, "Your great sword—the sword of your father—was hewn from the iron of this land. If you use Excalibur in the service of this land, it will bring back the spirit of those we have lost."

Arthur said quietly, "We can never bring back all those we have lost, not in body nor in spirit. The dead are dead forever."

"Are they?" Merlin said.

Merlin put his hand on Arthur's shoulder. Arthur did not flinch at the touch but, for reasons he could not exactly understand, he felt like weeping.

The grotto seemed to dissolve before Arthur's eyes. The years melted away like snow before a fire. Suddenly, the night was darker, filled with noise and terror and the acrid smoke of burning homes. As if peering through an enchanted mirror, Arthur saw himself at ten years old, clinging to his mother's skirts. He was surprised at how young she looked—younger than he was now. She was wailing with fear. The boy Arthur's eyes were clenched shut, desperately trying to block out the horror that surrounded them. The man Arthur knew that he was experiencing some kind of mystical vision, but he could not make it stop. Instinctively, he knew that he could not change the outcome of the events that were once again horrifyingly alive before him.

Arthur felt as if he were two different persons at

once: himself as an adult, and himself at ten years old. He was, at the same time, both watching the scene from a distance and experiencing it all over again; he was inside and outside the vision simultaneously. The sounds of battle surrounded him—clanking swords, shouted orders, cries of fury, screams of agony. He could feel the heat of the flames on his face and the trembling of his mother's body. When she wept, screamed or prayed, the sound was loud and close to his ear; he could feel the warmth of her breath and the trickle of her tears, which ran from her eyes and onto his own cheeks.

Arthur no longer knew if he was an adult or a child as he watched Roman soldiers hacking away at Woad warriors with spear and sword. He only knew that he had to save his mother . . . and save himself.

Suddenly, as he knew it must, a torch flew from the hand of his friend Ramus, the dying Roman legionnaire. Arthur felt the pain of Ramus's death all over again and watched helplessly as the torch ignited the rude wooden furniture of his home and then blazed into a small inferno when the flames reached the dry, tightly packed straw of the thatched roof. The child Arthur urged his mother to her feet; the adult Arthur tried to will her to get up and run out, determined this time to get her through the door and to safety. But though he frantically pulled at her, she hesitated. Arthur realized with the agony of grief that he could not change what was happening, that he could simply watch it again with its same inevitable end.

As it had happened so long ago, Arthur's mother pushed the child Arthur out the door as the flaming beams cracked and dropped, smoldering, to the floor. Once again, young Arthur found himself outside, screaming as he watched his trapped mother gaze wide-eyed in horror at the flames surrounding her. Once again, he determined to save her by racing through the forest toward the knights' graveyard on Badon Hill. And once inside the cemetery, Arthur again felt the darkness and dread of this place of death. The swords which served as gravestones were like a mute forest, planted by the seeds of doom. Lying beneath them was an army of knights. In life, there was nothing these hundreds of heroes could not have accomplished. But now, they could offer absolutely no assistance to the terrified child who searched frantically for his father's grave.

Watching himself pull the mighty Excalibur from his father's grave, Arthur's mind flitted briefly to the legend that had grown up around this desperate action. It was said that all the strongest and bravest knights in the land had tried to pull the mighty sword from an enchanted stone. But that only Arthur, his heart brave and pure, could remove it, and it was thus that God had chosen him to be the leader of men. Now, as ten-year-old Arthur yanked desperately at the hilt of the blade, crying pitifully, "Father! Please! Let loose your sword!" it occurred to Arthur the man that perhaps the event was almost as mystical as the legend claimed. It was

this night that irrevocably, if not magically, transformed a boy into a man, a son into an orphan, a child
into a fighter.

Again, as it had happened years earlier and was
continuing to happen tonight, the boy wrenched
Excalibur from the ground, fell flat on his back, and
then leaped to his feet, holding the heavy sword over
his shoulder, his small arms too weak to carry the
heavy blade. Then it was out of the knights' cemetery,
and back up the hill to his burning home, all the while
panting with fear.

The adult Arthur already knew what the boy did
not—that it was too late to save his mother. He saw the
determination on the boy's face, the readiness, if not
eagerness, to encounter a Woad and extract a payment
in blood for what he was going through, for what was
happening to his mother. But young Arthur encountered no Woads. As he arrived back at his devastated
village, they were once again retreating into the forest.
The darkness and their elaborate skin camouflage
caused them to vanish like wisps of smoke in the wind.

When Arthur again saw his burning house, the
ache in his heart was as painful—perhaps even more
painful—as it had been when he experienced it the
first time around. The hopelessness had taken root in
Arthur's heart and grown over the course of many
years; it affected every corner of his soul. The boy in
Arthur was still stunned by disbelief that God could
allow such an event to take place. Arthur the man had
had years to come to grips with God's cruelty.

As the sounds of battle drifted away, a disturbing silence cloaked the village. Even the roar of the fires had dwindled down to the sharp crackles of dying blazes, sounding at once as cheery as a hearth fire and as ominous as the final stages of a cremation pyre.

"Mother!" the boy shouted, his voice hoarse with sorrow and rage. "MOTHER!"

Arthur the man, tears now rolling full down his cheeks, whispered, "Mother . . . "

And then Arthur saw something that he had not remembered from that night of trauma and loss. A younger Merlin stood in the trees at the edge of the forest, looking at the frantic child Arthur with an expression of deep sadness and sympathy. As his fellow Woads ran helter-skelter back into the woods, Merlin walked slowly in the opposite direction, toward the village, toward the boy. The expression on his face showed the adult Arthur that Merlin realized he was too late to help the boy. He could do nothing but share the moment of pain with him. Merlin knelt and put a comforting arm around Arthur's shoulders.

Arthur looked fearfully at the Woad, afraid at first to be embraced by an enemy. But Merlin's kind gaze made the child realize that he was safe. He began crying again. "My mother . . . " Arthur said softly, his voice hoarse from weeping.

"Be brave, boy," Merlin said soothingly. "You must be brave . . . "

Before him, Merlin's sad face, so filled with sympathy, suddenly began to age. They were both back in the grotto, in the present. The past remained unalterably past.

Merlin said, almost to himself, "You were but a boy."

Arthur's eyes stung with tears and he said nothing.

"I am truly sorry," Merlin said. "I have also lost family to the enemy—my beloved daughter. Yet, though we have both paid a dear price, we have both been able to save our men. To fight."

Arthur slipped Excalibur back into its sheath.

Merlin said, "Do you know what I think a great leader is? A man who hates leaders. A man who would mistrust even himself in that position. A man who leads only because someone must."

"My trust is with my knights," Arthur said. "My responsibility is to get them home."

Merlin nodded wryly and said, "Yes, they still have homes. But exactly where in heaven or hell is Arthur's home? Does it exist in reality, or is it only in your mind?"

Arthur did not know quite how to answer this. He was not really sure himself.

Merlin said, "There comes a time when God sets the design of your life, Arthur. It is up to you to choose or to scorn the path that He sets before you." He pointed to the Woad families. "These people are your destiny."

Arthur shook his head and remembered his beloved

Pelagius. "There is no destiny," Arthur said, "there is only free will."

"The mistake you make is when you believe that destiny and free will are mutually exclusive," Merlin said. "They are not. Sometimes you must *choose* your destiny. Sometimes that is not God's job, but your own."

Arthur turned to respond, but, as he did so, he saw Merlin nod once. Then Merlin and the Woads who populated that mysterious grotto began to disappear, one by one, into the mist. The bioluminescent lights were snuffed out at the same time. After a moment, they were all gone, leaving Arthur alone in the dark.

THIRTEEN

❦

ARTHUR SLEPT ONLY FITFULLY FOR THE
rest of the night. His encounter with Merlin had
profoundly disturbed him. Here, back at camp, once
again lying beside his campfire, his horse tethered
nearby, Arthur was undecided as to whether the entire
episode had been a dream, some kind of magical
vision, or if he had actually traveled to that remote
grotto and truly stood face to face with Merlin and the
Woads. No matter which of these choices was true,
Arthur had no doubt that the meeting had enormous
importance and that he should heed the words of
Merlin, dream or not. As he desperately sought sleep,
his mind was alive with images of the Woads, of the
knights' graveyard, of his mother . . .

Even when he fell asleep, his consciousness

remained so close to the surface that even the slightest sound awakened him. As the cold light of dawn broke through the trees, Arthur heard a footstep quite close by. The instant he opened his eyes, the sounds of a desperate commotion erupted all over the camp. He tried to leap to his feet, disoriented, only to find a mercenary standing over him, sword raised in preparation for attack. As the soldier began to lower the blade, a startled look came over his face. As Arthur rose, Excalibur in hand, he saw the tip of a sword protruding from the mercenary's chest. A few yards behind, Lancelot, who had hurled his sword straight through the mercenary's back, nodded at Arthur, and then lunged for his bow and arrows.

There were now shouts and screams, some angry, some terrified, coming from all points of the camp.

Dagonet had been fast asleep when he was jumped by five mercenaries, but he was instantly alert. He pounded one soldier in the side of the head with the hilt of his sword, slammed another with his shield and —just as suddenly—stopped.

A few feet away, Marius gripped Lucan around the chest with his left arm and held a knife to the boy's throat with his right hand. Dagonet did not move a muscle. The other knights also were neutralized, glaring at Marius.

Marius shouted at the mercenaries, "Kill them! Finish them off! I will tell the bishop you were protecting us all from the demon knights! When we get back to the wall the bishop will support us against anyone."

The mercenaries also seemed to be frozen to the spot. Some looked puzzled. Others just stared at Marius defiantly. One of the guards straightened up. He said, "I am a soldier and I will follow orders. But I will not murder people in cold blood." He threw his short sword to the ground. Around the camp, a few other mercenaries also dropped their weapons, refusing to follow Marius's orders any longer.

Marius's face grew red with fury. He held the blade harder against Lucan's throat. The boy whimpered with terror and pain as a trickle of blood ran from his neck. "Kill them all!" Marius demanded. "Do as I say!"

An arrow slammed into Marius's chest. He gagged, staring in disbelief at the shaft, sunk up to the feathers. He looked up to see Guinevere holding a mercenary's bow. Marius tumbled backward, his face an image of shock. Dagonet rushed forward and lifted Lucan out of the dead man's grip.

Everyone else froze in their tracks as Guinevere loaded another arrow, raised the bow and pulled the string to her cheek. There was no question in anyone's mind that she knew how to use it. Slowly the mercenaries spread out. Guinevere pointed the new arrow at one of the guards and he stopped. The other mercenaries stopped, as well. They stood still, looking at her impassively. They knew, as she did, that it was only a matter of time before they got her. And this would not be murder, but self-defense. One soldier reached down for the sword that he had just dropped on the ground.

At that moment, Arthur stepped up beside Guinevere, pointing Excalibur at eye level. For a moment that seemed to be frozen in time, it was just the two of them, engaged in a staring match with a large force of trained killers. But in the space of that moment, the remaining knights lined up with Arthur and Guinevere, raising their bows or their swords, ready for action. The knights did not take their eyes off the mercenaries for long, but none of them could resist casting an admiring glance at Guinevere. There she was, a frail young girl, still recuperating from the tortures she endured at Marius's hands, standing erect with a seventy-five-pound bow at full draw, neither trembling nor moving a muscle. Lancelot laughed proudly at the sight. He slowly pulled his sword from its sheath and the silence was broken by the music of its metallic ping.

That was all it took. The mercenaries dropped their swords. Alecto ran over to Arthur's side. Guinevere altered the bow's aim ever so slightly and fired. Marius's soldiers flinched, but the arrow center-punched the circle where a limb had been cleaved off a tree. She looked at them without expression. Her point was made.

Casually, Guinevere slung the bow over her shoulder. She turned to find all the knights staring at her. Galahad and Gawain actually bumped into each other

—they were totally smitten with this remarkable girl.

Almost reluctantly, Alecto left Arthur's side and walked over to his father's corpse. He knelt there, staring at Marius's face. At first, he betrayed no emotion at all. Then, Fulcinia pulled her son into her embrace and Alecto burst into tears, burying his face in his mother's breast.

Arthur walked over to the mercenaries. "Did Marius offer you gold to overpower us?"

They all stared back at him, some defiantly, some guiltily. Finally, one of them said, "Yes." He almost smiled. "After all, we *are* mercenaries." He looked over at Marius's body. "He was the one who hired us and he was the one who gave us orders."

Arthur said, "I understand that. Now you must understand: I am the one who gives you orders from this point on. You will still receive the agreed-upon fee."

The mercenary said, "We could just ride off and leave you here. If the Saxon army is as large and fearsome as we have been told, perhaps it is a fight that we do not wish to engage in."

"Together we will be strong enough to defeat them," Arthur said. "But if you and your men should choose to leave . . . " he offered a friendly smile . . . "my knights and I—and Lady Guinevere—will kill you."

The defiant look disappeared from the faces of the mercenaries. They looked to their spokesman for some signal as to how this situation was going to play itself out. After a moment, the mercenary returned Arthur's smile.

"Perhaps you could," he said, "and perhaps you could not." He paused. "But I agree with you on one point," he said. "We are stronger together. We will ride with you."

Arthur reached out his hand and the mercenary took it. He turned to the others and said, "Get ready to move out. We still have . . . "

Suddenly Arthur held his hand in the air. "Quiet!" he ordered. He pointed into the forest. He and Lancelot drew their swords. Swapping hand signals, they each took cover behind a tree flanking the trail. They could hear the faint sounds of someone approaching. Guinevere ran over to the villagers, urging them to take cover. The knights and mercenaries armed themselves and braced for the impending attack.

Out of the woods, Tristran emerged, leading his horse. On the back of the horse were tied two Saxon swords, a shield and a bow.

The knights relaxed immediately. Bors said to Tristran, "How many did you send to Saxon paradise?"

Exhausted, Tristran could only hold up three fingers. "They were practically on our ass," he said in a hoarse voice, "so I had to kill them quick—it was no fun." Tristran looked at Arthur and said firmly, "We must leave—*now*!"

FOURTEEN

THE CARAVAN MADE ITS LABORIOUS WAY
across the open plain, wind whipping blinding
snow all around. Guinevere huddled in the wagon with
Fulcinia, Lucan and the other sick and wounded. All
together, buried under blankets, cloaks and whatever
else they could find, the little group created just
enough warmth to keep them from becoming numb
with the cold. Dagonet continued to steer the horses
pulling the cart. "For all I know," he thought, "we have
turned around and are traveling in the opposite direction." The rest of the knights and mercenaries on
horseback also had to trust that Tristran and Arthur
were leading them in the right direction. The snow created a nearly impenetrable curtain of white, and they
could only see a few yards ahead in the best of circumstances.

Alecto was riding a horse toward the rear of the column, his head covered in a hood and lowered against the freezing wind, his body bent with grief. Arthur dropped his horse back so that they were riding side by side.

"Alecto," Arthur said, "I am sorry for your loss." The wind howled eerily, like the moans of a ghost.

Alecto sniffed and said, "My father lost his way."

Arthur said, "Men stray, Alecto. The church is there to help us stay on our path."

Alecto looked at Arthur scornfully. "Path?" he said. "There is no longer any path in Rome! They need no path if our holy fate is predestined!"

Arthur said, "What are you talking about?"

"Arthur, do you not know?" Alecto said, his eyes blinking tearfully against the wind. "Free will is now a hated idea. What my father believed, so Rome believes. All of Rome."

"You mean that every man is a slave to the will of God?" asked Arthur.

"Yes!" Alecto said. "We are what we are created to be. We have no choice."

Arthur shook his head and said, "Pelagius went to Rome to teach that all men are free—that their fate is their own to choose . . . "

Alecto looked enraged. "Teach? How?" he said. "They killed Pelagius."

Arthur looked and felt as if he had been punched hard in the belly. For a moment, he was too breathless to speak.

"Killed Pelagius?" he gasped, finally. "When?"

"A year past," Alecto replied. "Germanus and others in Rome were damned by his indictments. They had him excommunicated and then killed."

Arthur felt helpless. Pelagius had been more than one of the great Christian philosophers, he had been Arthur's friend and mentor, the man who embodied everything great and promising about the church. News of his death was more devastating to Arthur than any other news could possibly be at this moment. Arthur had the odd sensation that someone had cut the lines that moored him safely to his beliefs, and now he was plummeting downward, out of control.

Alecto saw the effect the news of Pelagius's death had had on Arthur and was immediately sorry for breaking the news so callously. When he spoke again, it was with a voice tinged with pity. "The church hates freedom worse than hell itself," he said. "Arthur, the Rome you long for . . . that Rome now lives only in your dreams."

Arthur did not reply. Before Alecto could say anything else, Arthur pulled his horse to the side and let the rest of the caravan go on. He sat silently, staring into the distance, as the snowstorm swirled around him, burying him in a grave of white, freezing nothingness.

By the following day, the snow had stopped, but the gray sky hung low overhead and the temperature had dropped to well below freezing.

Arthur said to Tristran, "We have to find some kind of shelter soon." He gestured back to the villagers. Each of them wore every piece of clothing he owned. In many cases, even that was clearly not enough. "These people are going to start freezing to death."

"We are in luck," Tristran said. "There is a village not more than five miles from here. Surely we will find hospitality there."

"And if we don't?" Arthur said.

Tristran smiled and patted the crossbow in its holster. "Who would be hard-hearted enough to refuse hospitality to such as us?"

Word spread back through the caravan that respite was not far away. Heartened, the villagers began to walk and ride faster, longing for the moment when they could step indoors for awhile, perhaps even for the night, and to enjoy a hot meal, protected from the endless assault of this frigid wind.

But when they reached the village at around noon, it was clear to them that it offered no hospitality. What had once been a collection of small, tidy huts and a couple of public buildings, was now a nightmare of death and ruin. The buildings had been burned and the charred scraps were covered with snow. So were the mangled corpses. Together, they suggested a serene yet horrifying museum filed with exhibits of sculptures of pure white devastation. Here and there, faces first burned, and then frozen, stared out of the frost. There were men, women and children, dogs and horses. It was indeed like the day hell froze over.

"Saxons," Arthur said with weary disgust. "This is the path they took to cut us off."

Lancelot shook his head. "Destroying every village along the way," he said. He turned to Arthur, his face pale and gaunt. "Have you ever known me to fear anything—anyone?" He looked around at the awful sight and said, "Know that I fear now."

Arthur said nothing, but simply locked eyes with Lancelot. In the unspoken conversation between them was a never-ending debate about a troublesome word called "honor."

Lucan looked beyond the canvas cover of the wagon and gasped in horror at the horrible sight before him. He clung to Dagonet's arm and said, "Will this happen to us?"

Dagonet, riding beside Lucan on the cart, smiled with some effort and pointed to his own horse as a way of distracting the boy from this horror.

"Did I ever tell you that my horse was once a man?" Dagonet said heartily. Lucan looked at him with a mixture of confusion and fascination. Dagonet nodded. "That's right. A man who died bravely in battle. A man who came back . . . as this fine steed. To carry other warriors into battle."

He waved his arm toward all the other horses in sight. "They were all warriors!" Lucan laughed, now knowing that Dagonet was lying, but grateful for the fantasy. Dagonet pretended to be insulted by the boy's laughter. "It is true!" he insisted. "Sometimes at night, if you are very quiet and sneak into the stable you can catch them talking to each other. When we arrive back at the wall, we will go and listen, you and I. You would be amazed at the things they say to each other. Wonderful things."

Lucan said, "What kinds of things?"

Dagonet drew the boy closer to him. "Oh, mostly things that only a horse can understand. And mostly things that only a horse would be interested in. But all of these horses care so much for you, that I would not be surprised if they let you in on some of their horse secrets."

"Do you really think so?" Lucan asked.

Dagonet nodded seriously. "Just you wait and see."

The frail boy nodded and lay back on the floor of the cart, smiling dreamily. He added Dagonet's promise to his sparse supply of reasons to keep on living.

Riding close by, Galahad and Gawain had been listening to Dagonet's tall tales. Gawain said, "Has Dagonet ever spoken to you like that?"

Galahad laughed sharply, as though he were just realizing something. "I am not sure he has *ever* spoken to me," he said. "And if he has, surely never more than a word or two at a time."

Up ahead, Arthur, Tristran and Lancelot huddled for a conference. The other knights led the caravan into a thick grove of trees, where at least the freezing wind might be kept out. Immediately, some of the villagers went about making fires. It was difficult to find enough dry wood, and thick, black smoke rose from the struggling blazes. But warmth under any circumstances was most welcome at the moment.

"What do we do next?" Arthur said.

Tristran pointed up at the dense tree line that lay before him. "These are the last slopes of the Mountains of Mourne," he said. "Once we have crested this hill, we will encounter a large lake."

Lancelot looked dismayed. "How in God's name can we cross a lake? Is there a bridge? A ferry?"

Tristran almost laughed. "Feel the air. Look around you," he said. "I have a feeling that we will have no trouble crossing the lake without getting our feet wet."

Without a word, Arthur spurred his horse to a gallop and headed for what seemed to be the right vantage point from which to get the lay of the dense tree line before them. Tristran and Lancelot—and Guinevere—rode out after him. Arthur crested the hill first, but when he stopped, the others caught up with him. Together, they saw the lake just below them.

"You see?" Tristran said. "Frozen solid."

Arthur said, "Lancelot, go back and get the others. Tell them we are going down to the lake now and must cross it as soon as possible. The Saxons cannot be far behind."

Lancelot looked at the steep, narrow trail leading down to the lake. "If we can get all those peasants down this mountain without breaking all of their necks, it will be a miracle."

Arthur smiled enigmatically. "Miracles happen," he said.

Lancelot rode down the hill toward the caravan, to spur them into action. At a hand command from Arthur, Tristran and Guinevere began riding carefully down the other side of the crest, heading for the vast sheet of ice that lay before them. Soon, the caravan appeared at the top of the hill behind them. Slowly and painstakingly, the carts, horses and walkers began making their way along the mountain's edge with the forest on one side and a seven-hundred-foot cliff on the other.

Midway down, Arthur said, "Tristran, is there any other way?"

Tristran looked up toward his hawk, which hovered in a headwind. He shook his head. "None," he said. "But there will be trails on the other side."

Arthur sighed. "Then let's keep moving."

After a descent of several agonizing hours, the caravan broke out of the forest at the edge of the icy lake. The body of water was long and narrow. Arthur estimated that it was no more than three hundred yards across, but with no visible ends.

"Are you certain that this is a lake?" Arthur asked. "It looks more like a river."

Lancelot added, "A very still river . . . "

Tristran said, "It is indeed a lake. And I must say, I will be a happier knight when we are well on the other side of it."

Arthur alone rode down to the shore and looked around. It looked to him like the perfect place for an ambush. He carefully sized up the area, listening closely for any signs that the Saxons were lurking, ready to attack.

After a long moment, he slowly led his horse out onto the ice, stepping gingerly, alert to any sounds of cracking. With a determined look, Guinevere kicked her horse and followed Arthur onto the lake. Immediately the other knights—not to be outdone— followed. The farther out Arthur rode, the more the frozen lake groaned as the ice threatened to cave in. He stopped.

Arthur said to Tristran, "Are you *certain* there is no other way?"

"It has to be done, Arthur," the scout replied.

Arthur turned in his saddle and motioned for the caravan to come ahead. He waved his arms sweepingly in both directions, instructing them to spread out over as wide an area as possible.

As the villagers and the mercenaries advanced, the lake came alive with the warning sounds of creaking, groaning ice. Each knight eyed the shoreline ahead, periodically looking back from where they had come, always on the lookout for the enemy that they knew was on their heels.

Just as the caravan reached the center of the lake, Saxon drums echoed in the distance. Everyone stopped. Every head spun around. Arthur and Lancelot looked at each other with a kind of grim resignation. They knew that their luck had just run out.

Galahad said to Bors, "Here is a chance to give your poor horse a break from hauling your lard around . . . "

Bors pointed toward his buttocks and made a kissing sound at Galahad.

Gawain smiled and added, "It will be a pleasure to silence their horrible racket."

Dagonet stepped down from the driver's seat of the cart, handing the reins to one of the older boys from the village. Mounting his horse, he pulled his sword and rode over to join the other knights. As usual, he said nothing. His face was set in a grim smile; it looked like he was ready to welcome anything that might come.

As he stared off toward the forest, Lancelot's face lit up in one of his ironic smiles. The other knights found it difficult to tell whether Lancelot was eager for action or suffused with dread over what was about to happen. They decided that it was some combination of the two. He looked around at them and his smile widened. They all smiled back, in a display of bravado and camaraderie. It was Arthur whom they followed, but it was Lancelot to whom they looked for ultimate affirmation.

The smile eased off Lancelot's face, replaced by a

look of stern determination. He rode over to where Arthur sat on horseback. They rested in silence, side by side, while Arthur studied the tree line carefully as the drumming thundered louder and louder, closer and closer. Lancelot, too, looked straight ahead, calculating exactly where the Saxons would emerge and how they would attack. Without looking at Arthur, Lancelot said to him, "Orders . . . Commander?"

Arthur looked over at the villagers, who huddled around the carts, trembling more with fear than with cold. He called out, "Ganis!"

The young man ran over to Arthur's horse immediately, eagerly looking up into his face. "Yes, Arthur," he said.

"You will lead the caravan south," Arthur said to Ganis. "The main Saxon army is inland. If you track the coastline until you are well south of the wall, you will be safe."

"Arthur," Ganis said, his face strained with anguish, "please don't send me away. I can fight! I want to stay and fight by your side."

Arthur looked down at the boy and smiled. "And I would love to have such a brave warrior as you with me in the coming battle," he said. "But you will serve me better—serve all of us better—by doing what I ask." He pointed at the caravan. "These people need your help and your leadership. Their lives are in your hands."

Disappointed, but with his eyes shining with pride, Ganis nodded and said, "As you wish, Arthur."

Arthur spun around and looked at the mercenaries, standing in formation, bracing for the battle. "You will go with the caravan," he said.

The captain of the mercenaries stepped forward. "We do not walk away from fights," he said.

Arthur snapped angrily, "You will do what I say!" Suddenly, his face softened and he gazed into the captain's eyes. "The caravan may be lost without your protection. Alecto must be returned safely to the wall. That is your duty."

The captain looked at Arthur uncertainly.

Arthur smiled faintly and said, "Besides, look on the bright side—you may be walking away from this battle, directly into a much, much deadlier one."

The captain nodded and stepped back to rejoin his men. Arthur pointed a threatening finger at them and said, cocking his head toward Ganis, "This man is your commander. You will obey him as you would obey me. Am I understood?"

The mercenaries nodded, some of them reluctantly.

At that moment, Lucan jumped out of the cart and ran over to Dagonet, who knelt down to catch him. The boy jumped into Dagonet's embrace and wrapped his arms around his neck. The other knights were amused, and a little touched, to see their big, dumb brute showing such tender emotion.

"I'm staying with you," Lucan said, his eyes filled with tears.

Dagonet patted him gently on the back and said, "There now. This is no place for you. Wouldn't you rather be in the cart, where you can keep warm?"

"No!" the boy said.

Smiling warmly, Dagonet said, "Well, I would. So do it for me, will you?"

Lucan cried harder, "Please . . . "

Dagonet pulled him closer and kissed Lucan on the cheek. Then he put him down and gave him a push in the direction of the caravan. "You will be safe with them. Now go!" Once again, the boy threw his arms around Dagonet's neck. While trying to maintain his stern demeanor, Dagonet patted the boy on the back softly. "Remember," he whispered, "when we get back to the wall, you and I and the horses will have a lot to talk about."

Lucan smiled in spite of himself. Dagonet roughed up Lucan's hair. Then, with one last hug, Lucan ran back across the ice and jumped into the cart. Fulcinia immediately wrapped a blanket around him and Lucan sat there gazing at Dagonet, tears streaming down his face.

Suddenly, Fulcinia looked out on the ice in alarm. Her son was walking over to Arthur, a large sword in his hand. Alecto raised the sword before his face, presenting it to the knight. "I am able," he said. "I can fight."

Fulcinia cried out, "Alecto! No! Please!"

Arthur looked over at her and then dismounted.

He clasped Alecto on the shoulder. "You are a brave man," he said. "But you have a more important duty."

Alecto looked at Arthur gravely.

"There is one thing you must do," Arthur said. "The most important thing. You must get back to Rome."

Lancelot looked down at Alecto from his horse. "You are the reason we are going through all this," he said gruffly. "If you are not saved, what we are doing is meaningless."

Alecto looked up into Lancelot's stern face and then to Arthur's more compassionate one.

"He is right," Arthur said.

Lancelot said, his voice flat with anger, "So, if you don't mind—get going away from here!"

Alecto's face flushed with anger and embarrassment. Reluctantly, he wheeled around and walked away to join the caravan. Fulcinia smiled at Arthur gratefully and he nodded at her. He remounted his horse and surveyed the scene. The drumming was now louder and more insistent than ever. "Caravan!" he shouted. "Move out!"

Those civilians without horses either climbed into the carts or jumped up behind other riders. The mercenaries mounted and began to ride off in formation. As the carts began to roll, ice grumbling under their wheels, Horton glanced around to see if anyone was watching him and then started to slip off after the caravan.

But he had taken only a few steps when Galahad

touched his sword to Horton's back. "You are going nowhere!" he said, smiling. "We are going to need your mighty arm!"

The other knights laughed as Horton, dejected, stepped away from the caravan and walked over to stand beside Squire Jols.

Guinevere climbed off her horse and took out the mercenary bow. She noticed that all the knights were looking at her. Arthur started to say something, but before he could speak, Guinevere said defiantly, "You could use another bow. Deny it."

Arthur smiled. "I cannot."

Guinevere flexed the bow as if it were a child's toy. Arthur dismounted and stood between her and Lancelot. Jols and Horton stood with the horses a few yards farther back on the ice.

As the knights formed for battle, the civilian caravan crept slowly south down the length of the lake. The field of ice was bordered on both sides by steep cliffs. Dagonet looked at the disappearing cart wistfully, comforted by the knowledge that the narrow route increased the safety of Lucan and the others; the only way the Saxons could get to the civilians was through the knights. And, Dagonet thought with satisfaction, no one was going to get through the knights.

The knights took down their shields and swords. Bors and Tristran pulled their composite bows from their saddle holsters and slung the holsters over their backs. They wore both their swords and their regular bows on their backs as well, prepared to move from one weapon to the next as the battle demanded. But to start, they drew their crossbows.

Bors called out, "Feed us, Jols!"

Jols pulled a huge bail of arrows off a packhorse, flipped it open and cut the rope that bound the arrows together. He motioned to a reluctant Horton to help him pass arrows out to the men. Guinevere tested the string on her mercenary bow as Jols placed a pile of arrows at her feet.

Suddenly, the air grew silent. The insistent drumming had stopped. Guinevere and the knights watched the shore as Cynric's soldiers appeared at the edge of the frozen lake.

Arthur shouted, "Form a square! Horses to the rear."

The Roman Square was a maneuver that normally required a legion of soldiers, massed tightly in line after line, walled on all four sides by tall body shields. The square was normally used as a solid defense against almost any weapon, but the legionnaires could also march in close formation, turning their own massed bodies into a nearly unstoppable war machine.

The effect, Arthur knew, was not quite as imposing when the square consisted of only seven knights and one young woman. But faced with a battle out in the open against what was undoubtedly a much larger force of Saxons, it seemed like the only logical plan.

All of the knights had body shields lying on the

ice beside them, and they picked them up in order to get into the square. Jols ran forward and lay a long metal plate beside Guinevere. She looked down at it and shook her head. "I need no shield," she said.

Arthur said, "Pick it up, unless your body can repel arrows on its own."

Guinevere said, "How can I shoot my bow if my hands are filled with this huge piece of wall?"

"You will have plenty of opportunity to shoot," Arthur said. "For now, do as I say."

Scowling, Guinevere draped her bow across her back and picked up the shield. Watching Lancelot and Arthur on either side of her, she saw how to place it before her, helping to build a solid defensive wall. The knights formed their tiny square as the ice groaned and snapped beneath their feet. With each passing moment, the expectation that they were all about to be drowned became more and more insistent.

Arthur looked around, surveying the square. "Keep it tight!" he commanded. "Shoulder to shoulder!"

Jols and Horton pulled the horses to the center of the square, with shields on three sides. Jols knew that wise Saxon archers would bring down unprotected horses first, leaving the knights stranded out in the open, with no hope for escape.

When they spotted Arthur's knights in battle formation, Cynric's troops halted on the shore. Cynric, who had been traveling near the rear of the line, now rode up to take his place at the head of his soldiers. To his right was Geoffrey, the British scout. He surveyed the tiny group of knights out on the ice and smiled with grim satisfaction, knowing that he had finally outsmarted the enemy. This should be easy.

The opposing sides faced each other across the expanse of ice, checking each other out, waiting to see who would make the first move. It was eerily still. The groaning and rumbling had settled down significantly, now that the weight of the caravan was gone. Now that the Saxon drums had fallen silent, the frigid air was broken only by moaning of the winter wind, the sharp flapping of the Saxon banners and the ominous creaking of the ice.

Guinevere watched curiously as Bors attached a strange device to his arm. She had never seen a weapon like it. The contraption consisted of a thin wooden channel that ran from wrist to elbow, turning Bors's forearm into a highly flexible crossbow. Once it was attached, Bors took a very short arrow and loaded it in the string of his composite bow.

The knights stood ready. And across the lake, so did the Saxons. Cynric stared nervously at his enemy. His Saxon army greatly outnumbered the knights, but there was something about the preternatural calm exhibited by Arthur and his men. Cynric could not help but be suspicious that they knew something he did not know.

Arthur said in a low voice, "Hold until I give the command."

Lancelot glanced over at Guinevere. Her face looked stern and determined.

"You look worried," Lancelot said. "That is a great number of very lonely men out there."

Guinevere continued looking straight ahead. "Do not be afraid," she said. "I will not let any of them rape you."

Cynric watched the knights dig in. To get an idea of their distance, he turned to a crossbowman and gave him a signal. The soldier fired a single arrow toward the knights. The arrow landed far short of the knights and skittered past them on the ice. Cynric considered his predicament.

Out on the ice, Arthur, too, was considering options. "I believe they are waiting for an invitation," he said. "Bors, do you think you can do better than that Saxon archer?"

Bors laughed sharply and set the stubby arrow in the channel on his arm.

Guinevere looked at him with doubt on her face and said, "They are far out of range . . . "

Bors sneered at her and then took extremely careful aim—and fired.

One of the Saxons dropped to the ground screaming, the short arrow protruding from his face. Cynric, outraged, kicked the body of the squirming man aside and slapped a drummer on the shoulder. An irregular beat began and the Saxon line stretched to double its original length. Now they were three deep by seventy across. Together—almost as one—the Saxons slipped on leather helmets and began a death chant.

Arthur turned to face his men. "Hear me!" he said. "Aim for the wings of the ranks—make them cluster."

Guinevere wrapped strips of cloth on her shooting fingers. She readied the mercenary bow, testing the tension. She reached back without looking, took an arrow from the pile and nocked it.

Bors stripped off his sniper gear and reached for a normal-length arrow. All the knights were ready, with bows pulled back. Waiting, waiting . . .

At Cynric's command, the Saxons began to march forward, very regimented, in perfect rhythmic unison. They moved only three steps when the knights released their arrows. Saxons on the sides of the ranks were hit and fell, one after another, after another.

"Rapid fire!" Arthur said.

Guinevere, Tristran and Bors strung arrows and in an almost uniform motion, fired, then loaded and fired again. Three Saxons on the end of the line took arrows to the chest. Then three more. The stunning repetition of this spectacular marksmanship was beginning to unnerve the Saxons, especially those on the ends of the line, who were catching the brunt of the knights' rainstorm of arrows.

Cynric turned to the captain of his archers and shouted, "We are within range!"

The captain called out a sharp command and the

Saxons halted their marching abruptly. The belea-
guered soldiers on the ends of the line gladly closed
ranks as quickly as possible, so that now the infantry
line was four deep instead of three. Cynric nodded to
another officer, who shouted out orders to the Saxon
archers. With great discipline and precision, the
Saxons began to fire in sequence. The front row fired,
then knelt down to reload. As they did so, the line
behind them then fired and knelt, and then the third
and, finally, the fourth. Once the fourth row had fired,
the almost mechanized operation started all over
again. In an instant, the sky over the frozen lake was
darkened by a vast cloud of arrows.

The knights saw the first of the arrows speeding
toward them like black streaks of lightning. "Testudo!"
Arthur shouted. He turned to Guinevere and said,
"Pick up your shield and hold it to the front."

Just seconds before the first battery of arrows
reached them, the knights grabbed their shields to
form a Roman-style *testudo*, or "tortoise" defense.
Arthur, Lancelot, Tristran and Guinevere held body
shields directly before them, while Gawain, Galahad,
Bors and Dagonet held their shields overhead, forming
a nearly impenetrable wall and roof. Horton and Jols
ran forward to crouch among the horses under the
upraised shields to avoid the rain of shafts descending
upon them. Dozens of arrows fell down on the *testudo*
in wave after wave, and were harmlessly deflected,
clattering on the ice and skittering in every direction.

"Now!" Arthur ordered. "Remember! Fire at the flanks!"

At Arthur's command, the knights dropped their shields immediately and simultaneously picked up their bows. At once, they fired toward the shore. As before, the knights' arrows again dropped Saxons on the ends of the line, causing the survivors to instinctively crowd toward the center of the formation.

Cynric, frustrated, turned to his officer, who nodded and again shouted out his order to fire. And again, as each line of Saxon soldiers fired, the knights' shields deflected each arrow. Cynric's frustration turned to fury at this last straw. Cynric shouted, "Advance!"

The officer hesitated for a moment, and then relayed the command to his men. Immediately, the Saxons rose and started to move forward, onto the ice.

"Here they come!" Lancelot said. "Let's make them think twice about it!"

As the Saxons carefully advanced toward them, the knights dropped their shields to the ice and started rapid firing. As fast as they could release the drawstrings, the knights received more arrows, constantly fed by Jols and Horton.

More Saxons on the extremes of the line dropped, screaming in agony, arrows thudding into their chests, necks, faces. Even those soldiers were luckier than the ones hit in the legs. The arrows struck with such power that bones could be snapped instantly, or nasty gashes ripped through thighs and calves. Out here in the wilderness, far from even the primitive medical help that might have been available to them otherwise, these wounded could do nothing but writhe in agony and wait to die. Those with broken legs knew that the fractures were not fatal in and of themselves, but that their situation was hopeless nonetheless. Faced with a bleak future of lying in agony on the ice for hours before dying of exposure, most of the soldiers chose to end the pain themselves. They pulled out their own swords and, with trembling hands, cut long, deep swaths through their lower bellies, or across their throats.

Out on the ice, the soldiers who were still advancing toward the knights began to swap looks of real fear, seeing a tiny but seemingly undefeatable force before them and hearing only screams of the dying behind them. But terrified as they were, the Saxons were brave fighters who would not give up. Step by step they continued, slowly but surely getting closer and closer to the enemy.

Angrily, Cynric urged them on, shouting, "Advance! Move, you swine! Faster!" The Saxons picked up the pace, moving determinedly toward the knights. Arthur, Guinevere and the others continued to fire as rapidly as they could, picking off Saxons at the ends of the line with virtually every shot. The Saxons on the edges of the formation were rapidly growing tired of serving as the knights' favorite targets. As unobtrusively as possible, they started to fold back and toward the center of the ranks.

Three more arrows whistled in, hitting three Saxons perfectly in their heads. The men fell backward onto the ice at the same instant, looking ridiculously as if they had been tied together at the neck. All around them, other Saxons saw the triple kill and hesitated, looking on in shock as seemingly every one of the knights' arrows brought about the death of at least one of their fellow soldiers. The line slowed almost to a stop, but Cynric beat on his soldiers' backs with the flat side of his sword, urging them forward. "Move!" he growled. "Advance or be executed where you stand!"

Lancelot spoke out of the side of his mouth to Arthur, without taking his eyes off the advancing Saxons. "Their spirit is breaking," he said.

Arthur nodded and fired another arrow. "Yes," he said, "I think we should break it a little more."

Arthur turned slightly and shouted to his knights, "Rapid fire!"

Guinevere fired rapidly with her normal bow but noticed that Bors and Tristran were shooting almost two arrows to her one, firing them off toward the Saxons as quickly as Jols could feed them arrows. She saw that they were both using the short Sarmatian crossbows which could be reloaded and fired with amazing speed.

"Give me one of those," she said to Bors.

He grinned and tossed a spare composite bow over to her. She caught it and nodded her thanks.

"You'll like that one," Bors said. "Wait and see."

Guinevere gave the string on the Sarmatian bow a testing pull and found it to be far stiffer than any weapon she had previously encountered. Undeterred, she pulled it back and let an arrow fly. She watched with amazement as *two* Saxons were skewered by her single arrow. Guinevere gawked at the composite bow, not quite believing its accuracy and force. Bors saw her two-for-one shot and burst into laughter. "See?" he said.

Guinevere took full advantage of this amazing new toy, ruthlessly and rapidly firing point blank into the Saxons. She did not kill two warriors with a single arrow again—but she did not shoot without bringing down a Saxon.

Tristran drew his composite bow back so far it looked as if the tips would touch. When the arrow flew, it thudded right through a Saxon shield into the arm holding it.

The space between the Saxons and the shore was littered with corpses. But still they continued to advance, coming nearer and nearer. Galahad fired an arrow, bringing down an officer. "You have to admire their persistence," he said, to no one in particular.

Bors smiled unpleasantly. "I don't have to admire shit," he said. "I just have to kill the bastards!"

Jols had already sent Horton back to the packhorse for more arrows. When he did not return, Jols rushed over to the spot and was disgusted to find Germanus's secretary cowering on his knees behind the horse, babbling prayers in Latin. Jols picked up a short sword and shoved it into Horton's hands. "Want to live?" Jols said. "Stop praying and start killing!" Jols picked up a bundle of arrows and ran back to the knights. Numbly, still weeping, Horton followed him, holding the sword limply in his hand.

Under the withering fire from the knights' bows, the Saxons' advance had slowed considerably. Archers crouched and tried to fire back but were inevitably dropped by a knight's arrow before they could shoot. Arthur said to Tristran, "It looks like they might be ready to withdraw from the field." At that moment, a few of the Saxons actually turned and began sprinting back toward the shore.

Arthur held up his arm and called out to his knights, "Hold!" They all waited, arrows loaded. They watched the Saxons carefully, ready to respond to whatever it was they were about to try.

Cynric walked up to one of the Saxons heading for the shore and plunged a sword into his back. Then he turned and pointed the sword, dripping blood, at the rest of his soldiers.

"You can die here or there," he said. "It matters not to me."

Signaling to his bodyguards, who surrounded him immediately, Cynric himself headed back for the shore.

As he did so, he motioned to the drummers and called out, "Sound the attack!"

The drummers began pounding out a driving tattoo. The Saxon troops roared out their battle cry and started to trot forward, a wave of killers coming ever closer to the knights' square.

Watching the double-time advance, Arthur grinned with determination. He shouted, "Knights! Death in battle is the choice of fools and cowards!" Arthur pointed toward the approaching Saxons. "And here they come!"

From his safe vantage point at the rear of the line, Cynric could now clearly see that his ranks had bunched toward the center, as the men on the outside folded back to avoid being struck by the arrows of the unerring knights. Despite their charge, he suddenly foresaw the future—and it was a bleak one. The line hesitated and wavered, breaking around the edges, bunching up ineffectively in the middle. Desperately, angrily, Cynric shouted, "No! Hold ranks! Hold ranks!"

There was a thunderclap of cracking ice as the Saxons charged forward. Arthur heard it and held Excalibur over his head, pointing its mighty blade up at the dark gray sky. The knights looked at each other with grim, determined expressions. They all realized that their situation was virtually hopeless. But this was the way that they had all expected to die, and they greeted the possibility with calm acceptance. Only

Lancelot and Arthur, casting quick, sidelong glances at Guinevere, held any regret in their souls—and both for the same reason.

Arthur cried out, "Swords!"

Unquestioning, as one, the knights shouldered their bows and drew their swords.

With a savage cheer, the Saxons rushed forward with great speed. The ice creaked and groaned beneath the weight of their armored bodies. The knights' horses pushed forward, eager to join the fight. They stamped forcefully on the ice with their hooves, sending shock waves out in all directions. For an instant, the ice howled and shrieked like a dying dragon and everyone—knight and Saxon—braced himself for the inevitable.

But for the moment, despite the terrifying sounds, the ice continued to hold fast.

Their fears intensified with each pounding step they took, but the Saxons moved forward relentlessly, having no choice but to hope that the ice would continue to support them. The knights braced themselves. Despite the numerous casualties they had already inflicted with their arrows, they were still desperately outnumbered and knew that with each advancing step taken by the Saxons, they were in deeper and deeper trouble.

Suddenly a sound, slight but bone-chilling, split the air. A hairline crack zigzagged across the ice, drawing an ominous line between the two armies. The fracture was barely visible at first—but every warrior on the field saw it and waited helplessly for what seemed to be the inevitable moment when the crack would widen and the ice would collapse under their feet.

To Arthur, however, the charging Saxons presented a more immediate danger. Arthur called out to his knights, "Close ranks! Prepare for hand to hand!"

Almost everyone moved closer together, attempting once again to form an unbreachable Roman Square. But one knight did not take part in the human barrier. Dagonet tossed his sword over to Arthur and then, his mouth set in a determined frown, he grabbed his huge battle club, threw his leg over his horse and proudly cantered out on the expanse of ice.

Arthur watched helplessly as he rode away, calling sternly after him, "Dagonet! Get back here!"

The attacking Saxons watched this strange warrior's actions and were confused and more than a little unnerved. Yards before them, Dagonet casually dismounted. Before he went about carrying out his plan, he placed his face up against his horse's face. Dagonet said in a low, soothing voice, "We will ride together again."

The horse seemed to understand. Dagonet slapped it lightly but firmly on the flank and the horse immediately turned and trotted back to the line of knights. Behind him, the Saxons continued yelling like demons, screaming out the fury of battle and the horror of their imminent demise.

In the distance, Cynric smirked at Dagonet's bravado. He motioned for his soldiers to go ahead and bring him down. Dagonet raised his battle club and bellowed wordlessly at the Saxons as if he were a powerful beast issuing a personal challenge. The Saxons advanced at the quick step, eager to accept a fight with this madman, confident in their superior numbers.

Smiling broadly, Dagonet brought his club down hard on the ice. The boom and rattle of the blow reverberated to all points on the lake. The faces of the attacking Saxons blanched with horror, trying not to believe what they knew he was up to.

Arthur shouted to his knights, "Support Dagonet!"

Instantly, Guinevere, Bors and Tristran ran to the front and began to unleash arrows at the Saxons with uncanny speed and accuracy. Cynric watched helplessly as one after another of his men dropped from the trio's arrows. He was enraged that his men still had not reached Dagonet, who continued to beat powerfully on the ice with his battle club, all the while grinning maniacally. "Kill that knight!" he shouted. "Take him down—now!"

The handful of surviving crossbowmen in the Saxon infantry fired. Dagonet held his club high overhead, preparing to bring it down with all the power and fury in his body. But before he could, Dagonet was struck in the chest by three arrows. Stunned, he staggered backward. Then, to the amazement of the warriors on both sides, the crazed grin once again spread across his face and he brought his club down on the ice again with a thunderous crash. Instantly, he was struck by two more bolts and was knocked down into a sitting position. With an immense act of will, Dagonet struggled to his feet and raised the club once again in the air. This time, however, his body began weaving uncertainly.

Guinevere, Bors and Tristran kept firing, cutting down more Saxons, but never enough to stop the bolts flying toward Dagonet from the crossbowmen.

Arthur called out, "Lancelot!" Understanding immediately, Lancelot took Arthur's place at the head of the troops as Arthur moved out onto the ice toward his wounded friend. Running fast, his body bent low to the ground, Arthur dodged the numerous bolts that snapped off the ice all around him, cracking and popping.

Despite being pierced by five arrows, Dagonet stubbornly hung on to life. He reared back for one more blast and brought his club down on the ice just as the Saxons reached him. His final blow broke the surface and the ice began to crack and shatter in an ever-widening pattern. Dagonet had barely enough strength to stumble away, back in the general direction of the other knights.

Now, the ice howled like a wounded animal and began cracking in loud reports that sounded like thunder. The Saxons tried to turn and run, but the frozen floor under their feet began shattering and they plunged screaming into the freezing water. Some clung desperately to the sharp edges of the shattering ice field but the weight of their armor and the weapons they carried soon dragged them into the black depths of the lake. A few other Saxons managed to struggle back from the brink, and ran, panicked and screaming, back to the shore.

Across the widening chasm, Lancelot called, "Archers—fast fire!"

Guinevere, Tristran and Bors ripped into the retreating Saxons with fury. They took aim both at those in the water and those on the opposite side of the impassable gap. Arthur reached Dagonet just as the knight collapsed on the ice. Arthur knelt and lifted Dagonet's head. The second that he did so, Arthur was struck in the side by a bolt and flung sideways. Peering off into the distance, he saw with grim satisfaction that the archer who shot him was immediately brought down by one of Guinevere's arrows. Despite the blinding pain, he lifted Dagonet onto his shoulders and staggered back to his tiny army.

Beyond Arthur, drowning Saxons grabbed at jagged ice until their fingers, numb and bleeding, failed them and they sank beneath the surface. Others were swept underneath the great sheet of ice and pounded at it desperately as it held them under. Their submerged faces could be seen through the frosty surface, like distorted portraits of agony under glass. As if drowning were not bad enough, many of the Saxons who struggled under the water were struck by arrows which whisked down ceaselessly through the water around them.

Guinevere's arrow hit a Saxon drummer. Another arrow hit the drum itself and ricocheted upward, impaling itself in the drummer's throat. The last two surviving drummers glanced nervously back toward Cynric, anxiously hoping that he was about to give the order to retreat. The next arrow killed one of Cynric's bodyguards. Cynric eased backward, fighting panic. An arrow winged straight for him, but it died in flight, sticking in the ice at his feet. Fighting down the rising panic, Cynric raised his hand and gave a signal. With relief, the drummers began beating the retreat tattoo. The haggard Saxons stopped their perilous advance, turned and ran as fast as they could back to the security of the shore. The two drummers, continuing their pounding, ran with them. An arrow struck one of them in the back and he jerked forward, falling onto his drum, crushing it as he died.

At the first signs of Saxon retreat, Lancelot held up his hand. Immediately, the others stopped firing arrows at the running warriors, flung down their bows and ran out across the ice to help Arthur bring in Dagonet. Their wounded leader was struggling toward them, Dagonet stretched across his shoulders. Suddenly, as the knights and Guinevere reached Arthur's side, the air became eerily still. As they gathered around, Arthur gently lay Dagonet down. Wincing from the pain of the arrow in his side, Arthur sat on the cold ground beside him.

Dagonet's breath came in long, agonized gasps. Blood bubbled at his lips and his eyes seemed to be gazing at some frightful image far, far away. Arthur looked up at Guinevere hopelessly and she felt the salty sting of tears in her eyes. Lancelot shook his head sadly; it was clear to all of them that there was nothing that anyone could do to save him. Dagonet shifted his gaze ever so slightly until he was staring directly into Arthur's eyes. He could not speak, but it seemed to Arthur that Dagonet was pleading with him. He felt like covering his face and weeping, but with a mighty effort, he remained locked in that final gaze with his old friend.

Bors gently placed his hand on Arthur's shoulder. Arthur looked up at him and Bors offered him his sword.

Inclining his head toward Dagonet, Bors said to Arthur, "Free him. It was your promise."

Arthur's face blanched with anguish. He knew that Bors was right. He also knew that this was the most difficult and heartrending thing that he had ever had to do. Taking the sword from Bors, Arthur knelt over Dagonet and whispered in his ear. Dagonet seemed to smile a little and closed his eyes. With a quick thrust, Arthur ran the sword through Dagonet's throat.

Guinevere was now openly crying, as were

Tristran and Galahad. The others looked as though they had lost one of their limbs, or one of their organs. No one spoke for a long time; the only sounds were the howling of the wind and the distant voice of Cynric, berating his Saxon troops on the shore for their humiliating defeat.

Finally, Bors said in a hoarse voice, "We are six, now. Six."

FIFTEEN

❦

ARTHUR, GUINEVERE, AND THE KNIGHTS lingered in a circle around Dagonet's body for a long time, rendered immobile by their crushing grief. Bors took part in the vigil but, being the least sentimental of the knights, kept a practical eye on the far shore, observing the movements of Cynric's decimated army. He knew that they were in a quandary. The gaping holes in the ice, and the continuing presence of Arthur and company, made it impossible for the Saxons to advance across the frozen lake and continue toward Hadrian's Wall. Their only alternative was to retrace their steps and climb the treacherous pathway through the forest and up to the crest of the mountain. For hours, the Saxons gathered the corpses of their fallen and stacked them into three funeral pyres along the banks of the lake, alternating the bodies with layers of timber and fallen leaves. Once the pyres were constructed, three soldiers doused them with lantern oil and set them ablaze.

Instantly, the three grim piles began sending flames and dark, thick, acrid smoke toward the sky. The Saxon army marched away, back into the forest. Across the lake, the knights watched them leave. "All those dead soldiers," Gawain said bitterly, "and their commander did not even salute them for their bravery. He just walks away."

Galahad shook his head. "What kind of man treats his warriors like that?"

The gathering of the Saxon bodies had been accomplished as hastily as possible. The ground and the remaining ice on the lake were littered with weapons, helmets and three crushed drums covered in blood.

Arthur stood up. "It is time we were leaving as well," he said.

Guinevere continued to kneel by Dagonet's body. She peered up at Arthur with red, swollen eyes and said softly, "Will we bury him here?"

Lancelot answered firmly, "No. Dagonet left Badon Hill with us and he will return with us."

Arthur nodded. "Yes," he said, "there is a place for him in the company of heroes."

Gawain, Galahad, Tristran and Bors wrapped Dagonet's body in a blanket and gently draped it over his warhorse. Guinevere secured the blanket with ropes at Dagonet's head and feet. Then she and the knights mounted their horses and rode away from the lake, followed at a respectful distance by Jols and Horton, leading the packhorse.

Arthur and Guinevere rode slowly side by side, saying nothing. Guinevere could not take her eyes off him. She knew that Arthur must be in excruciating pain from his wound, but he continued to ride tall. For each of the knights, Dagonet's death was a sharp, painful blow, but for Arthur it was one of his life's most searing tragedies.

Tristran and Bors cantered up beside Arthur. "We have to go out again, to scout what lies ahead," Tristran said.

Bors nodded. "The civilians are moving too slow," he said. "The main Saxon army will catch them."

"No," Arthur said wearily. "We stay together."

"To attack them?" Guinevere asked.

Arthur shook his head. "We are in no condition to attack anyone at the moment." His horse stepped into an indentation in the ground, causing it to stumble a little. Even the slightest bump caused Arthur to wince with pain.

Guinevere could not believe that Arthur did not want to continue the battle on another front. "The Saxons can be beaten," she said. "You took their will!"

"I wasn't alone," Arthur said.

Guinevere said, "You and six other knights!"

Arthur looked at her sadly and said, "Who are now five . . . "

"What if you had a hundred?" Guinevere said.

"I *had* a hundred," Arthur replied. His voice sounded exhausted. "Their ghosts haunt the island."

The answer infuriated Guinevere, even though she herself did not exactly know why. Spurring her horse, she rode some distance away from the other knights to be alone with her thoughts.

Arthur watched her go, and then reined in and fell back to ride alongside Tristran and Bors. "Arthur," Tristran said urgently, "I know you don't want to attack again so soon, but we have to do something."

Bors nodded. "I believe we should create a diversion," he said. "Cut, slash and run."

Arthur closed his eyes tightly. The pain from the arrow was so intense that he wondered if he was about to faint. The two knights saw the blood on Arthur's side and swapped worried looks.

"All right," Arthur said, with a long sigh. "Tristran, you and I will get them to chase us. We can lead them away from the caravan."

Bors looked at Tristran with concern. He knew if he suggested that Arthur was too weak to carry out the plan, that Arthur would insist on it rather than exhibit any sign of weakness. Bors knew that he had to choose his words carefully. "You are no bowman, Arthur," he said. "This job should be handled from a distance."

Arthur followed their eyes and noticed the blood

on his side. He tried awkwardly to cover it up with his hand, but it was too late and he knew it. He realized that Bors and Tristran were looking out for his safety, but he also knew that Bors was right: Arthur was not nearly the bowman that these two were. Even if he were not wounded, he would clearly be the wrong man for the job.

Gruffly, Arthur nodded. "Kill who you can," he said. Bors and Tristran began to wheel away and Arthur called out to them, "But get back alive!"

"That we will!" Bors said, grinning. Then he and Tristran spurred their horses and galloped ahead at full speed. They passed Guinevere so fast that they seemed to be two whirlwinds sweeping across the wintry ground. Tristran gave her a friendly wave as they disappeared into the distance.

Guinevere looked back to see that Arthur was now riding alone, so she swung her horse around and galloped back to him. Arthur watched her approaching and sighed heavily. He did not feel like arguing anymore. As soon as she reached him, Arthur said without looking at Guinevere, "We need to catch the caravan."

Peeved and scowling, she rode off again. As soon as she was out of sight, Arthur reached into his coat and ripped off a piece of his shirt. He shoved the cloth up into his wound and nearly shrieked in agony. The pain made him feel faint, and he swayed in the saddle. Then, afraid someone would see him in his weakened condition, Arthur concentrated all of his will toward

sitting straighter in the saddle and looking like a commander. After a few moments, during which sharp
stabs of pain radiated from his wound toward every
part of his body, Arthur gained control of himself and
rode quietly, taking shallow breaths and trying to conquer his discomfort. When he thought that he could
continue his charade for a little longer, he rode to catch
up with the still angry Guinevere.

On the forest trail, Cerdic moved cautiously forward at
the head of the main Saxon column. Geoffrey, his
British scout, walked a few feet ahead, eagerly scanning the ground for any telltale signs. It seemed to
Cerdic that the man was as alert and relentless as a
hunting dog. As if to deepen the comparison, Geoffrey
suddenly dropped to all fours. Cerdic thought with
exasperation that he was doing everything but sniffing
the ground. It would not have surprised him to see
Geoffrey begin wagging his tail.

Turning to Cerdic, Geoffrey pointed straight
ahead. "Foot tracks!" he said. "They are up ahead!"

Geoffrey bounded to his feet and started walking,
bent low to the ground. At a hand signal from Cerdic,
the force behind him began moving again up the trail.
Rounding a bend, the path suddenly split. Geoffrey
stopped and gazed suspiciously at this fork in the road,
considering it carefully. Then he trotted the few yards
back to Cerdic.

"The tracks stop here," he said.

"What do you mean, 'stop here?'" Cerdic demanded. "Did they suddenly take wings and fly away? I know these knights are remarkable creatures, but . . . "

Geoffrey was of too literal a mind to respond to Cerdic's sarcasm. "No, I am certain they didn't fly away," he said seriously. "But something is not right." He looked all around, listening closely. There was nothing to hear but the soft moan of the wind through the trees.

"It may be nothing," Geoffrey said, "but it looks dangerous to me. I would ask that you remain here while I scout farther ahead. When I have determined that the path is safe, I will return."

Cerdic nodded impatiently. "All right, go. But hurry. And take some guards with you."

Geoffrey said, "If you please, sir, I will travel faster on my own."

"You will also be helpless if you are alone and attacked," Cerdic said. "Take guards with you!"

Geoffrey bowed slightly. "Yes sir, I will take . . . one guard."

Annoyed, Cerdic pointed to one of the Saxon soldiers and indicated that he should go with Geoffrey up the trail. The Saxon saluted his commander and trotted away, trying to catch up with the scout, who was already disappearing down the trail.

Geoffrey padded along as silently as possible, his

keen scout's instincts delivering clear warnings to him
at every step. Hearing the rustle of leaves, Geoffrey
froze in his tracks. The guard stopped, too, watching
the scout closely for any signs of danger. After a
moment, Geoffrey eased forward again, silently, the
Saxon soldier close on his heels.

At another slight sound, Geoffrey stopped and
turned in the direction of the noise. At that instant, an
arrow—clearly meant for him—whizzed by his shoulder and embedded itself in the chest of the soldier
behind him.

Geoffrey crouched low to the ground, tense and
alert. He looked frantically around in all directions,
scanning the trees and brush for any movement. But he
saw nothing and heard nothing. No more arrows were
fired. Geoffrey checked the guard for any signs of life.
Finding none, he rose and trotted back to report to his
commander.

In the trees, Bors and Tristran watched as
Geoffrey told an infuriated Cerdic about the stealthy
attack, and when the Saxons marched on, Bors and
Tristran followed at a short distance, moving soundlessly through the trees, knowing proudly that the
entire army now feared an imminent attack—from two
lone knights.

Running faster, they moved out of the forest and
up to the crest of a ridge. They had tied their horses in
a shallow canyon there some hours earlier, knowing
that the crest was the perfect vantage point from which

to watch the army pass. Tristran counted silently as the troops moved down the road. "Seven deep, thirty across," he said.

Bors grinned. "I would be terrified," he said, "if I knew how many that added up to be."

"Oh," said Tristran, smiling, "it is only a few hundred. I cannot think why it would be a problem for us to provide a detour for so few."

Bors said, "Well, then, let's do our work."

The two men ran down the slope to the place where they had hidden their horses from view. Bors unpacked a canvas filled with arrows and loaded his bow with five of them. Tristran jumped on his horse, filling his bow with four arrows.

Bors scrambled back to the top of the crest and aimed his bow almost straight up, pointing at the sky. When he did so, he traded a look with Tristran, who kicked his horse and, on the move, fired his arrows high into the air. Bors fired his arrows, reloaded and fired again. Tristran continued to gallop back and forth, doing the same thing—reloading, firing, reloading, always aiming for the clouds.

Down in the valley, the Saxon army trudged forward. Out in front, Geoffrey scanned the horizon and looked all around, alert to any danger. He was looking up at the crest of the hill to their right when suddenly, out of the sky, ten, then twelve, then sixteen arrows landed in their midst. One Saxon was skewered in the shoulder, another in the neck, another in the thigh.

Cerdic shouted, "Set up a defense! Prepare for attack!" The Saxon soldiers saw that they were under siege and immediately took a defensive posture, getting ready to face the enemy from any direction. The drummers began pounding out the alarm as swordsmen drew their blades and archers loaded arrows into their bows. Meanwhile, the arrows continued to rain down from various points along the ridge, and still the Saxons had not caught a single glimpse of who might be attacking them, or even precisely from which direction they were being attacked.

Hidden behind the crest of the ridge, Bors and Tristran continued to rain down arrows, always on the move. They were not taking time to aim, but were delivering their missiles in such abundance that they managed to take down Saxons with every shot.

Furious, Cerdic stalked up and down behind a line of Saxons. "Where are they?" he demanded.

The British scout pointed. "Dead south," he said. As he said it, an arrow came from the northeast, embedding itself in the back of one of the Saxons. Cerdic glared at Geoffrey angrily.

Tristran and Bors continued their assault, laughing wildly as they fired off arrows by the dozen. They felt as if they were playing the most thrilling game in the world, and so far, there seemed to be no way for them to lose. Bors kept firing from the ground while Tristran rode back and forth, always launching his arrows from a new position.

Finally, Bors fired the last of his arrows. He whistled to Tristran as he ran toward his horse. Tristran galloped over as Bors mounted and they both rode away, down the slope. The Saxons had never caught a single glimpse of either of them.

When the arrows stopped falling from the sky, the Saxons braced for another attack. After a while, when that attack didn't come, they jumped to their feet and moved double-time down the trail. Cerdic shouted, "Forward!" and they began to mount their attack on the "deadly" ridge above. But when the first Saxon warriors arrived at the area where Bors and Tristran had been, there was no one there. And no sign that anyone had been there.

Geoffrey stood with the puzzled troops, shaking his head.

"What is this?" Cerdic demanded. "A phantom army?"

Geoffrey shrugged, thoroughly confused. "They must have already moved out."

Cerdic sneered, "Yes, they must have! What kind of army can vanish in the space of a moment?"

Suddenly, a slight movement caught the British scout's attention. He looked over and his eyes widened.

"Look!" he shouted, pointing to a knoll about a hundred yards in the distance. Cerdic and the other Saxons focused their attention on the place he indicated. Bors and Tristran were standing there, smiling cheerfully, their bows slung carelessly across their backs. Tristran recognized Geoffrey as his counterpart in the Saxon army. He had nearly killed him in the woods a little earlier, but was now somehow glad that he had not. He nodded and, to his surprise, Geoffrey nodded back, acknowledging that he knew who Tristran was. But for the moment, Geoffrey did not feel much like an equal—he had the unpleasant feeling that he was being toyed with.

Cerdic did not notice these two consummate professionals paying their respects. He just wanted to bring the two annoying knights down. He held his hand in the air and bows were raised. With a chopping movement, Cerdic's hand lowered and the arrows flew.

Bors and Tristran watched calmly, in an almost detached manner. Then, as the arrows came near, they spun around quickly and ran north. Behind them, scores of arrows landed, falling harmlessly where they had just been standing.

Cerdic, now totally enraged, raised his fist. The Saxon warriors roared and charged after the two knights. Geoffrey ran along with them, but he knew that the two knights would be long gone before the Saxons ever arrived at the knoll. He wondered if such men could ever be caught.

Arthur and Guinevere were riding side by side when they reached the top of the hill overlooking Hadrian's Wall. Blood loss had made Arthur feel desperately weak but the throbbing pain in his side kept him alert. He and Guinevere had not had much to say. Earlier in the day, when they had caught up with the caravan, she had tied her horse to the cart and climbed in to comfort Lucan, who had just learned of Dagonet's death. Arthur could hear the boy's plaintive weeping, slightly muffled beneath the canvas cover of the cart.

But as they reached their destination, Guinevere had remounted and joined Arthur again. At the crest of the hill, they stood silent, as the caravan slowly crept by, making its laborious descent into the valley. The rest of the knights had been riding fanned out behind them, and one by one they joined Arthur and waited with him, watching the caravan move toward the wall, then through the massive gates of Hadrian's Wall, which were creaking open in welcome. Their mission had been accomplished. The knights had returned with Marius's family—if not with Marius himself—and now Bishop Germanus would have no choice but to give them their documents of freedom.

Out of the forest, meandering toward them as if they had just been out for a leisurely ride, Bors and Tristran took their places with their fellow knights, satisfied that their comrades had come through safely once again. Arthur looked at them with a questioning look. Bors nodded briefly and Arthur knew that they had been successful.

Once the caravan was inside the gates, Arthur clucked to his horse and started the slow descent. The others followed without a word. The knights

approached the gates of Hadrian's Wall, which were
open wide. Usually, when they returned home after a
mission, they felt elated, celebratory. They laughed
loudly, sang vulgar songs and looked forward to a
night of drinking and carousing with women. But this
time was different. They rode through the gates and
toward the fortress as if under a dark cloud of melancholy. They had lost brother knights in battle before—
many, many times before—but Dagonet should have
been free. They saw his death as a useless one. That
made them think, if only for the moment, that perhaps
their lives were useless as well.

The knights rode through the village and into the
fortress. As they dismounted, once again turning over
the reins of their horses to Jols, they watched the villagers emerging from the carts or getting off their
horses. Arthur could see that they were impressed by
their surroundings. Even Marius's estate was not as
towering and awesome as Hadrian's Wall and the
mighty fortress that defended it.

The mercenaries dismounted and stood in formation, awaiting their orders.

When he stepped out of the cart, helped by
Guinevere, Lucan saw Dagonet's body hanging over
his war horse. The boy choked back a sob and then
began to cry again. He walked over, reached up and
tenderly took the great man's hand and held it against
his face, all the while weeping bitterly. Guinevere
stood by Lucan's side and draped an arm around his

shoulder, comforting him as much as she could, but
feeling inadequate to the task.

Bishop Germanus emerged from his quarters—
that is to say, Arthur's quarters—and rushed forward,
smiling, his arms held wide in welcome. No one, however, seemed to return his enthusiasm.

Arthur noticed that as soon as she recognized
Germanus, Fulcinia wrapped her arms protectively
around Alecto, holding him close. She clearly did not
want to be embraced by Germanus, nor did she want
the bishop to touch her son.

"Fulcinia!" he said enthusiastically. "A thousand
welcomes!" He beamed at the boy and patted him
heartily on the shoulder. "Alecto!" he said. "How
pleased we all are to see you. What a fine man you are
becoming!" Alecto returned his look impassively and
said nothing. Fulcinia gripped him closer.

Germanus glanced around at the small crowd, and
his face took on a look of practiced concern. "But
where is your dear husband?" he asked Fulcinia.

"Marius has perished," she told the bishop, trying
for a tone of sadness in her voice. Then, brightening,
she added, " . . . but Alecto has survived!"

Germanus smiled happily and said, "Jesus be
praised! Against all the odds Satan could muster, you
have triumphed!"

In his own joy and satisfaction of the moment,
Germanus remained oblivious to the knights' mood.
The bishop motioned to a Roman guard, who handed

him a sheath of papers tied together with a string. Bishop Germanus proudly offered the bundle to Arthur. "Great knights," he said, "here are your papers of safe conduct throughout the Roman Empire."

Without looking at them Arthur handed the papers to Lancelot. Lancelot handed them out, making sure that, in addition to his own, Bors received those of his best friend as well. "For Dagonet," Lancelot said.

Bors looked at the papers and then at Germanus. "I am certain that Dagonet could not be more pleased at being given his freedom," he said. Germanus glared at him, incensed by his insolence, but said nothing.

At sunset, the knights gathered just inside the low fence of the knights' graveyard. Surrounding them were hundreds of burial mounds, some with rusted swords stuck in to the hilt, others with newer blades that, it seemed to the knights, had been placed there only yesterday.

Arthur, Guinevere and the rest of the knights stood quietly before Dagonet's grave. They had dug it themselves and each man had helped to fill in the dirt with his bare hands. When they had completed the somber mound, Arthur hammered Dagonet's sword into the ground, wincing with each blow from the pain in his side. Though the arrowhead had been removed, the wound remained raw and made itself felt with every movement. When Arthur finished pounding the sword, only its ornate hilt remained in sight.

The knights looked at one another, at a loss for

words. Lucan walked over to the burial mound, trying to hold back tears, his blanket around his shivering shoulders.

Gawain finally stepped up and spoke haltingly, occasionally stumbling over his words.

"He was not a man of many words, but . . . " he said, " . . . in his life, and through his deeds, he spoke as rivers flow: strong, deep, clear, endless."

Bors said softly, "Rest, old friend. We will ride again together soon enough."

Tristran knelt beside the grave and said, "What a proud army you now serve with—heroes all."

Arthur turned and walked away, across the cemetery, leaving Lucan and the knights to say their farewells. Guinevere watched him go. As he disappeared into the darkness, she rose and followed him.

When Guinevere caught up with him, Arthur was in a lonely corner of the graveyard. He sat very still on the ground, staring at a mound that was unmarked by a sword. Guinevere slowly and quietly approached him, reluctant to intrude on a private moment but too curious about this man to stay away.

"A grave with no sword," she said softly. She sat down beside him.

"It was my father's wish," Arthur said, "if he died on this island, to be buried with his knights. Now I carry his sword."

Guinevere asked, "He died in battle?" But she knew the answer.

"Now that your term of service is over, what will you do?" she asked. "Will you stay here? Go to Rome?"

Arthur shook his head. "Here?" he said. "There is nothing for me here. Nothing left. Only graves."

Guinevere said, "I can see why you would believe that, but I think you are wrong. You still have what you and your knights have done. You have your deeds. You have your memories."

Arthur looked at her with pain in his eyes. "What we have done?" he said. "We have only waged a war to protect a 'Rome' that does not exist."

Guinevere gestured toward the fortress and said, "You saved all these people when you did not have to."

Beneath his anger, Arthur was also genuinely mystified and confused. He said, "So many dead . . . Dagonet . . . Pelagius . . . for what?"

Guinevere said nothing.

"After all these years," Arthur said, "I am still astonished by the brutality of this age."

Guinevere said, "You and I will never be the gentle people who live in poems. We are blessed and cursed by our time."

He looked at her. The light was softly colored by the rich hues of the setting sun. Arthur leaned closer to her, feeling her breath on his face.

"What is it you fear, Arthur?" she said.

"Fear?" he said, puzzled.

Guinevere said, "I don't mean what do you fear as

a soldier, or as a Roman. I mean, what do you fear . . . as a man?"

Arthur considered the question for a moment. Then he looked at her and said "Killing without honor . . . or reason."

Guinevere nodded and said, "You are much like this country. Britons with a Roman father. This place, Arthur, this land, is the last outpost of that which your heart holds most dear. Whatever honor or reason there is left in this world . . . it is right here to be won."

Arthur looked closely at her brave and beautiful face, soaking up her words. In the windy mist of the day, Guinevere gently touched his cheek. After so much brutality and death, the two of them experienced an almost unbearable tenderness. There was in both of their hearts a keen yearning for more. But they both realized that this was clearly the wrong time and place. Arthur turned his face from hers and Guinevere stood up and walked away. When she was a hundred feet away she turned and looked at him once more. Arthur was still sitting silently, alone before his father's grave.

SIXTEEN

CERDIC'S TROOPS WERE ENCAMPED NEAR a burning village on the edge of the forest, a mile north of Hadrian's Wall. His troops had rounded up the captured villagers and were busily occupied in making their usual choices—which men to conscript into the army, which women and children to slaughter before the tortured eyes of their husbands and fathers. Cerdic, who normally enjoyed the entertainment of cruelty, watched the proceedings with little interest. Instead, he brooded darkly, preoccupied with thoughts of Arthur and his knights and Cerdic's own useless son. He should have known better, he told himself, than to hold out even the slimmest hope that Cynric would emerge victorious in a battle with Arthur, but at least the inept young man might have gotten himself killed, so that Cerdic could indulge in the fantasy that his son was anything other than useless.

But, to his chagrin, Cerdic had learned only hours earlier that Cynric had neither won the fight nor died in it. A Saxon messenger had come galloping into Cerdic's camp, swung down from his saddle and ran breathlessly to his commander to make his report.

"Sir," the messenger said, "I bear news from the infantry under Cynric."

Cerdic gestured impatiently. "Go on, then," he growled.

The messenger hesitated for a second, knowing that what he had to say was not apt to make Cerdic very happy. He swallowed nervously and then said, "Cynric's forces were joined in battle with the Sarmatian knights at the frozen lake at the foot of the Mountains of Mourne." The messenger stopped, hoping that this would be news enough.

Cerdic was red faced with anger. "Well?" he demanded. "Were the Saxons victorious?"

The messenger tried to avoid his commander's furious gaze. "No, sir," he said.

Cerdic sat down, his fists clenched. "How large was the Sarmatian force?" he asked at last.

"There were seven," the messenger said.

Cerdic's eyes opened wide in astonishment. "You must mean seven hundred."

The messenger was now more nervous than ever.

"No, sir," he said. "Seven." Then brightening, he added, " . . . and two servants. And a girl."

This was too much. "A girl?" Cerdic exploded, leaping to his feet again. "Seven Sarmatians and a *girl*?!"

The messenger said nothing, longing to be released from this interview.

Cerdic sat down again, deflated. He said at length, "How many Saxons lost?"

"That is difficult to say," the messenger said, choosing his words carefully. "There were three funeral pyres. But many drowned when the ice on the lake broke."

Cerdic's eyes blazed red with fury. "How . . . many . . . ?" he asked, his voice choked with indignation.

The messenger swallowed deeply again and then said, "I believe the number must have been . . . about one hundred and fifty lost."

He expected Cerdic to explode again at this news and he was right. Cerdic flew into a rage, jumped up and clutched the messenger around the neck. "Are you sure?" he said, growling. "Are you sure it was over half of Cynric's company?"

"Quite sure," the messenger said, trying to remain calm even as he was gasping for breath.

Abruptly Cerdic released him. In a quieter, though no less sinister voice, he said, "And what of Cynric?"

The messenger relaxed somewhat, happy to be offering good news to his angry commander. "Cynric is safe, my lord," he said.

Cerdic said, "Safe?"

The messenger almost smiled. "In his wisdom," he said, "Cynric commanded from the rear of the ranks. He was entirely unhurt."

Cerdic glared at the messenger and then said in a choked voice, "Get out of my sight."

The messenger was too shocked to move.

"Get out of my sight," Cerdic repeated, "or I will kill you!"

That was clear enough. The messenger immediately turned around and ran to his horse. Hurtling into the saddle, he galloped away to report back to Cynric.

Cerdic was nearly blind with rage. He pictured his pitiful progeny blithely watching the battle from safety at the rear of the lines. He pictured his son's large force being defeated by seven Sarmatian knights . . . and a *girl*. Had Cynric turned out to be a blackguard, a tyrant, a sadist, a thief, a rapist, none of these characterizations would have struck Cerdic as unreasonable. But a coward? The very thought sickened him. Cowardice was a stigma that blackened more than Cynric's character—it spread a stain onto Cerdic's reputation as well. The stain had to be removed, at any cost.

It was late in the day when Cynric rode into camp at the head of his decimated troops. They were all

weary, beaten and humiliated. Scowling, Cerdic
stormed over and stood, arms crossed tightly across his
chest, as his son dismounted. Cynric had known that
his father would have no sympathy for the defeat and
for Cynric's travails on the ice. But he was not quite
prepared for the fury that streaked Cerdic's face.

Cynric bowed respectfully to his father, and then
pulled out his dagger. He put the tip of the blade to his
own throat in what he believed was a ceremonious
gesture.

"I offer payment for my disgrace, my father," he
said with what he hoped was self-sacrificial courage.
"I deserve nothing less."

Father and son glared at each other. Cynric had
not believed that his father would actually take him up
on his suicidal offer, assuring himself that this brave
gesture would be enough. But now, observing the
seething anger in Cerdic's eyes, he wasn't so sure.

Cerdic said, his voice heavy with contempt, "If
you are not worthy to lead, you are not worthy of
death!"

Abruptly, Cerdic grabbed the dagger from
Cynric's hand and before anyone could make a move,
savagely slashed it across his face in two long, furious
strokes, carving a gory *X* that extended from Cynric's
forehead to his chin.

Cynric screamed in shock and pain. He almost
dropped to his knees, but Cerdic grabbed his shoulders, holding him steady to endure both the agony and

the humiliation. Cynric reacted without thinking, purely out of survival. He swiped the dagger from his father's hand and pointed it at Cerdic's neck. Cerdic stood motionless, calmly, contemptuously waiting. Through the red curtain of blood that flowed over his eyes, Cynric could see that his father was taunting him, mocking Cynric's weakness, daring his son to kill him.

The look in Cerdic's eyes froze Cynric. He could not kill his father now, any more than he could have killed himself a moment earlier. The knowledge of his impotence only intensified his own humiliation—and his father's disgust.

Cerdic calmly took back the dagger and Cynric fell to the ground, holding his hands over his bleeding face, wailing in pain and shame.

Cerdic turned to one of his first lieutenants and said loudly, so that all would hear, "You are more a son to me now." He handed the bloodied dagger to the lieutenant who received it, bowing to his commanding officer. Cerdic then gazed out at Hadrian's Wall in the distance. He was commander once again, father no more, consumed entirely by the business at hand. As he prepared to start dispensing orders to his troops, he ignored the young man curled up on the ground, screaming loudly and writhing helplessly in a pool of blood.

Cerdic said to his lieutenant, in a crisp, businesslike tone, "We need to make a display before we go to battle. We will give them a taste of what they will face if they choose to stay and fight."

The lieutenant listened very carefully, trying his best to block out Cynric's screams. And trying not to think of the possible consequences of being considered Cerdic's "son."

The sun had long since disappeared behind the hill to the west of the fortress. Arthur sat alone in his room. Many of his precious books were now gone, and the shattered fresco of Pelagius had been replaced with one of the Pope. Pelagius's fresco still lay in pieces in the corner, where Germanus had flung it in his rage. Arthur gazed at it sadly, thinking about his lost friend and mentor, trying to adjust to the reality that he would never again spend time in Pelagius's company, would never again debate him, laugh with him, learn from him. With a heavy sigh, he walked over to the corner. Alecto walked into the room and watched as Arthur carefully picked up the shards, placing them on the wooden table beside his bed.

Arthur sensed Alecto's presence in the room and turned to acknowledge him.

"Arthur," Alecto said at last, "I want to thank you for saving me. And my mother . . . and the others."

Arthur sat on the bed and began piecing the broken fresco back together again, like a large, simple jigsaw puzzle. "There is no need to thank me," he said. "You were just our passage out, nothing more."

Alecto smiled a little and replied, "It would have been quite difficult for you and your knights to leave if you had sacrificed your lives for us."

Arthur said, with only a trace of irony in his voice, "With free will, a man is able to choose his own fate."

Alecto looked out the window, unsure of what to say. Glancing at the fresco, he said, "I am sorry for your friend. It would not have happened if you had not come to save us."

Arthur said quietly, "Dagonet was a brave man. A good man." He looked up at the boy. "It is time for us all to be brave, time for you to return to your home and to your destiny."

Alecto sat down on the bed beside Arthur. "My destiny," he said, sighing. "I fear the world that awaits me."

"Then change it!" said Arthur. "Dagonet fought bravely for all of us here. But not every battle is fought on the battlefield. Pelagius fought his fight and was a casualty of that war. Your fight is in Rome. I hope that you will fare better than either of my friends."

At that moment, Bishop Germanus walked into the room, followed by Fulcinia and a Roman guard. The bishop nearly stopped in his tracks when he saw the shattered fresco on Arthur's table. Arthur, holding a piece of it in his hands, looked at Germanus without expression.

Choosing his words carefully, Germanus said, "I see that the boy has told you."

Arthur glared at him, saying nothing.

Germanus continued, "Pelagius's death was most regrettable. I decided to tell you nothing of it before you left on your mission. I knew that your deep affection for him would prevent you from—"

Suddenly, Arthur lunged for the bishop, sticking the tip of his sword to Germanus's throat. Germanus was outraged at Arthur's effrontery. He was fearful as well, knowing of the knight's deep affection for Pelagius. Germanus tried to take a step back but found himself blocked by the wall. "How dare you!" he said in a choked, infuriated voice. "Put down your sword or you will answer for it!"

Arthur did not budge but continued to hold the blade at the bulge of Germanus's Adam's apple, a murderous look in his eyes. Germanus looked sideways to the Roman guard and croaked, "Disarm him at once!"

The Roman guard did nothing. Germanus looked over at Fulcinia, hoping that she would step in to help. Without a word, she closed Arthur's door for privacy. Alecto smiled a little and sat down on Arthur's bed, watching the scene with amused interest. Germanus's eyes now clouded with terror. It was clear to him that everyone in the room supported Arthur and that he had no leverage at all.

"The Holy Father will hear of this," Germanus threatened weakly.

"Yes he will, Germanus," Alecto said. "My uncle, the Pope, will hear of many things."

Bishop Germanus looked at the boy with betrayed

eyes. "Young Alecto," he said in disbelief, "it is I who was appointed your official guardian."

"Were you?" Alecto said. "Or did you appoint yourself?"

Germanus knew better than to say more.

Alecto said, "Let my uncle hear the truth and decide."

Fulcinia closed her eyes as if to say, "Thank God." She and the Roman guard took their places beside Alecto. Arthur continued to stare hard into Germanus's eyes. Every instinct in his body urged him to plunge the blade of Excalibur through the bishop's throat and watch his body quiver and jerk on the floor as every drop of his blood seeped away.

But then Arthur relaxed. "I have only killed in battle," he said. "I have only killed brave soldiers who were fighting for their beliefs or their homes or their countries." He lowered the point of Excalibur's blade to the floor. "You," Arthur said, his voice laced with disgust, "you aren't worthy of standing in their company. I will not stain my sword with your impure blood."

Arthur stormed out of the room. The others remained there for a moment, still and silent. Then Fulcinia and Alecto left, the Roman legionnaire following close behind. Bishop Germanus stood with his back against the wall, breathing deeply, trying to regain his equilibrium. Finally, with one last bitter glance at the fresco of Pelagius, he left.

Arthur walked aimlessly along the wall of the fortress, eager to clear his head in the cold night air. Turning a corner, he saw Guinevere standing at one of the parapets, gazing over at the forest south of the wall. She could see what others could not: The Woad army had arrived. She smiled to herself with pleasure, suddenly flooded with thoughts of home and family. Of her father . . .

Arthur stood beside her for a moment, looking off at the forest—and seeing only the forest. Finally, he said, "When we leave tomorrow, the last Roman legions will already be gone. You must come with us. It is the only way you will be safe."

Guinevere turned to Arthur, her face ruddy and her eyes bright in the brisk air. Her expression told him that she was wrestling with secret thoughts. Arthur expected her to protest or to suggest an alternate plan of action or simply, as was her wont, to argue with him just out of reflex. What he did not expect was her next question.

"What is death, Arthur?" she asked. "Where do I go after this little time I have called my life?"

"Why do you ask me such a question?" Arthur said.

Guinevere replied, "You are a Christian, are you not? I thought that you must have some knowledge of the subject."

Arthur looked off into the distance. "I only know what I have been told . . . by those who have lied to me all my life."

Guinevere said, with an almost desperate tone in her voice, "What? No fairy tales?"

Arthur looked at her. He realized that right now, at this moment, she was not a fearsome warrior or a brave Amazon—only a young girl who feared that she would soon be dead.

"You are not going to die tomorrow," he said gently. "You do not even have to fight. You know that, don't you?"

She shook her head, battling her young-girl tears. "You are wrong," she said. "I must fight."

"Why must you?" Arthur asked. "This is not your battle. These are not your people."

Guinevere said, "Oh, but my people *are* here." She pointed into the distance, toward the forest. Arthur looked in that direction, but still saw nothing but the darkness of the woods.

"I am the last of a high family and the first woman of my people," Guinevere said. "I am a leader and I must fight. I *will* fight. My father, if he lives, will be here with the dawn."

Arthur stared at her. "Your father?" he said. "What are you talking about?"

Guinevere nodded. "My father," she said softly, "is your greatest enemy . . . "

Instantly, Arthur knew who she meant. He could even see the Woad commander's features in Guinevere's face. Now that he noticed it, he could not imagine how he had missed it all this time.

"Merlin . . . " he whispered.

Guinevere just looked at him, smiling sadly.

The news neither surprised nor outraged Arthur. Indeed, what troubled him most at the moment was not so much the fact that Guinevere was Merlin's daughter, but remembering what Merlin had said to him that enchanted night at the dreamlike grotto. Were Guinevere's people his people as well?

Guinevere lightly touched her fingers to Arthur's face. She said, "I can touch your face. That is what the gods have given me, the greatest gift. A night to touch you."

She took his hand and placed it on her cheek. As Arthur looked deeply into her eyes, she lowered his hand to her heart. He felt it beating beneath her breast, its rhythm quickening by the second, like faint war drums calling him to action. Arthur took Guinevere by the hand and led her back down the long corridor to his room.

Without a word, they made love on the hard mattress of Arthur's rude cot, the dying embers from the hearth bathing their naked bodies in a warm golden light. They did not attack each other hungrily, with the fervor of passion long withheld and then ignited. Instead, Arthur and Guinevere clung softly to each other, as if each had found the only possible place of safety and peace and beauty in the world. Arthur held himself over her, basking in every shiver of pleasure as if it were his last gasp of air, his final sip of wine. Guinevere lay back, her hair spread behind her in waves like a dark, magical lake. As they moved slowly and rhythmically together, her hands explored his body, her fingers tracing the sword scars that crisscrossed his back like a map of violence, pain and betrayal. As she felt the urgency of the moment building up within her, leading her to what she knew would be a searing moment of perfect bliss, she vowed to herself to protect Arthur if she could, and to die beside him if that was what fate held in store for her tomorrow.

Afterward, they lay quietly, wrapped in the warmth and comfort of each other's arms. Guinevere tried to think only of the peace and pleasure of the moment. But her mind was filled with unbidden and disturbing images. She knew that they were being sent to her by her father. In her vision Guinevere could see and hear Woads in the forest, preparing for battle. They danced to the insistent throb of their war drums, applied the intricate coloring of camouflage to their skin, sharpened their blades and strung their bows. Merlin . . . *Father* . . . watched calmly, knowing his people would triumph, no matter what came. He sent his love to his daughter across the miles, and his promise that they would meet on the morrow.

Guinevere and Arthur drifted into a restful sleep as the last embers died in the grate. But suddenly, they were jolted awake by a furious pounding on Arthur's door. Arthur leaped from his bed, grabbed Excalibur and rushed to open the door.

Squire Jols stood in the hallway, an excited gleam

in his eye. "Arthur," he shouted, "the Saxons! You must come to the wall!"

Arthur and Guinevere dressed quickly and rushed down the corridor and up the steps to the top of the wall. There, the people of the fortress, the other knights—including Lancelot and the mercenaries—watched in horrified fascination as a huge flaming cross blazed in the dark of the field beyond the Wall. The massive flame crackled and roared. No one had encountered such a thing before, but they all knew what it meant. The Saxons were promising total defeat, utter annihilation.

Bishop Germanus was the last to arrive at the Wall. He took one look at the burning cross and shook his head in despair. "This is a godforsaken place," he said. "This is not for Romans."

Lancelot said, unable to keep the sneer from his voice, "This is not your fight any more than it is ours." He turned to Arthur and said, "Arthur, we are ready to leave."

Arthur did not take his eyes from the flames. "I am staying," he said quietly. "This is my fight."

Lancelot looked at him in disgust. "I knew it!" he said. "In the beginning, I feared you would betray us." Arthur looked at him with pain behind his eyes. "But now," Lancelot said, "you betray yourself."

Arthur realized that Lancelot, staring at him with such anger, knew him too well. In this moment, Lancelot and Guinevere were two opposing forces fighting for Arthur . . . and they knew it, even if Arthur did not. Lancelot turned angrily and stormed away. Arthur and Guinevere watched him go. Neither said anything. Then Arthur, too, walked away, down the stairs of the wall and out of the fortress gate. He did not stop until he reached the silence and darkness of the knights' graveyard.

At his father's grave, Arthur knelt with Excalibur in his hand. He carefully laid the great sword on the burial mound. He sat there in silent communion with his father for so long that he lost all track of time. Perhaps he was there for hours. Perhaps the sun abandoned this bloody earth and he sat in darkness on the spot for days or weeks.

Even before he saw the figure standing before him in the gloom like a graveyard ghost, Arthur sensed its presence. Looking up, he saw Merlin looming there, motionless. He was backed by four Woad warriors.

Merlin said quietly, "These people will follow you if you choose to lead."

Arthur rose, holding the shimmering blade of Excalibur before him.

"Each night," he said, "as I lay in bed, my father would tell me stories of how this blade was hewn." He fingered the hilt of the sword, the carving of a double profile of a man, facing right and left.

"The gods I know are pagan," Arthur continued. "But I know little else about them. The gods of my forefathers . . . "

Merlin shook his head and said, "They are not your father's gods, Arthur. Those are the gods of your mother, the gods of the Celts." Merlin smiled. "*Our* gods . . . "

Arthur turned the sword over, exposing the gold crucifix medallion on the other side of the hilt. He said, as if to himself, "But this . . . this represents the God whom I came to love . . . " Arthur ran his fingers over the medallion, thinking of Pelagius and Germanus, of the Holy Father, and the many betrayals he had suffered at the hands of Rome.

Arthur stared at the sword for a moment. And then, abruptly, he sheathed it and looked at Merlin. By the action, Merlin understood that Arthur had made his decision. He nodded with satisfaction, but Arthur looked at him with some lingering suspicion.

"Tell me this, Merlin," Arthur asked. "Where will you be when the swords crack and the dying scream?"

Merlin waved his arm out into the night. "Everywhere," he said.

SEVENTEEN

❧

THE CRACK OF THE TWIG WAS SO FAINT that it almost did not register as a sound; few people would have heard it, no matter how closely they might be listening. But the two Woad guards were not ordinary people. At the soft snap, each of them looked alertly into the blackness of the predawn forest and when they saw the shadowy movement of the intruder, they pounced forward as one, holding their spears before them.

"Stop there or die," snarled one of the guards.

"Harold," said a cheerful voice. "I knew you would be the first friend I would meet. And who is this with you . . . Arrian?"

The Woad guard peered closer at his prisoner and his face brightened into a wide smile.

"Guinevere!" Harold said. "The gods be praised!"

His friend Arrian laughed gleefully. "We thought you were dead!"

Guinevere kissed each of the young men on the cheek and put a hand on a shoulder of each. "And just who could kill me?" she said, smiling.

The two Woads embraced her happily. "Not I," said Harold. "Of that I am certain."

Guinevere said, "Is my father well?"

Arrian said, "He is as he always is."

"But he will be even better," Harold added, "when he sees you. He probably gave you up for dead long ago."

Guinevere started walking through the woods. "No," she said, "I do not think he did."

They escorted her into the thickest part of the forest. The narrow path suddenly opened up into a large clearing, in the center of which raged a huge bonfire. Around it were gathered dozens of Woad families, roasting meat for their dinner and applying their camouflage and battle paint for the upcoming fight. When Harold and Arrian stepped into the bright circle, Guinevere between them, Harold called out, "We have caught a dangerous warrior, whom we have made our prisoner!"

Several people looked up at them with shock and concern. But the moment the Woads recognized Guinevere, excited smiles broke out on their faces and they rushed to her side, burying her in an avalanche of kisses and embraces.

Then a loud voice came booming across the

camp. "If it took only two of you to capture this prisoner," the voice said, "she must have been asleep—or else she is not the warrior she once was."

Guinevere broke free of the mob of well-wishers and rushed over to her father, tears stinging her eyes. Merlin opened his arms wide and she flung herself into his embrace, burying her face in his chest.

Merlin kissed Guinevere on the top of her head and said softly, "Welcome back, my darling daughter." He looked up at the crowd and said, "Soon we must fight. But right now, let us celebrate the return of our beloved Guinevere." To Guinevere he said, "We often despaired, but we never gave up hope. Come, there are things we must discuss."

A woman ran forward and placed a bowl of pheasant stew and a crust of bread in Guinevere's hands. "You must be starving after your ordeal," she said.

Guinevere took the food and smiled at the woman. "Thank you. You cannot know how much I have longed for the hospitality of my people."

Merlin led her away to a large fallen tree a short distance away from the crowd. They sat down and Guinevere ate a little of the stew. Merlin looked at the cuts and bruises on her face, and at her fingers, still swollen from their dislocation. His face creased in anguish.

"We did not know where you were," he said. "If we had, I would have come for you, even if it had cost my life and the lives of every one of our people."

Guinevere nodded gravely. "I know you would have," she said.

"Thank the gods that Arthur was led to the place of your imprisonment," Merlin said. "And thank the gods that he did not know that you are a Woad."

Guinevere was surprised to hear this. "You know that Arthur rescued me? How?"

Merlin smiled enigmatically and said, "I have spoken to him on more than one occasion."

This surprised Guinevere even more. "You have spoken with Arthur since he saved me, yet you did not make yourself known to me?"

Merlin gently put his arm around Guinevere's shoulder. "It was not the right time. I saw that Arthur had a special feeling for you. And I knew he had a life-long hatred of our people. I had to makes things happen in a certain order, otherwise all might have been lost."

Guinevere said, "But . . . "

Merlin interrupted her. "I did see you one night," he said, "in camp. You were asleep, and I watched you for hours from a tree. My heart was so filled with gratitude that you were alive. It took all of my strength not to rush over to you and take you in my arms."

Guinevere embraced her father. "I wish you had . . . "

Merlin patted her on the back lovingly and said, "I wish that our reunion could have come at a happier time. But tomorrow, we must go into battle. I would like for you to stay out of the fight. I could not bear to lose you again so soon after finding you."

Guinevere looked at him in shocked disbelief. "You cannot ask such a thing of me," she said. "And if you order me, I will disobey you."

Merlin protested, "But Guinevere . . . "

"No," she said. "I owe it to my people to fight by their side. I owe it to you." Guinevere cast her eyes downward, not quite sure how to say the rest. "And . . . I owe it to Arthur."

"Because he saved you?" Merlin asked.

Guinevere looked into her father's eyes. "Because I love him," she said.

The sun crested Badon Hill, south of Hadrian's Wall. Its soft golden rays spread slowly across the ground, down the hill and toward the fortress, illuminating the caravan that was rolling slowly into the light. The caravan was smaller than the one that had arrived the day before. This one consisted of a cart, which carried Alecto and Fulcinia, and the ornate coach of Bishop Germanus, in which he rode with his secretary Horton. For his part, Horton was highly relieved to have this dangerous episode over with and to be heading back to the beauty, civility and luxury of Rome.

A second cart carried a few of the villagers and servants who were there to make life easier for the nobility. Lancelot and the other knights escorted the caravan, riding in a protective formation around the vehicles, keeping an especially close eye on Alecto and his mother.

But though the caravan may have been of modest size, the group of Roman legionnaires marching behind it was not. They were the last of the troops that had defended the Wall's fortress, the last of countless thousands of legionnaires who had been stationed there over hundreds of years. Now, to the disbelief of most of them, they were leaving. It was truly the end of an era.

The line moved slowly up the slope of Badon Hill. Atop it, Arthur sat astride his great horse, adorned in full battle gear, waiting for the caravan to arrive. Jols waited by his side, on his own horse.

Arthur shook his head as if he could not really grasp the reality of the situation. He said to Jols, or perhaps to himself, "Rome, leaving Hadrian's Wall. Leaving Britain for the first time in four hundred years."

Jols sat straighter in his saddle and said, "This changes everything, doesn't it, Arthur?"

Arthur looked at his squire, a little bemused by the question.

"Yes," he said, nodding thoughtfully, "I suppose it does."

Jols said, "Then, may I ask something of you?"

"Of course, Jols," Arthur said. "What is it?"

Jols pulled himself up to his full height in the saddle and took a deep breath. "I am not a knight," he said. "Only a lowly squire."

"Hardly lowly, Jols," Arthur said, smiling affectionately.

Jols said, "But I can fight! And I will never give up. I would die in battle sooner than desert you."

Arthur looked at the young man and nodded. "You have a great heart, Jols," Arthur said. "Great enough for two knights."

Jols smiled but waited for Arthur to turn him down.

Arthur said, "Go to the Wall. I need a steady arm to brace the people in this fight. I know I can count on you."

Jols swelled with pride. "You can trust me to my very last breath, Arthur," he said. "That is my eternal pledge to you." Happily, Jols turned his horse around.

"Wait!" Arthur cried. Jols returned to his side, his eager face showing that he was more than ready to receive an order. Arthur reached into his saddlebag and brought out a long sword with a narrow blade. Its hilt was carved in a simple spiral pattern and the tip was slightly rounded instead of honed to a sharp point.

Arthur handed the blade to Jols hilt first. "This is called a spatha," Arthur said. "It is a Roman cavalry sword." Jols wrapped his hand around the hilt and gaped at the spatha wordlessly, his eyes wide with wonder. "However," Arthur said, "I expect it will work

just as well on the walls of the fortress as on the back
of a horse."

Jols could barely get the words out, "Th . . . thank
you, Arthur."

Arthur nodded. "As you say," he said to Jols, "you
are not a knight." He grasped Jols's shoulder and
squeezed affectionately. "But every knight has to start
somewhere, yes?"

Jols nodded. He was slightly panicked to feel his
eyes filling with grateful tears. "Yes!" he answered.
And before he shamed himself before Arthur by weeping like a baby, he once again wheeled his horse
around and galloped back toward the fortress.

Down the hill, alongside the caravan, Bors raised
his hand to Arthur and bellowed his battle cry. Arthur
returned the call. Soon the cry echoed from all of the
knights, sounding across the countryside like the
dying song of a great beast of battle.

When Bors and the rest of the knights reached the
crest of Badon Hill, they gathered around Arthur. None
of them seemed able to find words appropriate to the
moment. The exhilaration they felt at being granted
their freedom after all these years was tempered by this
unexpected farewell to their leader, the man they had
followed into every kind of battle horror, the man they
all loved as a brother, as a father. Now, he was remaining here to fight while they rode back home, to safety,
to what might, against all odds, turn out to be long
lives. None of the knights could find the right words, so
they said nothing. Arthur and Lancelot looked into

each other's eyes. Each of them remembered the details—some violent, some hilarious—of a life spent together on the frontier. It was too much to say; the pain of their separation was too great to verbalize.

The two warriors traded a final look, and then each of the knights nodded their farewells to Arthur. One by one, they passed over the crest, heading toward home.

When they had disappeared from view, Arthur looked down the hill toward the Wall's fortress. In his mind he made an inventory of all the points of their plan of defense. Hay bales had been set along the walls and at various points around the town, to be set ablaze at just the right moment of the battle. The villagers who could fight, as well as the mercenaries, were at their positions, poised to surprise the Saxons, who had just watched the army march away and were now convinced that the fortress was virtually undefended.

And in both the fortress and the forest, the great secret weapon, the force that the Saxons did not expect: the Woads. They included Guinevere, whom Arthur had not seen since well before dawn, when she had slipped over the Wall and rushed to the tree line to join her father and her people.

Cynric, accompanied by Raewald and his personal swordsmen, emerged from the forest and formed ranks down the field from his father's force. The fortress was their destination, but both Cerdic and Cynric had the foreboding feeling that there was a lurking danger in another direction. Shading their eyes, both father and son looked up toward the crest of Badon Hill. There they saw nothing but the glare of reflected sunlight glinting off brightly polished metal. They both knew that someone clad in armor was alone at the top of that hill. But neither of them realized that it was Arthur, astride his horse in full battle gear, shimmering in the brilliant glow of the rising sun.

The British scout Geoffrey rode to Cerdic's side. Pointing in the direction of Badon Hill, he exclaimed excitedly, "The Roman auxiliary has left the wall!"

Cerdic said impatiently, "Yes, we watched them march away. But what of the knights?"

"They are leading a caravan out of the fortress, headed south," Geoffrey said. "Your demonstration of force has driven the fighters south with their tails between their legs."

Cynric squinted as he looked over at the fortress. "So no one defends the Wall?" he asked hopefully. "There will be no resistance?"

The British scout shrugged. "There are a few dozen villagers," he said. "They may be armed with pitchforks and harvest scythes. But they will certainly not be equipped to offer any kind of resistance to your mighty army."

Cerdic nodded, and then looked at Geoffrey with ill-concealed disgust. "You will not join the attack," he said. "You may watch the slaughter of your people from some hiding place."

Geoffrey looked down, willing himself not to show Cerdic the shame he felt.

"After we take the Wall," Cerdic said, "I will need your abilities again."

The scout nodded curtly and rode away. Perhaps one of those villagers would make a lucky shot, he said. Perhaps Cerdic would be one of the battle's casualties. Geoffrey did not think such an outcome was likely, but he was comforted by the thought.

Cerdic rode over to where Cynric and Raewald waited. "Ready the troops for immediate attack," Cerdic said to Raewald, pointedly ignoring Cynric. "The attack should only take a matter of moments."

Raewald nodded his assent. "What of the Roman family?"

Cerdic said, "They are in a caravan heading south, guarded by the knights. We will take the fortress as quickly as possible, station a small company here to occupy the fortress and then we will turn south to overtake that caravan and avenge my son's humiliation." He glanced at Cynric and continued, "We will learn today that it is no great feat for Saxons to annihilate a handful of Sarmatian scum."

Cynric, his face marked by the festering X carved there by his father, simply glared at Cerdic, furious but not daring to respond to the insult.

Raewald glanced upward toward the crest of Badon Hill. From where they sat, Cerdic and Cynric could still see nothing on the slope but a faint metallic shimmering. Raewald saw the same thing, but instantly recognized what it was. He pointed toward the glint. "See!" he said. "On that hill . . . "

Cerdic looked up and scowled. "What is it?" he demanded

"It is a knight," Raewald said. "His armor shines in the sun."

Cerdic squinted, shading his eyes with his hand. Finally, he managed to make out the shimmering figure of Arthur. "A knight!" he snarled. "I was told that all the Sarmatian knights were to be gone!"

"They are gone," Raewald said. "All save that one." He then added dismissively, "A single knight, a tiny fly on the back of your great army."

Cynric looked at Arthur, as still as a statue, and felt a chill of foreboding. He could not help but wonder if perhaps the Saxons were walking into some sort of trap set by the canny Sarmatians. His father could be dismissive about the abilities of the knights, but Cynric had faced them and knew how dauntless and deadly they could be. Even one knight was a threat too significant to ignore. But Cynric knew if he articulated such thoughts, it would only make him seem weaker and more cowardly to Cerdic. And so he said nothing.

Cerdic said to Raewald, "Is it Arthur?"

"I do not know," Raewald answered. "But if I had to venture a guess, I can think of only one Sarmatian knight who would remain here alone."

Cerdic looked thoughtful. "Something isn't right." He turned to Raewald. "Perhaps we should speak with this knight."

Raewald nodded. "As you wish," he said. Raewald turned to one of his lieutenants and ordered him to bring a large piece of white cloth. When the lieutenant returned with the fabric, Raewald affixed it to his lance. He said to Cerdic, "I will be back soon to report the results of my mission to you immediately."

Cerdic shook his head. "No," he said. "I am going with you."

"It may be dangerous, sir," Raewald said.

Cerdic cast a contemptuous look at him. "Let's go," he said.

The slowly spreading light of dawn had now reached every part of the landscape. It seemed to Arthur that he had not moved a muscle for hours, sitting patiently on his horse, intently watching the field before him, alert to any movement from the army below. But he knew that today would be the day. There would be no more hesitation. Looking down on the Saxon force, Arthur's hand instinctively dropped to Excalibur's pommel. He caressed the steel in anticipation.

Then, in the distance, came the sound of Saxon drumming. From the hill Arthur could see Cerdic approaching on horseback, followed closely by Raewald bearing the white flag of truce.

Arthur gently spurred his horse, and together they galloped down from Badon Hill. When he arrived at the fortress, he ordered the soldiers to open the gargantuan main gate of Hadrian's Wall. They rushed to carry out the order and Arthur settled in, knowing the operation would take some time.

Raewald and Cerdic watched the complicated operation from the other side of the wall. Cerdic dismounted and Raewald started to do the same.

"No," Cerdic said. "Stay here. I will speak to this Roman alone."

Raewald protested, "Is that wise?"

Cerdic peered at him, dangerous amusement in his eyes. "Do you doubt my wisdom, Raewald?"

Raewald blanched a little. "I do not, sir."

Cerdic nodded. "Good." He began to walk forward, toward the Wall.

Creaking and groaning, almost painfully, the huge doors finally slowly swung open. Arthur rode through alone. To the watching Saxons, he seemed magnificent and imposing. Many of them—especially those who had faced him on the lake of ice—wondered if perhaps the magical legends about him were true after all.

From the opposite direction, Cerdic approached on foot.

The two leaders reached each other at about a hundred yards beyond the gate. Both Arthur and Cerdic paused for a moment, each sizing up the other. Finally Cerdic, like a lion fixed on his prey, stepped closer to Arthur, who remained mounted.

Arthur's horse began to stir, nervously scuffing the ground with his hooves. He seemed to sense Cerdic's danger and ill will, as if he were a wild beast to either kill or flee from. Because Arthur's horse was as brave and stalwart as Arthur himself, fleeing was not an option.

Cerdic put his face close to the horse's. The two of them stared each other down, beast to beast. Cerdic said admiringly, "Exquisite. They are perfected creations, are they not?"

Arthur remained silent, simply fixing his stare on the Saxon, waiting to hear what he had to say. Cerdic began to circle the horse as they spoke. It looked to Arthur as if he were sniffing out his prey, planning the details of his oncoming conquest.

"I am Cerdic," he said. Arthur did not reply. Cerdic continued, in a pleasant conversational tone, "You are the Roman I have heard so much about. Of course, I can scarcely be expected to believe most of it. Legends and tall tales." He smiled condescendingly.

Arthur kept staring at him.

"But Rome is gone," Cerdic said. "We watched the legions march away from this place this morning, deserting Hadrian's Wall after all these years. They have left this fortress to us—to the Saxons—without a fight . . . without even a debate."

Arthur said nothing.

Cerdic continued. "So now that Rome has deserted you . . . for whom do you fight?"

Arthur said, "I am no Roman. I am Arthur. And I fight for my people."

The easy smile left Cerdic's face. Perhaps he

sensed a stronger, more committed Arthur than he bargained for.

"All who try to prevent me from passing that wall will perish," Cerdic said. "All. Did you not come out here to beg a truce?"

Arthur said, "I came to see your face so that I alone may find you in battle."

This was not the answer that Cerdic expected. Momentarily, the confident expression dropped from his face. But Arthur's recklessness only seemed to harden Cerdic's resolve.

"How do you know my belly shooters will not cut you down?" Cerdic asked. "Here and now?"

Arthur replied calmly, without taking his eyes from Cerdic's face, "They are out of range." He smiled now for the first time. "For that matter, how do you know I will not kill you where you stand?" He lightly touched the hilt of Excalibur. Cerdic saw the movement and took a second to examine the weapon.

Cerdic managed to come up with a smile at the threat. He was about to reply when Arthur simply turned his horse and rode slowly back toward the gate. Cerdic watched him ride away for a moment. Then, his smile broadening, he turned and walked back over to where Raewald waited with their horses.

Cerdic mounted and watched Arthur ride up the hill. Then he turned to Raewald and said, with great satisfaction in his voice, "Finally a man who is worth the trouble of killing."

Raewald asked, "It was Arthur?"

Cerdic nodded. "The famous Arthur." He grinned. "He has a wonderful sword. I look forward to owning it before this day is over."

He began riding back toward the Saxon lines. Raewald ripped the white banner from his lance and let it flutter to the ground. Then he followed his commander back to the ranks of his army.

EIGHTEEN

WHEN CERDIC REACHED THE FRONT LINES again, Cynric rode out to greet him. Cerdic looked past him—or, as it felt to Cynric, *through* him—and shouted an order to Raewald: "Prepare the troops!"

Before he moved to carry out Cerdic's order, Raewald pointed toward Hadrian's Wall. Both Cerdic and Cynric looked over at the massive structure.

"See," Raewald said. "They have not shut the gates again. Do they not realize that we are about to attack?"

Sure enough, the huge gates stood wide open. There was no sign of life in the space between the gates and the fortress—and no signs of life in the fortress, either.

Cerdic's brow furrowed with concern as he pondered the meaning of this. There was dead silence all across the plain, so quiet that Cerdic found himself speaking almost in a whisper. "He has a plan, this Roman," he said.

Inside the fortress, Jols brandished the Roman cavalry sword before him, beaming with pride. He had polished it to a high sheen and with a whetstone had honed the tip and edges to razor sharpness. He was keenly aware that a soldier helping to organize the defense of the Wall against a savage enemy should not be so giddy. But Jols was just as aware that his life had changed radically, and for the better. Even if he died in this battle, and that new life lasted only an hour, he would perish knowing that he was a warrior and no longer just a servant.

Suddenly, a mighty noise from across the field drew Jols's attention to the area to the north of the Wall. Up on Badon Hill, Arthur heard it, too, and rode over to the crest to see what was happening. In line after line, hundreds of Cerdic's troops poured rhythmically out of the forest like a flood, marching straight for Hadrian's Wall. The drummers marched out front, beating an urgent rhythm that echoed ominously through the valley. Just behind them, lines of swordsmen formed most of the second rank, each holding his blade in readiness across his chest. They were followed closely by the dreaded crossbowmen, marching with arrows already loaded, prepared to fire at the first order.

A young Woad ran up to Jols and said, "Everything is ready here." He smiled. "These Saxons will find something behind these walls that they do not expect."

Jols said, "Thank you. We can handle things inside if you want to go back to your people. It's your choice."

The Woad warrior nodded. "We have always preferred fighting in the open. These confined spaces are not where you will find the Woad at his best. The gods be with you." Jols nodded his thanks and the Woad ran down the stairs, calling for his fellow painted warriors to join him. By the time they reached the outside of the fortress, there were dozens of them, all running, inexplicably, without making a sound. They rushed over to the south side of Hadrian's Wall and climbed over. All of the Saxons were on the north and the Woads ran single file at the base of the wall, keeping out of the enemy's sight until they could make a dash for the far forest to join their main force.

Atop Badon Hill, Arthur was able to survey all the troop movements, both inside and outside the fortress. From down on the plain, the strident sounds of drums, horns and hundreds of marching feet reached him. He mounted his horse and galloped down the hill in order to see to the last-minute preparations. At the huge gate, Arthur rode past Jols and several mercenaries who were pushing a pair of catapults inside the fort. "Jols!"

Arthur shouted. "Set those out on the forest edge! Facing the main gate."

"Yes, Arthur!" cried Jols, grinning from ear to ear.

Arthur rode around the fortress, satisfied with the preparations that had been made there. Now there was only one thing left to do. Arthur turned and rode back out of the fortress and up the hill. When he reached the summit, he raised the Draco standard—what he and his knights called the Sarmatian Dragon.

The dragon was like an enormous wind sock made of dozens of pieces of colorful fabric sewn together in a tubular fashion. At various points along this sleeve, hoops were placed to keep its shape. At the end of the standard was a fearsome head with a special device placed in its mouth that made it screech and scream when the wind blew through it. Different companies created different heads: dogs, lions, wolves, bears. Arthur and his knights had always preferred the dragon. There were those who believed the knights had actually slain dragons during some of their incredible adventures, and it amused the men to take this terrifying mythical beast with them into battle.

The Draco standard was constructed so that as long as it lay still, it looked like nothing more than a pile of laundry. But streaming from a high-placed flagpole, or carried atop a charging battle horse, the dragon came to life, flying through the air like a kite and shrieking like a monster.

Far on the other side of the hill, the knights continued following the caravan. Each of the men was lost in private thought, but had they spoken to one another, they would have discovered that their minds were working in unison, all consumed by the same subject. As Lancelot rode along, he focused on the faces of three village children who stared back at him out of the last wagon. They bore no real expression—they were simply gazing at him curiously. But to Lancelot it seemed they were glaring at him contemptuously, challenging him to stop acting like a coward and go back and do what had to be done.

In the distance, the knights could hear the faint sounds of the Saxon drums and horns. Then another noise joined the cacophony—the eerie screech of the Sarmatian Dragon. Suddenly, the knights' horses began to neigh and tug frantically at their reins, stamping the ground; they knew a battle was brewing and they wanted to fight. Bors's horse spun him in a furious circle and Bors laughed uproariously. "Didn't Dagonet tell us that they were all warriors?" he shouted. Lucan, from his place in one of the wagons, joined Bors's laughter. "Do these horses have to tell us our duty?" Bors yelled.

Almost instinctively, the knights gathered into a circle, looking at one another expectantly. They saw no reason to talk about anything—they all knew what they had to do. Lancelot looked from one face to another, then nodded firmly and rode toward the supply wagon, bringing it to a halt. Once it had stopped,

Lancelot dismounted and started gathering arrows, packing them into his own quiver as tightly as they would fit. The other knights dismounted, too, and began tearing the tarp off the wagon and pulling out their battle gear.

When they were armed and ready, Bors embraced his three sons, one by one in order of size. He lifted the baby from Vanora's lap and kissed it tenderly on the cheek.

An outraged Bishop Germanus jumped out of his carriage, with Horton scurrying along behind.

"Are you all mad?" Germanus shouted. "We must leave—move south now!"

Everyone ignored him. Alecto rode his horse to where the knights were making battle preparations. "Tell Arthur I will honor his name in Rome," he said.

Lancelot said, "I will tell him."

Fulcinia had stepped from the wagon and waved at the knights, her eyes shining. "May God be with you all," she said.

Germanus nearly gagged when he heard those words. He turned his bile on the knights. "Can't you see?" he said desperately and angrily. "God has pre-destined that the Saxons shall win! No force on earth can defeat them! God has spoken!"

Lancelot hefted his mighty shock lance and aimed it directly at the bishop's nose.

"My lance has spoken as well!" he said. "It is pleading with me to plunge it into your heart."

Germanus stared at the point of the lance, only an inch away. He tried to look defiant, but failed. He backed up cautiously, ready to break into a run if Lancelot followed him. Instead, Lancelot simply turned and mounted his horse.

"Animals!" Germanus yelled, spitting with each word. "Pagan beasts!" He wheeled around and he and Horton bolted for the wagon. Bors rode up behind them and shouted at Bishop Germanus, "If my family does not make it home safely, I'll find you, Bishop. And by your God, I'll skewer you! Believe it!" Germanus just kept running, staring straight ahead, beginning to wonder if these savages were going to slaughter him then and there.

Bors wheeled his horse around and then said, almost to himself, "Damn it, maybe I *will* be governor after all!" As he rode past the cart in which Vanora and his children sat, he called out, "No matter what happens, keep going. One way or another we will be together. That I swear to you!"

Germanus and Horton ran faster. When they reached the coach, they jumped inside and pulled the flap down. Meanwhile, Alecto helped his mother back into their own wagon. The knights galloped off into the distance. When they had disappeared, the caravan began moving again, slowly making its way back to Rome.

Arthur sat on horseback carefully smoothing the Draco standard. He had given it a test run and was gratified to see several of the Saxon soldiers look up the hill with shocked expressions at the weird noise. Now he planned to carry it with him into battle, holding it high over his head as it screamed out its cry of Sarmatian victory.

From behind him a voice spoke. "And will you bear the Sarmatian Dragon yourself, Arthur? Is that not a job for Squire Jols?"

Arthur gaped at Lancelot with surprise. Then his face broke into a happy grin. "Jols is squire no more," Arthur said. "Someone had to take your place on the field of battle, and Jols has always been a greater warrior than you, anyway."

Lancelot laughed. "True enough!" he said.

Now they sat side by side on horseback. Arthur began to acquaint Lancelot with his battle plan. He said, "The sun is at our back. This hill is . . . " Arthur stopped suddenly, staring at the edge of the forest south of the Wall.

Guinevere stood there, her face made up with Woad dye, camouflaged like a guerrilla fighter. Dressed in the tight leather outfit of a female warrior, she waited calmly with her Woad fighters. That night, seemingly so long ago, when she was bathing in the wagon, Lancelot had seen more of Guinevere's flesh than at this moment—but not much more. The leather dress was clearly designed for speed rather than modesty.

Both Lancelot and Arthur stared at her in awestruck silence. Neither man had declared his love for her to the other, but each of them knew what his friend felt. That knowledge did not evoke anger or jealousy—just understanding between them. They also knew, however, that this would have to be sorted out someday. Just not today.

After staring at Guinevere for a very long time, Lancelot finally said, "Beautiful, beautiful—I never saw anything like it before. She is . . . "

Arthur completed his sentence, " . . . perfect."

Arthur noticed with a shock that the rest of the knights had arrived, arrayed in full Sarmatian battle gear. They waited patiently as Arthur and Lancelot stared off into the distance at some fascinating sight, but a loud snort from one of the horses broke the spell. Galahad laughed as Arthur turned with a start to look at them. "Fine warriors," he said. "The Saxon army could have ridden up behind you and neither one of you would have noticed."

Gawain looked down the hill and saw Guinevere, understanding immediately what had preoccupied the two knights. "Now there," he said, smiling lewdly, "is a warrior I would like to meet on the field of battle. Well, not *battle* exactly . . . " The other knights laughed and Arthur immediately put on a stern expression.

Tristran pointed. "Look yonder," he said.

Behind Guinevere there now stood four women. All of them seemed to be younger than Guinevere but were all uniformed as she was, and they all looked just as fierce. It seemed to the knights that the women served as Guinevere's bodyguards. They had never seen women warriors before. They knew if the other young women were half the fighters that Guinevere was, that the Saxons were in real trouble.

Galahad said, "Oh, to be outnumbered by *that* legion!"

Lancelot looked around sternly at them. "It is time to fight, friends," he said, "not to carry on as if you were in a tavern."

Bors said, "Then let us fight and win, so we can get to that tavern all the sooner!"

The knights' horses were also dressed in their finest, each with an opulent saddle blanket and head-dresses adorned with silver spikes. Their hooves glinted with razor-sharp battle anklets. Arthur's was the simplest horse of all. Lancelot's horse, however, wore the entire hide of a bear, giving the terrifyingly surreal effect that the horse's neck emerged from the full-fanged mouth of the bear's head.

It was the tradition of Sarmatian knights to deco-rate their full-length body shields with images of battle, mythological figures or of one of the many pagan gods. Each of Arthur's knights had created his own unique battle image. Gawain's shield sported a painting of a full moon, backed by clouds. Bors's depicted a light-ning bolt with a horse's head. Galahad's showed the morbid image of a mountain of skulls. On Tristran's shield was the picture of a lion whose teeth and claws were arrows. A red dragon roared from Lancelot's shield. And Arthur prepared to go into battle with the image of Christ on his shield. But Arthur's Christ was not the meek, loving figure of the scriptures, but a God of war, with wild, Medusa-like hair and burning eyes. This savage Christ held before him a bloody cross, which he wielded as if it were a broadsword.

Everything was in readiness. Arthur looked around at his knights—his friends—and said, "I wish you had not come back." He smiled and added, "But I am so very happy that you have come back. Thank you." The knights said nothing in return. They were eager to present themselves as fierce fighters, not sentimental types. Each knight suspected that if he were to express his true feelings of loyalty and camaraderie at this moment, the others would respond with jeers. Yet each man instinctively knew that the others felt as he did.

The knights lined up beside Arthur, who held the Draco standard high in the air in his left hand. The wind was beginning to fill its cloth body with air again, and it looked like a sleeping monster, slowly awakening in fury.

Arthur held up his right hand, and below, at the edge of the forest, the Woads, who looked as though they were getting anxious, sank back into the shadows.

As the Saxon army waited in readiness, Cerdic and Raewald studied the gate, working out their strategy for attack. Cerdic looked up from the huddle and called out, "Cynric! Prepare your light infantry. Send them through the gates."

Cynric was surprised at the order—and proud.

Cerdic saw his son's reaction and enjoyed the moment. Then, with the keen pleasure he always felt when he stuck the blade in, Cerdic added, "No. Not you. Just your men." Cynric's face blanched in painful shock.

"You will stay with me," Cerdic added, his voice laced with disgust. "In safety."

"Father," Cynric said, whining slightly, "please let me lead my men into battle. I will lead them to victory, I pledge it!"

"As you led them to victory on the lake?" Cerdic said with contempt. "There is still one knight left. I am not sure but that even he could destroy your force single-handedly." Cerdic smiled. "At least he could if *you* were in command."

Cynric could barely stomach this final humiliation. His father was blithely preparing to kill off Cynric's men, and Cynric himself was to be denied that glory. And the exchange had happened in plain sight, overheard by the entire Saxon army.

Up on Badon Hill, the knights swapped looks. They felt the old pride and eagerness, the longing for battle. They sometimes gave lip service to living long, peaceful lives and dying in bed as old men. But truly, this was the kind of moment they had all been born for, the sort of situation when they felt strongest, most in control—happiest.

Arthur stabbed the pole from which fluttered the

huge Sarmatian dragon into the ground and turned his horse to face the five men.

"Knights," he said. "In our lives, we roam the earth. Missions, quests, battles, crusades. Our duty compels us to keep moving. But whither do we wander? We forever seek home, but we will never find it. Home is for others, not for us. For when the great gods created knights, they decreed that death would be our share. Our lives are nothing more than dew that dries in the morning sun!"

Now the fifteen-foot dragon battle standard rose as if flying, its long, tubular body filled with air, its serpent tail whipping in the breeze. Its dragon face, decorated with bright reptilian blue and orange scales, sparkled in the sunlight. Best of all, it was beginning to make its horrendous sound, hissing and moaning like a genuine beast from hell.

The knights' horses pawed the ground impatiently and arrogantly tossed their heads, resplendent in their head armor. They seemed to be listening to Arthur's words along with the knights. Arthur noticed their attentive gazes. He thought with amusement that perhaps Dagonet was right and that their horses were warriors reborn.

Arthur looked down lovingly at his own steed and said quietly, "God took a handful of the south wind and he created the horse. And He said, 'My power shall be with you wherever you are. I hold you above all beasts, making you lord of them all. Able to fly without wings, you are destined to carry your masters into eternity!'"

He patted his horse affectionately on the side of the neck, and then looked up at his men and smiled. Arthur pulled Excalibur from its sheath and held it aloft. Bors grabbed his horse's ears and planted a kiss on the top of the animal's head. The horse was as unsentimental as the knights, and tossed his head angrily at the display of affection.

Lancelot also drew his sword and looked into Arthur's eyes. "Here," he said. "Now."

Tristran joined the others in a rousing cheer of camaraderie. Then his sharp eye noticed something. He rode over beside Arthur and pointed down the hill with his Sarmatian bow, which he held at full draw. "Look yonder," Tristran said. "There, at the great oak."

Geoffrey, the British scout, was slinking beneath the tree, his eyes on the great wall. He moved quickly, like a cautious animal.

Arthur saw him and said, "Do you suppose he is trying to determine the strength of the fortress?"

Tristran said, "Perhaps. I do not believe we should let him take such information back to the Saxons, do you?"

Arthur said, "I do not." He smiled, giving Tristran an approving nod.

Tristran adjusted his bow ever so slightly . . . and released.

Geoffrey had moved behind the tree, believing

that he would remain unseen both by those in the fortress and on the hill. As the scout was peering out through a space between the branches, Tristran's arrow passed through the tiny opening. The tip thudded into his left eye and emerged out of the back of his head. Geoffrey lay sprawled on the ground, his arms and legs spread wide. The arrowhead kept his head from lying flat, with the result that he appeared to be straining to look over his feet.

Tristran lowered his bow and took a moment to admire his shot. Arthur looked at him with incredulous pride. The other knights cheered lustily and Galahad pounded him on the back. Tristran holstered the bow and then said with a smile, "Every story has an end."

NINETEEN

❈

STANDING JUST BEHIND CERDIC AND Raewald, Cynric watched miserably from a distance as the Saxons' light infantry passed through the ominous open gate of Hadrian's Wall. Once inside, they spread out with machine-like precision on the plain facing the fortress. As they continued to march toward it, the Saxons saw no signs of life behind the walls. But even over the rumble of their marching, they could hear the hiss and shriek of the Sarmatian dragon from its perch up on Badon Hill. The sound was unnerving, but the force of men who bore the Draco standard seemed even more ominous to the Saxons. They had faced these same men on that terrible day on the icy lake and had fallen in bitter defeat. Now there were far fewer Saxons—and only one fewer

Sarmatian knight. Nervously, the marching men kept
their eyes on the ridge, feeling safe only as long as the
knights retained their distance.

Cerdic and Raewald watched in anticipation as
their forces entered the gates. Neither of them had yet
noticed the arrival of the other knights up on the hill,
but Raewald continued to scan the area, looking for
any sign that the fortress was a trap, or that another
force may be waiting in another direction. He had a
sinking feeling of dread that he could not shake. But
while Raewald seemed concerned, Cerdic just seemed
interested, as if watching a mildly interesting theatrical
performance.

"I do not know what is behind that wall," Raewald
said, unable to keep a worried tone from his voice,
"but if Cynric's light infantry encounters a strong
defense, this may not be as simple as it looks."

Cerdic said dismissively, "It is just another village, like all the others we have swept through on our
way here. That it stands behind a big stone wall makes
no difference. We will see the smoke from our fires
any moment now. Without Cynric to command them,
the light infantry should do much better today."

Suddenly, the air was filled with a loud creaking
sound. Cerdic and Raewald reacted with a start as the
huge gates of Hadrian's Wall swung shut just as the last
of the Saxon troops marched through. Raewald's hand
instinctively went to his sword. "What is this . . . ?" he
whispered.

Cynric gaped at the sight in shock, his scarred

face wearing an expression of anguish. For his part, Cerdic seemed more curious than concerned. The lives of Cynric's men meant less than nothing to him. He was simply baiting the trap, attempting to gauge the size and ferocity of the enemy's bite.

The Saxon light infantry had marched confidently through the gates, only to discover that the field between Hadrian's Wall and the fortress was completely empty of men or weapons. The lieutenant at the head of the column looked around carefully at the walls, alert to any signs of impending attack. There was nothing—no sound but that of their feet stomping across the hard ground and the unnerving shriek of the Sarmatian Dragon.

Then had come the rusty scrape of the gates being closed behind them. Before the Saxons could react, mercenaries and armed villagers leaped at them from where they had hidden behind the open gates. Up on the fortress walls, Jols signaled to Ganis, who helped the village children set fire to bales of hay and shove them over the edge, where they rolled toward the Saxons, blazing mightily, then slowed to a stop, forming smoldering heaps. From the forest, at Guinevere's signal, the Woads unleashed a barrage of arrows. The thick clouds of smoke from the hay bales gagged and blinded the infantry as they struggled to form a defensive position, but dozens were instantly felled by the arrows or struck down by the swords and lances of the mercenaries.

Arthur turned to his men and said, "All is going

according to plan. Let us go amongst them." Spurring his horse and raising Excalibur to eye level, Arthur galloped down the hill, the knights following in close formation. Bors grabbed the Sarmatian Dragon and held it aloft. The wind ripped through the standard, intensifying its shrieking. To the light infantrymen who saw the knights coming, it was a chilling sight. The knights, with their terrifyingly decorated shields and elaborately armored horses, drew nearer and nearer before becoming shrouded in a cloud of black smoke. The Saxon infantry could see virtually nothing. Then arrows poured out from the smoke, mowing down the front line. The second line looked around in panic, trying desperately to anticipate where the next assault would come from.

Suddenly, the knights broke through the swirling black cloud, shock lances leveled, Arthur holding Excalibur high over his head. Behind them came a small army of screaming Woads and determined mercenaries.

Blocked from view on the far side of the wall, the battle came to Cerdic, Raewald and Cynric only as a roar of horrendous sounds, of agonized screams, of the hellish whinnying of horses, the clash of steel and the snap of bowstrings. They could only imagine the carnage. Cerdic glanced at his son with smug satisfaction. Cynric no longer had an army with which to threaten to overtake his father. The young man looked at the mighty wall, desperately wondering where there was redemption for him. Perhaps, he thought, if he could kill someone whom even his father would consider worthy, then Cerdic would consider *him* worthy as well. Failing that, Cynric thought darkly, perhaps he could simply kill his father.

Behind the wall, the battlefield was a wild, demonic vision distorted by smoke. To the Saxons, the knights on their armed chargers seemed to be creatures straight out of a nightmare, drifting in and out of their field of vision, attacking the confused and demoralized Saxon infantry, always coming in from where they were least expected.

The Saxon lieutenant took an arrow to the gut, falling to his knees beside the wall. The battle went on furiously without him and as his life's blood trickled slowly from his body, pooling on the dirt beneath him, the lieutenant watched the knights as if they were phantasmagorian beings from another, more terrible, world. They seemed to be superhuman, implacable. With dimming eyes, the lieutenant watched Arthur swinging Excalibur, bringing down on either side Saxons, who dropped headless or gushing blood from where an arm had been a second earlier. Beside Arthur, Bors calmly fired deadly arrows from his bow, each finding its home in the chest or neck or belly of a Saxon infantryman. Lancelot wielded his shock lance, impaling men as if they were chunks of beef on a dinner knife. Tristran carefully, almost surgically, sliced through Saxons with his sword, the blade so sharp that many of the unfortunate soldiers never even felt the cut that killed them.

The wounded Saxon lieutenant slumped backward, still clutching the arrow in his stomach. He knew that he was dying. Anything, he thought in his final seconds on earth, was better than the scene that was now playing out before his horrified eyes.

Outside the fortress, the sounds of battle were heard to abruptly stop, leaving only a strange, terrifying silence. Nervous, Cynric looked to Raewald and then to Cerdic. Raewald stared straight ahead, shaking his head in dismay. But the stoic Cerdic was not frightened. He looked over at the wall with a kind of benign interest, apparently only curious about what was going to happen next. It seemed to Cynric that his father was actually *enjoying* this.

With a loud, metallic groan, the massive gates slowly began to swing open again. Issuing from the opening came a thick cloud of acrid, black smoke. It spread out onto the plain, low to the ground like a nasty fog. For a long time, the smoke was the only thing that came through. Then a lone Saxon soldier staggered out of the cloud. Cerdic and Cynric could see that he was barely alive; it looked as though he had been used for testing blades. Struggling to stay upright, the wounded Saxon limped laboriously across the open space.

"We should help him," Cynric said.

Cerdic looked at his son with the expression of disgust that was so familiar to him. "A soldier comes to his commander," he said. "A commander does not go to a soldier."

Raewald started to show his dismay. "But sir . . . "

"Silence!" Cerdic hissed. "Or you will take his place."

After a torturous interval, the wounded man at last arrived before Cerdic. Cynric gasped when he saw the man up close: His face had been mutilated worse than Cynric's own. His uniform was black and soggy with smoke and blood.

"The knights are demons!" the Saxon said in a hoarse, terrified voice.

"Are you the only survivor?" Raewald asked.

The Saxon acted as if he had not heard the question. He said desperately, "They have blue devils fighting with them!"

Cerdic said angrily, "How many defend the fortress?"

Again, the Saxon stared straight forward, as if he were still seeing the horrible sights from which he had just escaped. If he heard Cerdic, he made no indication of the fact. Instead, he pointed back toward Hadrian's Wall. "That is the gate to hell!"

Cerdic had heard enough. If the man was going to offer nothing more useful than this, there was no point in continuing the interrogation. Lifting his battle axe

high in the air, Cerdic brought it down with a sickening thud on the Saxon's head, slicing his skull in half
like a melon. Raewald looked on with a grim, sickened
look on his face. Cynric wanted to turn away, to run, to
scream. He wanted nothing more than to cover his
eyes, to escape from the grisly vision before him. But
he stood there as calmly as possible, determined not to
let his father see his weakness.

Cerdic said to Cynric, "Your infantry has again
been inadequate to the task. They proved to be as useless as you." He turned to Raewald and said, "Prepare
the army to attack. This ends now." Raewald hurried
away, beginning to shout orders to the leaders of each
division.

At the tree line, lower on Badon Hill, Guinevere
waited with the Woad army, her young, female bodyguards behind her, braced for action. All the tribes
were there, gathered for what they knew would be
either a glorious victory or their final defeat. Guinevere could see them faintly through the smoke. She
saw that the leaders of each division were watching her
carefully, ready for her signal. Guinevere looked up
and down the line, hoping to catch a glimpse of her
father. But he was nowhere to be seen.

Suddenly, in the distance came ominous sounds—
beating drums, blaring horns, marching boots. Now it
was the Woads' turn to imagine what was coming. It
sounded to them like the biggest army on earth.

Cerdic, Cynric and Raewald rode together in the

midst of the massive Saxon force. At Cerdic's signal, the Saxon army immediately formed a shield wall facing Badon Hill. When the Woads caught sight of the Saxons, they reacted with the calculated fury of warriors. They began to beat their spears against their shields furiously, howling and screaming. The deafening din they made came close to drowning out the Saxons.

With another signal from Cerdic, the Saxons stopped—and so did everything else. The drums ceased to beat, the horns went silent, the boots stood still. It took a few moments before the Woads noticed the Saxons' stillness. Line by line, they became quiet themselves. Now they simply stood staring at each other, each side sizing up the opposing force. The only sounds were the anguished groans of the dying Saxon light infantry men, which littered the field all around. The luckier ones had been killed instantly by Tristran's arrows and Arthur's sword, but others had been carved up and left to suffer a very slow and agonizing death.

In the center of his army, Cerdic signaled again, and the main Saxon force, comprising crossbowmen and swordsmen, moved slowly and deliberately forward. Calling a pair of lieutenants to his side, and pointing left and right, Cerdic commanded, "Secure our flanks." He pointed straight ahead. "Crossbowmen, to the center." He gestured to the archers with their longbows and said, "Bowmen, watch the wall at our back." Then he turned to his son. "Cynric," he said, pausing

for a moment to toy with his son one last time, "take
your force of swordsmen to the left and form a flank
there. Raewald, support him."

Cynric nodded gratefully and hurried off, leading
his men across a battlefield that was still black with
smoke from the smoldering bales. A Saxon lieutenant,
on Cerdic's orders, formed a right flank.

On Badon Hill, near the cemetery, Arthur again
waited with the knights, calmly watching the approach
of the enemy force.

"That is quite an army," Lancelot said, standing
beside him. "This may not be another day on the lake."

Bors snorted. "There was never a Sarmatian
knight who ever lived," he said, "who could not beat
Saxons ten to one."

Galahad grinned and pointed. "True enough," he
said. "But I believe they outnumber us by at least sixty
to one."

Bors dismissed him with a wave of his hand.
"Then I suppose we will just have to work a little
harder," he said.

Arthur looked around at his friends and their
mounts. The horses' armor was splashed with blood.
The knights' faces were black from the smoke of battle, their blades dripping and stained with the blood of
Saxon warriors. Observing it all, Arthur did not appear
frightened or unnerved. To the other knights, he
seemed calm, almost happy—perfectly in his element.
His demeanor made them calm as well. Looking down

on the massive army, each man realized that this time, the odds were probably too great. But they were ready. More than that, they were eager.

Nearby, Merlin stood facing the Saxon center. Behind him was an army of his seasoned warriors. Concealed in the trees and camouflaged with cut branches and bushes were the Woads' catapults, armed and ready to fire.

At the tree line, Guinevere readied her bow. Her bodyguards unsheathed their short swords and watched closely, awaiting Guinevere's order to attack.

Inside the fortress, Lucan peeked through a door at the villagers, who tensed in a high state of readiness. Some of them were armed with swords and spears. Others carried axes, pitchforks, shovels and any other kind of farming implement that they could turn into a weapon. A village woman saw Lucan looking through the door and quickly shooed him inside to safety, pulling the heavy door closed behind him. Lucan wanted a weapon, too, but he knew the adults would not give him one. More than anything, he wanted to kill the Saxon devils, to avenge the death of Dagonet. He looked through a crack in a shuttered window, knowing that he would have to be satisfied only with *watching* Saxons die. Outside, at the wall itself, Lucan saw Ganis and several more armed villagers crouching nervously, waiting for the battle to begin.

The Saxons under Cynric who formed the left flank came to a trench. They stepped in, attempting to cross it, and immediately became bogged down, ankle-deep in what had appeared to be mud. They could lift their feet from the sludge only with great effort. "This ain't mud, men," said one struggling Saxon. "Look! It's pitch!"

"Pitch?" said another. "Why would anyone fill a trench with pitch?"

By now, some of the soldiers were seriously mired in the thick, black sludge. The Saxons cast concerned looks at one another.

"Sir!" one of the lieutenants said, "we should probably turn back and find another way to cross this plain."

Cynric sneered in his direction, "What mighty warriors you are, worried about getting your feet stuck in the mud."

"It isn't mud," said one of the soldiers. "It's pitch—"

"Silence!" Cynric ordered. "Keep quiet, unless you want to this trench to become your grave."

The Saxons said nothing more. Heedless of the sticky mire, Cynric continued to push the men on across the trench and into position. Raewald slogged through the thick, gooey mess, looking down at it suspiciously. He thought the soldier had asked a perfectly valid question: Why *would* anyone fill a trench with pitch?

TWENTY

❧

ON THE EAST EDGE OF THE FOREST, Guinevere looked over at Arthur. Somehow, he seemed to feel her gaze across the distance and looked back at her. For a long moment, their shared look said everything that their voices could not. Then Arthur nodded and waved to her. Nodding back, Guinevere set fire to an arrow and carefully nocked it in her Sarmatian bow.

As the Saxons continued to march forward across the battlefield, the moaning of their wounded brothers became louder and more insistent. Around the mass of bodies, the ground was so soaked with gore that it resembled a crimson swamp. Stepping through it, the soldiers felt the blood bubble up from the earth, soaking their feet. The terrible sounds, the horrible smells,

marching through a sea of blood . . . The Saxons were
trained fighters and had been through many ghastly
experiences, but this was proving to be too much for
many of them; they were openly terrified.

And above the groans of the wounded came the
continuing screech of the Sarmatian dragon. The
Saxons looked up at it in all its terrible beauty, roaring
like a beast of death and waving its tail. Standing
before the dragon, motionless, were Arthur and his
knights.

Cerdic stared at the knights and their wind-filled
mascot. For the first time in this engagement, an
empty pocket of fear hollowed out his stomach. They
were back. All of them. Not just Arthur, but the entire
force that had defeated Cynric's men on the lake.
Cerdic scanned the battlefield, which was littered with
the corpses of his Saxon light infantry. When he had
sent them in, they seemed like acceptable losses. Now
their defeat seemed portentous. Cerdic had an ominous presentiment that things were about to go very,
very badly for him and his army.

At the cemetery, Arthur unsheathed Excalibur
with a flourish and held it straight overhead. The great
sword sparked in the sunlight.

Seeing it, Guinevere shot off her fire arrow.
Instantly, fifty more Woad archers shot their flaming
arrows as well.

One Saxon officer crossing the trench was hit
square in the face with Guinevere's arrow. Fortunately,

the arrow tip perforated his brain, killing him instantly so that he did not have to feel the agony he might otherwise have experienced when his hair and facial skin burst into flames. Nor did he have to suffer as many of his fellow soldiers did when his body dropped limply into the sticky murk, immediately igniting the black pitch and causing the trench to erupt in a horrendous wall of flame that shot north like a grounded lightning bolt, bisecting the battlefield. The Saxons crossing the trench were cooked before most even had a chance to scream. Others quickly jumped away from the ditch, their pitch-covered feet blazing furiously, the flames quickly spreading up their bodies. Their dying screams could barely be heard over the thunderous roar of the inferno. The massive snake of burning pitch, combined with the already smoldering bales, turned the battlefield into a nightmare.

The wall of fire had cut off the left flank—along with Cynric and Raewald—and the surviving Saxons were now facing Guinevere and her Woads all alone. The center formation, controlled by Cerdic, faced Badon Hill and the knights. The right flank, to the west, under the command of the Saxon lieutenant, now faced the fortress.

Guinevere waved her hand and her Woads unleashed a barrage of arrows. When she gestured again in the other direction, a second line of Woad archers released more flaming bolts. Woads on the Saxon flanks let fly arrows, slinger stones and spears.

Smoke billowed on the wind in every direction. The whole battlefield was black as night.

On the fortress walls, the village children braved the Saxon arrows and hurled torches over the side to the hay bales that were piled high, blocking the stone steps to the wall. Several of the children were struck by arrows and fell back, but others rushed forward to take their places. The burning hay, whipped by the wind, spread across the battlefield, raining sparks down on the Saxons' heads.

Like a mighty force of nature, Arthur and the knights once again charged down Badon Hill. Arthur extended Excalibur at arm's length. Behind him, Lancelot, Gawain and Galahad rode with swords leveled straight ahead. Bors held the Draco standard high, its body whipping violently in the wind, the scream of doom emanating from its fierce dragon's head. The knights' horses snorted threateningly with each thundering hoofbeat.

At Hadrian's Wall, Ganis and the villagers heard the screaming of the Sarmatian Dragon and the pounding hooves of the battle horses. Turning to see Arthur and the others, they raised their weapons aloft, waving them over their heads, cheering the knights' attack, and ready to meet the Saxons on their own ground.

As the knights passed, Guinevere and her Woads tossed aside their bows and drew their swords, holding them aloft in salute. Then Guinevere gave the signal, and with a terrifying roar, the Woads charged out of the forest, following the knights across the field and into the heart of the battle.

Guinevere and her troops rushed directly for Cynric's division and immediately found themselves blocked by a seemingly impenetrable wall of thick black smoke from the burning pitch. Guinevere led her Woads directly into the swirling darkness, screaming for Saxon blood. On the other side of the cloud, Cynric watched helplessly, cut off from the main battlefield by the flames, unsure who was about to emerge from the smoke, and from where.

Further down the tree line, Merlin's Woads tripped the pair of catapults as Merlin himself stood off to the side, keenly surveying the battlefield.

Ganis crouched on the Wall with the armed villagers, waiting. Jols rushed up to join them on the parapet, proudly holding his precious Roman spatha before him. He arrived there only an instant before Saxon forces rushed the steps, roaring their battle cry as they ran upward.

Jols signaled to Ganis and shouted, "Now!"

Ganis nodded in reply. Wielding torches, he and the villagers quickly set fire to more bales of hay and then hurled the burning bundles down onto the lower steps behind the Saxons, cutting off their retreat. Then they rolled more burning bales down the steps, mowing the screaming Saxons down in a fiery avalanche.

The knights charged at full gallop, straight through the cemetery and out toward the open battleground. The knights rode directly at the Saxons' shield wall. The first line of Saxon swordsmen braced themselves for the impact as the approaching knights rushed toward them. Behind them, the Saxon drummers continued to pound away, their drumming joining the rumble of hoofbeats across the battlefield to form an earth-shaking thunder.

Arthur signaled with Excalibur and the knights moved immediately into their dragon formation. Arthur rode point, archers Tristran and Bors rode on the flanks, and the others rode in single file, ready to spread out at the moment of impact. Over their heads, the two massive fireballs launched from the Woad catapults streaked like comets toward the Saxon lines.

The fireballs crashed into the soldiers manning the shield wall, scattering panicked Saxons in every direction like game pins. The fireballs hit with the force of a cannonball, and exploded upon impact with the ground, showering flames over the area. The versatile weapon offered a variety of ways in which a man might be killed, and various Saxons fulfilled each of the possibilities: Some were crushed, others were perforated by shrapnel and still others were ignited by the flames and died frantically trying to escape the deadly fire.

Cerdic watched dozens of his men die in the space of thirty seconds, but he continued striding forward without hesitation. When one of the flaming balls came bouncing along the ground, taking out Saxons left and right, Cerdic calmly sidestepped it, completely fearless.

"Close ranks!" he shouted. "Steady, men!" His soldiers were heartened by his bravery and began rallying to his side, loudly bellowing their Saxon battle cry.

Bors rode his horse at full speed through the crowd. He lowered the screaming dragon like a lance as his horse slammed into the terrified swordsmen. The other knights leveled their shock lances at the Saxons, scattering them like toys. The Sarmatian dragon lodged in a Saxon's chest, its mighty cry stifled as its head was crushed by the impact. Saxons dropped from sword and lance. A few ran in panic, looking desperately for safe haven and finding it nowhere. Still others tried to crawl away from the danger, but the horses' razor hooves stomped down upon them. Those soldiers who were not crushed were ripped to shreds within seconds.

Arthur chopped and hacked his way through the lines. Blood poured from Excalibur as if it somehow bled on its own.

Yelling with bone-chilling ferocity and brandishing short swords, the Woads charged in directly behind the knights. The Saxons, already crushed by the knights' cavalry charge, were ill-equipped to meet this next challenge, and the Woads waded through them, hacking away mercilessly. At the same instant, two more catapult balls slammed into the Saxon center, leaving another alley of mutilated and burning corpses.

The Saxon drummers continued to pound out

their battle tattoo as the soldiers rushed to fill the gap
made by the catapults' flaming missiles. A Saxon
drummer stopped beating the drum when an arrow
thudded into his chest. He looked at it with deep
curiosity before keeling over. His drum rolled down a
slight slope. A Woad warrior, running madly through
the smoke, tripped over it and fell flat on his face,
breaking his nose. Enraged, he stood up, hacking at
Saxon swordsmen left and right, making them pay for
his pain.

Guinevere picked off a Saxon commander with
her Sarmatian bow. Using their longbows, Tristran and
Bors, twisting in their saddles, steering their horses
with their knees, fired repeatedly, taking out Saxon
crossbowmen two at a time. Galahad waded through
the soldiers on his horse, running them through with
his sword. Several Saxon bowmen regrouped, nocked
their bows and fired a volley of arrows into the attacking mob. A dozen Woad warriors dropped to the
ground, dead. Seeing this, their fellow Woads raised
their swords and headed straight for the little cluster of
Saxons, chopping them to pieces.

Now the Woads were on both sides of the Saxon
line, ripping into them from two directions at once.
The Saxons struggled to advance, but the black smoke
blinded them. "Regroup!" Cerdic shouted above the
battle's roar. "Move forward! Move forward!" The men
could barely see Cerdic, but they could hear his orders
and they tried to move in the direction of his voice.

Again and again, Cerdic shouted out orders, determinedly inching his army along.

On the wall, Jols, Ganis and the villagers had repulsed the Saxon attack. Jols shouted to Ganis, "There is no more to do here! Let us join Arthur on the field!"

Ganis nodded and lifted his sword for all the villagers to see. "Get off the Wall," he cried. "Fight! Fight!" He rushed down the blackened steps, which were still smoldering from the hay fires, and leaped over the burnt corpses of the Saxons. After a few moments, he realized he was alone. Pausing, he looked back. The villagers stood at the top of the Wall, looking apprehensively at the scene of death and mayhem before them. Ganis smiled encouragingly and shouted, "What? Do you want to die of old age? Let us do to the rest of the Saxons what we have already done with these!"

There was only a moment's hesitation. Then, with a loud cry, the villagers rushed down the stairs and followed Ganis out onto the field. Jols was there first, almost giddy with the thrill of being in battle at last. He held his spatha before him threateningly, not quite certain what to do first.

A few yards away, a crossbowman aimed carefully at Jols, lining up the former squire in his sights. Jols saw him, and instead of running to safety, reached for one of his short throwing spears. Thinking, "Now's my chance at last!" he flipped the spear up and out of

its case, and with a single smooth motion, hurled it
through the air. It skewered the crossbowman, whose
weapon rattled to the ground, the arrow skitting harmlessly across the earth. Jols grinned with delight. Ganis
saw the move and his eyes widened; he was most
impressed with the skills of this young warrior.

On the east battlefield, Guinevere reached back
into the quiver to find that she had run out of arrows.
Flinging her bow to the ground, she drew her sword
from its sheath and shouted, "Come on! Follow me!"
She ran straight at the Saxon left flank, followed by a
dozen male Woad warriors, and the four tough young
girls who served as her bodyguards. Guinevere saw
instantly that Cynric and Raewald were in charge and
she immediately honed in on them. The two men were
too far apart to attack simultaneously, however, so
Guinevere had to make a quick choice. She picked
Raewald, since he was bigger and looked more powerful. Raising her sword, she screeched a battle cry. But
before she had run ten yards, a small group of Saxon
archers let fly at her and her company. Four of the
Woad men fell. Guinevere dove sideways to avoid an
arrow. By the time she got up, Raewald was gone.

The small group of children that remained on top
of Hadrian's Wall continued to hurl rocks, spears, furniture—anything they could find—onto the Saxons
below. They worked in relative safety since most of
them were so short that their heads barely cleared the
wall. They had to lift items above their heads in order

to throw them over the side, and though a steady barrage of Saxon arrows continued to clatter away at the
rock wall, the children had little cause for fear. Some
of them, in fact, seemed delighted, treating the brutal
activity as a kind of game. Two of the older boys made
a mark in a piece of wood every time they brought
down a Saxon soldier with a rock or a chair. At this
point in the battle, their scores were nearly tied.

Gawain powered into the Saxon horde, guiding
his horse into a spin as it kicked the soldiers and sliced
at them with its razor hooves. Bors looked over at the
damage Gawain's horse was doing and laughed loudly.
"Which is the knight and which is the dumb beast?" he
yelled across the battlefield. Gawain grinned in
response. At that instant, a Saxon crossbowman got off
a long shot. The arrow hit Gawain in the side and
knocked him off his horse. He hit the ground hard and
lay there stunned for a moment, the arrow protruding
from his side. He could see that several Woads had
already taken care of the Saxon archer and, with great
effort, he stood up and walked back over to his horse.
Gawain took a deep breath and broke off the arrow,
close to the point. A white-hot bolt of pain shot
through him and he grimaced and fought to continue
breathing. His horse seemed to sense that his master
was in trouble and stood very still among the chaos as
Gawain struggled back into the saddle, whimpering
involuntarily in agony. His horse was not the only one
to come to his aid. As he remounted, a group of Woads

gathered around Gawain. They stood in a circle around him, facing outward, swords raised, protecting him as he took a moment to conquer his pain.

Arthur spotted Cerdic across the mass of Saxons and headed straight for him, eager to introduce the leader to Excalibur's wrath. Passing Gawain at a distance of about twenty yards, he waved his arm and shouted, "Come with me!" But suddenly he noticed that Gawain was swaying uncertainly in the saddle, a dark mass of blood on his side. The Woads surrounding him were fending off the Saxon swordsmen who were moving in for the kill like sharks who had detected the scent of blood. But there were too many Saxons and too few Woads. Arthur forgot about Cerdic and wheeled his horse around, crashing into the Saxons with hurricane force, knocking most of them flat. Rearing and kicking savagely, Arthur's horse drove them away from Gawain. The Woads followed the retreating Saxons, firing arrows into their backs. Some of them simply overtook their enemy, leaped on the Saxons' backs and hacked at them with their short swords as they fell to earth.

Arthur rode to Gawain's side. "Are you all right?" Arthur asked. "Can you continue?"

Gawain smiled grimly and nodded. "I was just about to take care of all those Saxons when you came barging in.."

"Sorry," Arthur said. "I just didn't want you to have them all to yourself."

A few yards away, Lancelot galloped full-bore down the Woad lines as they howled and cheered him on. He spotted Arthur and Gawain and pulled to a stop beside them, out of the fray. Seeing that Gawain was wounded, Lancelot shot a troubled look at Arthur.

Arthur said to Lancelot, "We were just taking a short rest."

Lancelot nodded and said, "I have always maintained that you were all far too lazy to be knights. I don't know about you, but I am ready to end this thing."

Gawain smiled bravely, pretending that he wasn't in pain, hoping that Lancelot and Arthur would not notice how badly hurt he was. "Then what are we waiting for?"

Lancelot pointed. "It looks like we're waiting for Galahad." They all turned to watch Galahad come galloping up, breathing heavily. He was covered in blood but seemed to be fine. Arthur realized, with relief—and pride—that it was Saxon blood that stained Galahad from head to toe. As Galahad reloaded his bow, he noticed the blood on Gawain's side. He looked at Arthur and the others but said nothing. Then he studied Gawain closely. Gawain returned the look with no expression but determination.

All of the knights acknowledged each other. Arthur said, "It is time to go." The others nodded, knowing that Arthur's statement was probably truer than he knew.

Lancelot said, "It is indeed. Let us show these Saxons how Sarmatian knights do things."

Gawain's face was white with pain. He said in a soft voice, "Whatever gods you claim, may they be with you."

Arthur turned his horse so that they were facing the main force of the Saxons. The other three knights formed a tight line on either side of him, placing Arthur in the center. He raised Excalibur, then pointed it forward and began to ride hard toward the enemy.

Together, for the last time, they charged.

TWENTY-ONE

❖

CERDIC SAW THE KNIGHTS THUNDERING toward him. He shouted at his drummers and they began pounding a hard staccato as the Saxons formed lines of defense and turned their shields to face the attacking knights. The four knights rode in a perfectly straight line, side by side. Cerdic saw that Arthur was among them and felt an equal measure of dread and pleasurable anticipation at the thought of meeting him face to face on the field of battle.

As the knights thundered toward them, the Saxons braced themselves behind their shields and grasped the hilts of their swords so tightly that their knuckles turned white. Arthur carried Excalibur, and Lancelot, Gawain and Galahad brought out their shock lances, aiming them low.

The knights crashed through the Saxon shield wall, blasting the soldiers aside, trampling some of them under the relentless hooves of their mighty horses. Three Saxons lay writhing on the ground with shock lances sticking out of their bellies or chests. The knights immediately drew their swords, turned their horses, and headed to the Saxon line, which was now scattered in disarray.

Rallying quickly, the Saxons charged forward with their long spears. The knights turned their horses quickly in order to avoid the tips of the weapons. Arthur turned his horse too hard and the animal reared and stumbled, hurling Arthur to the ground. He rolled twice and then got to his feet immediately. He grabbed a shield from a dead Saxon for protection and began swinging Excalibur with deadly fury.

Gawain dismounted to help Arthur. As his feet thudded to the ground, he felt another blinding jolt of pain from the arrowhead in his side, but he ran anyway, rushing to Arthur's side. Both of them were hurt, but neither ceased fighting for an instant. With the malevolent persistence of demons, Gawain and Arthur advanced steadily on the Saxons. Though they were only two against a much larger force, they drove them back.

At that moment, the enemy was joined by two dozen reinforcements and, through the strength of their numbers, they began closing in hard on Arthur and Gawain. The two knights walked carefully backward, slicing at every Saxon who came within range of their swords, but they knew it was only a matter of time before they became overwhelmed. Just when things got desperate, Arthur heard a familiar gallop. Lancelot and his terrifyingly costumed horse plowed into the Saxons. The horse trampled some while Lancelot slashed at others with his twin blades. Then he, too, dismounted and stood beside Arthur and Gawain, dealing death to Saxons two or three at a time.

As Arthur fought savagely with a Saxon officer, he heard Lancelot shout, "Arthur! Down!" Without hesitation, Arthur lunged straight ahead, knocking the officer off his feet. Before the Saxon could throw him off, Arthur placed Excalibur's blade on his throat and pushed down hard, using both hands. He nearly severed the Saxon's head from his neck and then rolled off the twitching body to see what Lancelot had warned him about. He saw two crossbowmen falling to earth. One was riddled with Woad arrows; the other had one of Lancelot's short swords stuck in his back where Lancelot had hurled it from ten yards away.

Arthur briefly waved his thanks and then got to his feet and rushed at the nearest Saxon, bringing him down with a single swipe of Excalibur's blade. Only a few feet away, Arthur's horse continued to fight on, even without Arthur in the saddle. He spun wildly, kicking the enemy, stomping down hard with his front hooves, leaving numerous trampled Saxons in his wake.

Far from Arthur's sight, on the west side of the battlefield, Bors and Galahad dismounted. Bors pointed and shouted, "There!" They ran toward a small animal pen, now empty of the pigs and cows that had lived there until recently. The pen stood directly in front of the advancing Saxon line and the soldiers had to break formation to move around it. Bors and Galahad saw immediately that they could occupy the stinking little swamp, using its rough wooden walls as a tiny fort from which to fire on the Saxons. As the enemy moved around on either side, they found themselves on the receiving end of a rapid barrage of arrows fired by Bors on the left and Galahad on the right.

Unaware of the grisly fate met by their predecessors, more Saxons poured into the fortress, then were stopped by the scene inside. There lay dozens of charred corpses, burned by the fiery bales of hay dropped on them by the villagers and their children. Before the Saxons could get their bearings, eight mercenaries quickly moved in to close the gates behind them. Those soldiers closest to the gates turned quickly at the sound but were immediately overcome. The others ran headlong up the charred, grisly stairs. When the last of the Saxons lay dying, one of the mercenaries shouted to the top of the wall, "The scorpions! Now is the time!"

The "scorpions" were deadly weapons that had been too large for the Romans to take along when they abandoned the fortress the day before. They resembled giant crossbows and worked on the same principle. The bowstring was drawn back tight and attached to a trigger, then loaded. When the trigger was pulled, the scorpion sent its ammunition flying. But where a crossbow shot arrows, the scorpion fired six-foot-long lances. The weapon was not only deadly, but also highly accurate and reliable.

At the order of the mercenary, the villagers uncovered all of the scorpions atop the wall. Two large ones were situated on the tower tops, and two smaller ones, pointed inside the fortress, sat on the lower wall. At the order of "Now!" the villagers fired both of the smaller scorpions directly into the mass of Saxons trying to climb the steps inside. One lance skewered two at the same time and the other nearly cut one Saxon in two. All the bodies were hurled backward, knocking several of their comrades down the stairs.

The two large scorpions fired their missiles into the Saxon main force, dropping several men at once. As quickly as the scorpions were fired, the villagers reloaded and fired again. By the side of each huge weapon lay stacks and stacks of lances—hundreds of them. As far as the villagers were concerned, each one of those lances was destined to puncture at least one Saxon's body. They fired in relays to keep from becoming exhausted by the endless work.

Guinevere had singled out Raewald for attack, but when she lost sight of him, she saw that she had, in turn, been singled out by Cynric, frustrated by failure and half mad with the heat of battle. As hard as it was for him to accept the fact that a woman was acting as a commander, it was nevertheless clear to him that Guinevere was directing the attacking Woads. Cynric reasoned that if she were brought down, her savage forces would probably disintegrate into disarray.

Cynric turned to his swordsmen and pointed in Guinevere's direction. "Men!" he shouted. "Let us bring down this Woad bitch!"

Seven of Cynric's swordsmen rushed forward with him to attack Guinevere's line. She watched the tide rolling in her direction, her Woads rooted grimly to the spot behind her, ready to stand and fight. "Steady," she said. "Let them come to us."

Two-handed, she ripped her sword across the face of the first Saxon who reached her. The other Woads then stepped in front of her, slashing wildly at everyone who approached. The Saxons found Guinevere's female bodyguards particularly unnerving, especially as they watched soldier after soldier fall under the expert blows of their swords.

Over on the west side, Cerdic's larger force was proving ineffective against the relentless attack of the knights and their steeds. Since his Saxons were not having much luck bringing down the knights, Cerdic came up with an alternative plan. He shouted, "Kill their horses!" Immediately, the Saxons began stabbing with their swords at the horses' bellies. As fearless as they were with their own lives, the knights were fiercely protective of their mounts. Frantically, the knights spun their horses, trying their best to avoid the Saxon blades while using their horses' razor hooves to slash back at them.

One Saxon grabbed Gawain's foot and pulled him off his horse. The knight landed on the ground with a thud. The impact sent an agonizing bolt of pain through his body from the arrowhead in his side. Gawain screamed in a mixture of rage and agony, and with a supreme force of will, he pulled himself to his feet. Continuing to wail like an unearthly demon, he laid into the Saxons with his two-headed mace. Although he brought down one Saxon after another, they continued to surge toward him in a tide.

A few yards away, Galahad rode his horse through the crowd of soldiers, swinging his bronze battle axe left and right, brutally knocking the Saxons down on all sides.

Arthur's horse, still fighting along, reared high on his back legs, coming down hard on one Saxon head after another. When he reared again, a Saxon archer fired a bolt directly into his massive chest. The horse dropped to the ground with a pained whinny. With a cry of rage, Arthur rushed over to his beloved steed, slashing a path through the Saxons with Excalibur. Galahad rode by to cover his back as Arthur dropped to his knees and laid a hand on his horse's side. He drew back his hand covered in blood, and Arthur felt the sting of tears in his eyes. The horse breathed heavily for moment and then lay still, his dead eyes staring out at the battle before him. With a bellow of fury, Arthur jumped to his feet and waded into the Saxon throng, slicing back and forth with Excalibur, mowing down Saxons as if he were harvesting wheat.

Galahad saw Lancelot nearby and shouted, "Lancelot! Arthur is on foot! Help him!"

Immediately, Lancelot rode to Arthur's side. There the two friends fought side by side, one on horseback, the other on foot.

Guinevere continued to fight fiercely and desperately on the west side of the battlefield. Cynric had been directing the attack on her, but he remained some distance away in relative safety. Anytime a Woad made a dash forward to bring him down, one of his Saxon swordsmen ran interference.

Guinevere cut and slashed left and right. As she felt that she was about to be overwhelmed, she noticed that her bodyguards were nowhere to be seen. Suddenly, a Woad warrior on her left went down, a horrible sword gash in his forehead. Instantly, two Saxons backed her up against a tree. She was bleeding from a slash to her cheek and felt faint from the unending exertion of battle. But she brought her sword directly up into the stomach of one Saxon and spun him around on the other, knocking him over. Before he could get back up, Guinevere brought her sword down on his head.

Raewald sprang forward from behind the tree and swung his sword, attempting to decapitate her. Guinevere caught the motion out of the corner of her eye and ducked just in time. His blade hacked a large wedge from the tree trunk. He immediately turned around and took another swing at her. She parried Raewald's blows and jabbed at him with her own sword, but he smashed her with his shield. Guinevere charged him again with sword outstretched, but Raewald hit her blade so hard with his own that he knocked her flat on her back. She had to roll over quickly to avoid Raewald's sword as he honed in on her chest. Guinevere jumped to her feet and ran a short distance away to gather her wits. She knew suddenly that he was too good and too powerful for her to handle alone.

Luckily, she did not have to. As Raewald advanced on her, Guinevere's four female Woad warriors suddenly sprang from the forest, screaming like banshees. They immediately surrounded Raewald. Desperately, the Saxon spun around, trying to defend himself from an attack that was coming at him from every side. One of the women cut an ugly gash across his back. Though wounded, he fought like a bear. He spun and slammed the woman aside with his shield. As he did this, a second Woad girl stabbed him in the shoulder. Raewald slashed at her with his sword but she dove out of the way. The third Woad warrior sank a knife into Raewald's side. He made another weak swipe with his

sword, but missed entirely. In agonizing pain, Raewald
was also furious, not only at being defeated by females
who were little more than children, but also because he
saw Cynric standing nearby with members of his
guard, calmly watching the scene, doing nothing to
help.

As the women continued to stab and slash at the
exhausted fighter, Guinevere pulled a garrote from her
belt, snagged it around Raewald's throat and with all
her strength pulled him backward. Raewald collapsed
on top of Guinevere, gagging and gasping for breath.
Two of the Woad girls stood back while the other two
plunged their swords into his chest. His body jerked
convulsively for a few seconds as blood spurted sky-
ward like a crimson geyser, drenching Guinevere.
Then the twitching stopped and Raewald lay still. Two
of the Woad women pulled his body off Guinevere and
helped her to her feet.

In another part of the battlefield, two muscular
Saxon crossbowmen stood calmly on the field, unleash-
ing arrows at the Woads and mercenaries rapidly and
accurately. Tristran saw them and spurred his horse,
charging forward. His horse leaped over one of the muscle men. As it did so, Tristran hooked his bowstring
around the man's throat, dragging him down to earth.
He continued urging his horse to gallop ahead, pulling
the helpless bowman behind, his body bumping across
the rocky ground, until he was thoroughly strangled.

The second crossbowman swung his loaded bow

around and fired, hitting Bors in the chest. Bors struggled to stay in the saddle and as quickly as he could, he raised his own bow, bringing the man down with a single well-aimed shot. Tristran rode over to Bors, a look of concern on his face.

"You're hit!" he cried.

"I'm all right," Bors said. He tried to smile but the searing pain in his chest turned the grin into a grimace. "Let's kill them all!"

Like some magnificent animal, Bors reared back in his saddle and unleashed arrow after arrow into the Saxon ranks as he continued to use his knees to steer his horse. But though his arrows cut a deadly swath through the enemy, there were simply too many of them. Within moments, Bors and his horse were surrounded. He knew there was no way to escape. He stopped firing arrows for a brief instant and simply stared at his attackers. The hopeless situation and the painful wound in his chest made him angry enough to spit. And, as they closed in on him, their blades flashing in the sun, that's exactly what he did.

Arthur pushed forward, still on foot. He was supported now only by Tristran, on horseback, who kept up a rapid fire of arrows into the mass of crossbowmen.

Suddenly, Tristran spotted bigger game than the foot soldiers who were falling so rapidly under his arrows. About fifty yards away he saw Cerdic, the greatest Saxon warrior on the battlefield.

Cerdic noticed Tristran at the same time, watching in furious fascination as the archer killed one crossbowman after another as though he were at target practice. Cerdic was impressed by the knight's courage and prowess—so impressed that he decided to kill this one personally. Cerdic yelled to his men and made a fist, first holding it in the air and then pulling it to his chest. Responding to the signal, the surviving crossbowmen packed together toward the center of the field, forming a protective circle around Cerdic.

A group of Woads noticed Cerdic and rallied immediately, making an attempt to power into his position. Cerdic watched them come at him, and when they were within reach he leveled them with his battle axe, fighting the Woad warriors like an enraged bull.

Tristran dismounted and tossed his bow aside. He drew his broadsword and began cutting his way through the crowd toward Cerdic. A small horde of Saxons attempted to intercept him, but Tristran beat down warrior after warrior. One after another they dropped to the ground screaming, suddenly missing arms or legs. Those who were not screaming had just been deprived of their heads.

Cerdic smiled grimly as he watched Tristran approach. The Saxon commander grabbed his highly decorated round shield and his battle axe, and then stepped forward to meet his foe. Two Woad warriors came at him at a full run and he swung hard, slicing deep gashes through each of their chests in one uninterrupted swipe of his axe. All around, Saxons, Woads and mercenaries fought like wild animals. Cerdic saw that he would have to carve a path through this sea of battling humanity before he and Tristran could meet. Tristran continued to carve his way through the Saxon soldiers toward Cerdic, never taking his eyes from his enemy's face.

Behind Tristran, only one crossbowman remained standing. Preparing to fire into the crowd, the archer was astonished to see Bors staggering toward him, covered in blood. A few yards away, Bors's horse stood among a pile of dead Saxons, stamping impatiently. The crossbowman hurried to load his weapon, desperately racing against time to bring this devil down. But Bors stopped calmly in the field, raised his already nocked bow, and fired the arrow directly into the Saxon's chest. The distance was so short between them that the arrow's force drove it straight through the archer's body, only a ruffle of feathers protruding from his breastplate.

With a smile of grim satisfaction, Bors turned back to his horse. He gave a short whistle and the steed galloped toward him. Suddenly, a Saxon archer unleashed a dart that hit Bors's horse in the withers, just below his long neck. With a low groan, the horse fell onto his side and lay still. Screaming in rage, Bors tried to run to his beloved mount, but a small squad of Saxons sprang up before him and attacked.

Finally face to face, Tristran and Cerdic lunged at

each other, the sword of one parried by the battle axe of the other. They bounced off, dropped back to size each other up, then crashed together again.

For several brutal moments, the battle was give and take. Tristran gained the advantage when he drew back his sword and sheared off a quarter of Cerdic's shield with one massive stroke. Cerdic staggered backward from the force of the blow. Then he quickly rallied and rushed forward again, holding the hilt of his battle axe with both hands, ready to swipe it at Tristran's head with every ounce of strength in his body.

Tristran braced himself with legs set wide apart as Cerdic came at him with everything he had. He leaned back with the blow, lessening the force of its impact and staying upright. Cerdic swung the axe back and forth. Tristran could feel the air on his face in the wake of the weapon as it passed within inches of his nose. Then Cerdic tried swinging the battle axe up and down, beating savagely at Tristran's body shield, the heavy axe blade landing with loud, bone-rattling thuds. Tristran feared that one of the blows would break the arm that held the shield and decided to go in for a quick kill. He made a high, wide sweep with his sword, aiming directly for Cerdic's head. Cerdic ducked slightly in a quick move that saved his life. His helmet went flying off from the impact of Tristran's blade, which ripped a painful gash in Cerdic's ear.

Blood trickling down the side of his face, Cerdic chopped into Tristran's shield again, still holding the battle axe with both hands. At the same time, Tristran thrust at Cerdic's chest, straight through the missing chunk in the Saxon's shield. Tristan's blade hit first, but skidded harmlessly off Cerdic's breastplate.

Cerdic's blow split Tristran's shield, striking him hard in the neck. The powerful impact dropped the knight to the ground. Tristran lay on his back, stunned and unable to move. In shock, he felt very little pain, but when he tried to move his left arm, he heard a cracking sound and felt a sharp stab run through his neck. He knew his collarbone was broken, and that it probably was not the full extent of his injuries.

Cerdic walked over to the fallen knight and kicked away his sword. Suddenly, with his right hand, Tristran pulled a knife and sat up, stabbing at Cerdic. But the thrust was too weak and the dying knight moved too slowly. Ruthlessly but calmly, Cerdic slashed Tristran across the chest. Wincing with the blow, the knight fell back, trying vainly to hold himself up with one arm. He reached for his knife with his other arm, but the limb would not move and he realized the attempt was useless.

Too exhausted to fight anymore, Tristran collapsed. The thought flitted across his mind that this moment should be terrifying or agonizing or perhaps just terribly sad. But it was none of those things. Tristran experienced it all with a kind of detached acceptance. "So this is death," he thought. He noticed that Cerdic was standing over him, one foot on either side of his prone body. But Tristran did not want, in his last seconds of life, to have to look at the evil visage of the Saxon commander. Instead, he turned his eyes to a place beyond Cerdic, to the fast-moving clouds, floating majestically in the wind above the treetops. The thick smoke of the battle fires made the ground dark, murky and acrid. But above, the sky was a brilliant and promising blue.

Cerdic raised his battle axe high above his head and brought it down with a sickening thud.

Across the field, Arthur watched in horror and rage as Tristran died at Cerdic's hands. He immediately headed toward Cerdic, wading through the Saxons, drenched in the blood of those he had killed and those he was continuing to kill as he stormed forward like a relentless fighting machine. One of the Saxons sank a dagger into Arthur's shoulder. With a roar of fury, Arthur dropped Excalibur to the ground and then turned and grabbed the Saxon around the neck with his left hand. Reaching behind him with his right hand, Arthur yanked the blade out of his shoulder, taking a second to recover from the blinding pain of the wound. Then, looking straight into the Saxon's terrified eyes, Arthur plunged the knife into the warrior's chest and dropped his limp body to the ground. He picked up Excalibur and started slashing again, continuing to fight his way toward Cerdic.

Satisfied that Raewald was dead at the hands of Guinevere and her savage female warriors, Cynric and his bodyguards now bravely stepped up to hem her in. Now that she had been weakened by constant fighting, Cynric saw the possibility of victory. He relished the opportunity to face down Guinevere on the field of battle; it was his one chance to kill a Woad commander and redeem himself in the eyes of his father.

Cynric turned to his bodyguards and pointed toward the Woad women. "Get them! Leave no one standing!" Then, his sword drawn, Cynric advanced upon Guinevere.

Lancelot and Gawain on horseback met a Saxon counterattack of a half dozen warriors and slaughtered them all with fierce, decisive thrusts of their swords. From his saddle, Lancelot could see over the wall of flame. Instantly, he saw that Guinevere was in trouble. Lancelot jumped his horse through the fire and arrived nearly airborne in the midst of the Saxons; those watching looked at him in awestruck fear, as if he were an avenging god. The impact slammed one of Cynric's bodyguards aside and before his horse had even come to a stop, Lancelot flew from the saddle, a sword in each hand, swinging violently at every Saxon within reach. His first thrust brought down one of the soldiers nearest Guinevere, causing Cynric to turn and unceremoniously flee the area. He saw Lancelot as an ideal target and the perfect foe—but not face to face. For his part, Lancelot barely even noticed that Cynric had ever been there, concentrating instead on bringing down bodyguard after bodyguard. With Guinevere slashing at them, and Lancelot and the four female fighters coming from virtually every direction, the Saxons did not stand a chance.

Running away, Cynric saw how he might still have a chance to wring a victory from the disaster. He stopped to pick up a crossbow from the battlefield, and then maneuvered around until he stood at a safe distance behind Lancelot. The knight turned toward him, felling the last of Cynric's bodyguards with his sword, and then turned back toward Guinevere. Cynric took advantage of the brief window of opportunity to aim the crossbow and let fly an arrow. The tip of the arrowhead landed square in Lancelot's back and he staggered forward, falling face-first in the dirt.

Guinevere screamed, "Lancelot!"

Arthur heard the scream and looked across the battlefield. When he saw that Lancelot was wounded, he also shouted out his friend's name; his and Guinevere's cries echoed each other in sorrow and horror.

Lancelot struggled to his knees, bleeding profusely from the wound in his back. Cynric walked forward, now holding a sword in his hand. This, he thought with satisfaction, would be the coup de grâce. He would finish off the haughty knight with one heroic swipe of the blade. Lancelot was still facing Guinevere, whose tear-filled eyes were staring straight into his. He smiled grimly at her and, without warning, spun around, pulling his short lance from its back sheath. Before Cynric could react, Lancelot threw the lance at him with all the force remaining in his body. Cynric watched Lancelot throw the spear as if in a dream. It seemed to be lazily drifting in his direction through the air, but he was powerless to move out of its way. The lance landed in his belly, propelling Cynric backward with its force. Cynric lay flat on his back, a shocked expression on his face. Blood bubbled up around the embedded tip of the lance.

Lancelot struggled over to him. Dropping to his knees beside the dying Cynric, Lancelot lifted him up by the collar, bringing the Saxon's face so close to his own that it seemed they were about to kiss. Lancelot spat blood into Cynric's face and said, "You have made this land sacred with my blood!" He pulled a short sword and considered slitting Cynric's throat. "No," he said to the gasping man, "I'd rather see you suffer as long as possible." Roughly, he threw Cynric's body aside and, with great effort, stood up. Cynric lay there, weakly trying to pull the lance from his stomach. There was too much blood, however, and every time he tried to grip the shaft of the spear, his hands slipped ineffectually.

Looking once more at Guinevere, Lancelot took a step toward her. Just for a moment it looked to her as though he was going to be all right. He stood upright; he was even smiling. But before he could take a second step, he crumpled to the ground. Saxons immediately surrounded him like vultures. Lancelot stabbed upward, embedding his sword in a Saxon's groin. And

with one last powerful arc of a swing, he swept his
broadsword low across the ground, severing the legs of
another Saxon at the ankles. The man dropped to the
ground, screaming in agony.

Now the Woads rushed to the scene, driving away
or killing the other Saxons as Guinevere ran over to
Lancelot and knelt by his side. She gently lifted his
head and held it in her arms, trying to urge life back
into his body, looking desperately for whatever spark
remained in his eyes. Her tears dropped onto his face,
leaving tracks of white through the grime of smoke
and battle that stained it. Looking up into her eyes,
Lancelot could say nothing. A breath puffed from his
mouth in a crystal sphere and mist of blood. The crimson bubble burst … and Lancelot lay still.

Still standing over Tristran's body, Cerdic surveyed the battlefield. As the many fires began to die
down, he saw that Raewald's forces had been destroyed.
Enraged, he looked up to see Arthur striding toward
him, his grim eyes filled with death. Cerdic once again
picked up his huge battle axe.

At that instant, several Saxon warriors hurled
spears at Arthur. He raised his shield just in time to
deflect them but two of the spears pierced the surface,
knocking Arthur backward with their force. He lay
still, and at first the Saxons thought the mighty knight
was dead. There was a long moment of silence as the
Saxons looked at one another uncertainly, not quite
sure what to do next. But Cerdic was not uncertain

about anything. With a satisfied smile, he strode toward Arthur from across the battlefield, holding his battle axe high.

Jols rushed to Arthur's side and threw down his sword, trying desperately to revive his stunned friend. "Arthur . . . " he whispered urgently. "Arthur . . . get up . . . "

A shadow loomed over the distraught Jols. Cerdic drove his axe full force at the young man's head. Inches before impact, Arthur thrust his decorated shield into place. Cerdic's axe crashed into the burning cross borne by Arthur's wild warrior Christ. Jols rolled out of the way and jumped back to his feet. He knew better than to try and intrude on one of Arthur's fights, but stood nearby, in case his friend needed him.

Arthur stood up and shoved Cerdic backward with his shield. Bleeding profusely and struggling to put one foot in front of the other, Arthur leveled Excalibur and glared at Cerdic. For what seemed an eternity, the two silently acknowledged each other and the arrival of the moment that each had longed for.

Suddenly, Cerdic raised his axe, and the two ultimate warriors smashed together with a thundering crash. At first it looked like they were as evenly matched as had been Cerdic and Tristran. They both leaped back instantly. As they repositioned, blood oozed down Cerdic's face from a slash on his forehead. Cerdic felt a split-second surge of panic—he had neither seen nor heard the sword stroke that cut him.

Like ice, an emotionless Arthur rotated Excalibur so that Cerdic could see the cross on its hilt facing him. It was as if the burning cross with which Cerdic had started this battle had returned to exact its revenge upon him. The two men cautiously circled each other in the midst of hundreds of bodies. All around their private skirmish, individual battles continued to rage.

The blue skies over Badon Hill were quickly turning dark as storm clouds swirled in. A lone figure stood on the slope, intently watching the personal battle within the greater fight. Instead of leaning on a staff, as was his wont, Merlin leaned on a battle spear. To anyone who might have seen him, high on his hill, Merlin looked like an imposing god of war.

Below, Arthur and Cerdic continued to circle each other. Cerdic parried—Arthur countered—but they did not even touch. Each of the warriors was so good at the craft of battle that they knew when a stroke was useless. They also knew they had plenty of time.

After numerous feints, they finally lunged for each other again. The sky was nearly as black as night now and as their weapons raged, a massive streak of lightning split the sky while thunder cracked and roared. It seemed to Arthur that God was accompanying the epic fight with his most powerful and portentous music of war.

They were slowly moving nearer to the pitch-filled trench. Dark, ugly flames and thick, suffocating smoke still poured from the ditch, forming an impassable wall. Both Cerdic and Arthur knew that they would have to stop there, that this was where their personal battle would end, one way or another.

Feeling the searing heat of the flames against his back, Cerdic swung his axe high and came down for a do-or-die chop. Arthur sliced sideways with Excalibur at the same moment and severed Cerdic's axe head from the shaft, sending it flying through the air. The sudden loss of his weapon stunned Cerdic and he stared at the useless axe handle in his hands. Before he could react, Arthur made the most of his momentary advantage. He swung Excalibur with a collapsing, spent-strength lunge. With a sickening crack Cerdic's head flew from his body, hitting the ground and rolling. The corpse stood there for a moment as if it could not decide what to do. Then with a resigned air, the body dropped backward into the flames of the trench. Arthur walked over to where Cerdic's head lay staring upward in mute surprise. Without a word, he nudged the skull with his toe and it, too, rolled into the fire and disappeared.

Arthur leaned on Excalibur, exhausted and demoralized. He might otherwise have felt pride in his defeat of Cerdic, but all he could think of was Tristran . . . and Lancelot . . . and Dagonet. All around him, Woads and villagers surged forward against their enemy. The Saxons continued to fight, but their will was failing. Arthur saw that some of them were beginning to run across the battlefield toward the gates of Hadrian's Wall, hoping to escape in the land beyond.

It became unthinkable to Arthur that any of the Saxons should survive. He felt that all of them were guilty for the deaths of his friends, and all of them must suffer the most severe punishment possible. Wearily, he turned to the Woads and the surviving mercenaries and shouted in a hoarse voice, "No quarter!" Then, louder, as if his fury were giving him new strength, he yelled again, "Destroy them all! No prisoners!"

The ragged remains of the Saxon force heard Arthur's cry. It shattered what was left of their resolve and they broke ranks and began their quick retreat toward safety beyond the Wall. Most of them did not make it very far. Within seconds they were surrounded by a mob consisting of Woads, mercenaries, villagers and three knights. Panicked, without hope, without leadership, the Saxons fought blindly.

Leaning on Excalibur for support, Arthur watched the massacre through pained eyes. He was still watching when the field fell quiet and he knew that the Saxons had been defeated.

TWENTY-TWO

❖

GALAHAD AND GAWAIN LIMPED THROUGH
the carnage of the battlefield, looking carefully at
each fallen warrior for one specific face. Galahad saw
him first. He clasped his friend on the shoulder and
pointed to Tristran's body. His head had been split
open, but his eyes still gazed serenely at the sky. Both
of the knights knelt beside their comrade, waiting for
the first devastating wave of grief to pass. After a
time, they rose wordlessly, lifted Tristran into their
arms and carried his body to the waiting Arthur.

Bors limped across the field to his fallen horse,
his face stricken by his loss. The battle had forced him
in the other direction and he had tried repeatedly to get
back to his companion. But it was only now that he
could pay his respects to the martyrdom of his closest

friend. He stood looking at his horse for a moment and then knelt, nearly crying, gently stroking the steed's neck and murmuring words of endearment. Without warning, the horse snorted loudly and rose to its feet. It stood there uncertainly, favoring the leg just below the arrow, bloodied but alive. Overjoyed, Bors let out a loud shriek of delight. He jumped to his feet and wrapped his arms around the horse's neck, hugging and kissing him enthusiastically.

Arthur surveyed the field grimly. It was all over— there was no one left to kill. Blue bodies, smoke, black leather Saxons: It all looked like nothing so much as the aftermath of hell.

Then Arthur saw Lancelot's horse pushing at Lancelot's body with his muzzle, urging him to get up, to come back to life. Guinevere still knelt there, holding the fallen hero's head in her arms. Bors limped over to join them, carefully leading his horse behind him. In a moment he was followed by Jols and Ganis, both of whom had come through the battle virtually without a scratch. And then Gawain and Galahad stepped up, bearing Tristran's body in their arms. They knelt and gently laid him beside Lancelot.

Arthur bent over and reached down to touch Lancelot. The movement aggravated his own pain, making him plop suddenly onto the ground. He grimaced but said nothing. Affectionately, stroking Lancelot's hair, Arthur looked out across a nearby field of blue-bells. The storm had passed, and the afternoon sun was breaking through the clouds, spreading its golden warmth.

Without letting go of Lancelot's head, Guinevere reached over and gently laid her palm upon Arthur's cheek. His stoic resolve seemed to evaporate under her touch and Arthur began to sob, from loss, from physical pain, from sheer exhaustion, from spiritual emptiness. Through his tears Arthur saw Lancelot's childhood dragon medallion, splashed with the great knight's blood. Arthur had seen this medallion around Lancelot's neck every day of his life. His fingers softly traced the design.

As he fingered it, Arthur whispered, "Lancelot, you were the truest of us all." He looked over toward Tristran and the tears fell thicker from his eyes.

"My brave knights," Arthur said to his two dead comrades, his voice choking, "I have failed you. I neither got you off this island nor shared your fate."

From behind him, another voice spoke. "Their fate and yours are separate, Arthur," said Merlin. "They have always been."

Arthur rose and Guinevere rose with him, helping him to stand, embracing him both out of affection and to serve as his support. Jols stepped forward with a cloth, trying to stanch the blood seeping from Arthur's wounds. Merlin also stepped forward to help steady Arthur. The Woads and the villagers gathered around, nearly all proudly bearing the wounds of battle.

"Merlin is right," Bors said, "they chose their fate,

Arthur. As did all of us." Bors finished placing a rough bandage on his horse's wound and slowly eased himself into the saddle, alert to any signal that the movement was hurting his bloodstained companion.

Arthur looked at Bors and said, "Where to now, my old friend?"

"It is time to get my family back," Bors replied. "That caravan moves so damned slow. I should be able to catch up with it, even with this worthless old horse." The horse snorted as if protesting the insult, and Bors patted it lovingly on the neck. He took a long last look at his friends and without saying anything else, Bors turned his horse and rode away at an easy trot. Guinevere and the knights watched sadly as he disappeared up and over Badon Hill.

Hours later, as dusk fell over the knights' graveyard, Arthur stood before two fresh earthen mounds. At the head of each grave, a long sword had been thrust into the ground, marking the final resting places of Tristran and Lancelot.

Except that Lancelot was not actually in his grave. Arthur had not forgotten his promise to his friend. A few yards away, on the outskirts of the cemetery, Lancelot's body was being consumed in the raging flames of a funeral pyre.

Galahad looked somberly at the grave and then at the funeral pyre. Then he said, "And you, Arthur? Where do you go next?"

Arthur shook his head sadly. "Nowhere. With this,

our adventure is over. There are no more knights of the
Round Table. No more deeds to accomplish or quests
to fulfill. No more . . . "

"You are wrong, Arthur," Merlin said. "Your most
challenging adventures still lie ahead. Your greatness
yet lies before you."

Arthur looked at the Woad commander. "It is you
who are wrong, Merlin. I have no greatness. Perhaps I
never did have."

Merlin stepped up to Arthur and clasped his forearm. "In you," he said, "has come together all the best
that was Rome. In you is all the greatness that Britain
shall become."

Arthur said nothing, but continued staring into the
flames that were taking Lancelot's body from the
earth. His ashes swirled in graceful eddies above the
fire before falling gently to the ground like snow.

Lucan stepped up to a third burial mound. Only
days old, it still seemed as fresh as the two new ones
that joined it today. The young boy stared at the grave
as if his heart were breaking. Suddenly, a look of
determined fury came over his young face. He grabbed
the hilt of Dagonet's sword and pulled as hard as he
was able, groaning with the strain. Dagonet's sword
did not move—it did not even quiver in the earth.
Lucan tugged and tugged until his strength failed him.
Finally, he faltered and fell to his knees, tears streaming down his cheeks. Guinevere left Arthur's side to
kneel beside the weeping child.

Arthur walked over to him and also knelt. He stroked the hair back from Lucan's forehead in the way that he had once seen Dagonet do it. Lucan looked at him with a tortured expression of loss and hopelessness.

"You know where the sword is," Arthur said softly. "When you are stronger, come back for it."

Lucan's face brightened, if only slightly. He would return and one day he would carry Dagonet's sword into battle. One day he, too, would wear the proud title of knight. Arthur smiled at the boy. He knew, too, that the future was now gazing up at him, small and frightened, but alive and determined. Taking Guinevere's hand in his own, Arthur knew that Merlin was right, that his greatest adventures did lie ahead of him.

Merlin looked around the group, studying each face. "And to you who still live," he said, "who race above the long earth and over all the plains on swift horses, delivering mankind from pitiful death—fly to the crests of our swift lives, and gazing over sword and lance, bow and shield, blaze a way through the midnight to your home."

AFTERWORD

THE VICTORY OF ARTHUR AND HIS KNIGHTS at Badon Hill was so complete and so devastating that the Saxon army retreated forever from Britain.

This one fantastic victory by brave knights of flesh and blood gave birth to an enduring legend, the undying tales of King Arthur, whose mythic exploits continue to echo through time. Yet, as fantastic as the legends are, they rise from this one heroic moment when Arthur, Lancelot, Guinevere and a handful of brave knights changed the course of history and wrote a new future for Britain with their spirit and their blood.